RAVES FOR JAMES PATTERSON

"PATTERSON KNOWS WHERE OUR DEEPEST FEARS ARE BURIED... THERE'S NO STOPPING HIS IMAGINATION."

—*New York Times Book Review*

"JAMES PATTERSON WRITES HIS THRILLERS AS IF HE WERE BUILDING ROLLER COASTERS." —Associated Press

"NO ONE GETS THIS BIG WITHOUT NATURAL STORYTELLING TALENT—WHICH IS WHAT JAMES PATTERSON HAS, IN SPADES."

—Lee Child, #1 *New York Times* bestselling author of the Jack Reacher series

"JAMES PATTERSON KNOWS HOW TO SELL THRILLS AND SUSPENSE IN CLEAR, UNWAVERING PROSE." —*People*

"PATTERSON BOILS A SCENE DOWN TO A SINGLE, TELLING DETAIL, THE ELEMENT THAT DEFINES A CHARACTER OR MOVES A PLOT ALONG. IT'S WHAT FIRES OFF THE MOVIE PROJECTOR IN THE READER'S MIND."

—Michael Connelly

"JAMES PATTERSON IS THE BOSS. END OF."

—Ian Rankin, *New York Times* bestselling author of the Inspector Rebus series

"JAMES PATTERSON IS THE GOLD STANDARD BY WHICH ALL OTHERS ARE JUDGED."

—Steve Berry, #1 bestselling author of the Cotton Malone series

"The prolific Patterson seems unstoppable." —*USA Today*

"Patterson is in a class by himself." —*Vanity Fair*

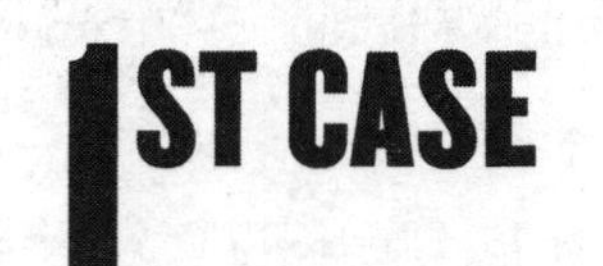
1ST CASE

For a complete list of books, visit JamesPatterson.com.

1ST CASE

JAMES PATTERSON
AND CHRIS TEBBETTS

GRAND CENTRAL
PUBLISHING
New York Boston

For Angela Hoot, of course
—JP

For Jonathan
—CT

Grand Central Publishing
Hachette Book Group
1290 Avenue of the Americas, New York, NY 10104
grandcentralpublishing.com
twitter.com/grandcentralpub

Originally published in hardcover and ebook by Little, Brown & Company in July 2020
First trade paperback edition: August 2021

Grand Central Publishing is a division of Hachette Book Group, Inc. The Grand Central Publishing name and logo is a trademark of Hachette Book Group, Inc.

The publisher is not responsible for websites (or their content) that are not owned by the publisher.

The Hachette Speakers Bureau provides a wide range of authors for speaking events. To find out more, go to www.hachettespeakersbureau.com or call (866) 376-6591.

ISBNs: 978-1-5387-1497-3 (trade paperback), 978-0-316-41819-5 (ebook)

Printed in the United States of America

LSC-H

Printing 1, 2021

Forensic Media Analysis Report

Case agent: William Keats, ASAC, FBI Field Office, Boston, MA

Evidence marker #43BX992

Media: iPhone 11, serial 0D45-34RR-8901-TS26, registered to victim, Gwen Petty

Recovered file: Unknown source mixed-media electronic message transcript. Source investigation pending.

I want to touch you. Your face, your skin, your thighs, your eyes. I want to feel you shiver as my hands explore every part of you.

I want to hear you. Your voice, whispering my name. Your breath in my ear. Your soft moan as I give you everything you want, and so much more.

I want to taste you. Your lips. Your kisses. Your beautiful flower, opening to my touch, my mouth, my tongue.

I want to take in the scent of you. I want to smell the perfume of your hair. The musk of your desire, bringing us closer, always closer.

More than anything, Gwen, I want to see you. Face to face. Body to body. I could pour my heart out with words forever, but words will never be enough.

It's time we finally met, don't you think?

Please say yes.

CHAPTER 2

THEY TOLD ME ahead of time to prepare myself for the dead bodies. But nobody told me how.

When I pulled up outside of 95 Geary Lane in Lincoln, all I knew was that a family of five had been killed and that I was supposed to report to Agent Keats for further instruction. Talk about jumping into the deep end, but hey, this was exactly the kind of assignment I'd been jonesing for. On paper, anyway. Real life, as it turns out, is a little more complicated than that.

"Can I help you?" a cop at the tape line on the sidewalk asked.

"I'm Angela Hoot," I said.

"Good for you," he said.

"Oh." I'd forgotten to show him my new temporary credential. I held it up. "I'm with the FBI," I said.

I could hardly believe the words coming out of my mouth. Me? With the FBI? Not something I ever saw coming, that was for sure. I certainly didn't look the part, and I didn't feel like I belonged there for a second.

Neither could the cop, apparently. He eyeballed me twice, once before he even looked at the ID, and once after. But that seemed to take care of it. He handed back my card, gave me an if-you-say-so kind of shrug, and lifted up the yellow tape to let me into the crime scene.

"Watch out for the smell," he said. "It's pretty bad in there."

"Smell?" I said.

"You'll see."

It hit me on the porch steps, before I was even through the front door. I'd never been anywhere near a dead body, much less smelled one, but what else could that acrid nastiness be? A gag reflex pulsed in my throat. I switched to mouth breathing and fought the urge to run back to my safe little cubicle in Boston.

What was I doing here? I was a computer jockey, not some *CSI* wannabe.

Up until two hours ago, I'd been a lowly honors intern at the Bureau field office, focusing on cyberforensics. Clearly, I was here to look at some kind of digital evidence, but knowing that didn't make it any less bizarre to walk into my first real crime scene.

The house was almost painfully ordinary, considering what I knew had gone down here just a few hours earlier. The living room was mostly empty. I saw all the expected furniture, the art on the walls, the fan of cooking magazines on a glass coffee table. Nothing at all looked out of place.

Most of the action was centered around the kitchen straight ahead. I'd noticed police officers stationed outside the house, but inside, it was all FBI. I saw blue ERT polo shirts for the Evidence Response Team, techs in white coveralls, and a handful of agents in business attire. Voices mingled in the air while I tried to get my bearings.

"No signs of a struggle," someone said. "We've got some scuff marks here on the sill, and over by the table..."

"Looks like the back door was the point of entry. Must have shot this poor guy right through the window."

"Yup."

They all sounded like they were discussing the score of last night's game, not a multiple homicide. It just added another dreamlike layer to the whole thing.

The lights were off in the kitchen, and one of the techs was using some kind of black light to illuminate spatters on the linoleum floor. It was blood, I realized, fluorescing in the dark. I could just make out a half empty glass of milk on the table, and a sheet-covered body on the floor, next to a tipped-over chair.

I was still standing in the doorway, silent until one of the bunny-suited techs brushed against me on his way out. I started to speak and had to clear my throat and try again, just to get the words out.

"Excuse me. I'm looking for Agent Keats?" I said to him. Even then, my voice sounded so small, so unlike me. I wasn't used to feeling this way, and I didn't like it one bit.

"Sorry, don't know who that is," the guy said, and kept moving. Somehow, I'd expected for everything to make sense here, and that I would know what to do as I went along. Instead, I was left standing there with a growing sense that I'd been dropped off in the wrong nightmare.

"Hoot, up here!" I heard, and turned to see one of my supervisors, Billy Keats, at the top of the stairs. Thank God.

He hurried down to meet me. "You ready for this?" he said, handing me a pair of latex gloves matching the ones he was already wearing. I put them on. His demeanor was all business, and his face was grim.

"I'm okay," I said.

"You don't look it."

"I'm okay," I repeated, as much for myself as for him. If I said it enough, maybe it would come true. And maybe my stomach would stop folding in on itself, over and over, the way it had been doing since I'd arrived. "Where do you need me?"

"This way." He led me up the carpeted stairs, briefing as we went. "We've got one of the victims' cell phones in a Faraday bag. They're just clearing the body now."

The body. Some person who had been alive yesterday, now just "the body."

But that other phrase—*Faraday bag*—was like a piece of driftwood, something I could latch on to in the middle of all this unfamiliarity. At least I knew what I was supposed to do with *that.* A Faraday bag blocks out any digital signals and preserves the device in question exactly as it was found until it can be forensically examined.

"Eventually, I'm going to want you to cover every machine in the house, but this phone is going to be your primary concern."

We passed two open bedroom doors along the upstairs hall. I told myself to keep my eyes straight ahead, but they didn't obey the impulse. Instead, I stole a glance into each room as we passed.

Through the first door, I saw something truly horrendous. A woman lay on her back on the king-size bed, eyes wide-open, with a small but unmistakable dark hole in her forehead. A halo of blood stained the pale-blue pillowcase under her hair. Outside of the few family wakes I'd been to, this was the first corpse I'd ever laid eyes on. The sight of it seemed to jump right into my long-term memory. No way I'd ever forget that moment, I knew right away.

As awful as that tiny moment had already been, it was the bunk beds in the next room that really split my heart down the middle. Each bunk held a covered body, draped with a white sheet. On the lower bunk, I could see one small hand sticking out, spiderwebbed with dark lines of dried blood, which had also pooled on the rug.

Jesus. This just got worse as it went along. The tightness from my stomach crawled up into my chest. I didn't want to throw up anymore: now I wanted to cry. These poor, poor people.

"Hoot? We're in here." I looked over to see Keats already standing outside the last door on the hall. He stepped back to make way for two EMTs rolling out a gurney with a black zippered body bag on top. Beyond them, I could see what looked like a teenage girl's room, with a floral comforter and an LSHS Warriors banner.

As I came closer and got a full look, one thing jumped out at me right away. I didn't see any blood. Not like with the others.

"What's her name?" I asked Keats, looking back at the gurney as they moved it down the hall. Somehow, I needed to know who she was.

"Gwen Petty," Keats said. "Mother Elaine, father Royce, and twin brothers Jake and Michael. But if anyone in this family had information we can use, it's going to be this girl."

I only nodded. There were no words. Or maybe there were too many, racing around inside my head. It was hard to know anything right now.

"Come on, then," Keats said. "Let's get you to work."

CHAPTER 3

"WHY ISN'T THERE any blood in here?" I asked as soon as we stepped into Gwen Petty's bedroom.

I always ask a lot of questions, especially if I'm nervous. Facts are always reassuring. And if I didn't know what I was doing, well, at least I could ask questions. Always that.

Keats ran a hand over his jaw like he was trying to decide how much to say.

"It looks like he shot the others, but our best guess in here is asphyxiation," he said.

"Jesus."

"Yeah. Whoever did this had strong feelings about Gwen, one way or another."

I could feel some kind of empathetic tightness in my chest. Did that mean Gwen Petty had been strangled? Something else? What were her last moments like?

I couldn't help the morbid thoughts cascading like lines of code through my mind. It was force of habit, in the worst possible way. So I tried to focus on the room instead—on what I could actually do.

I walked over to a built-in desk in the corner. A whole collage of photos was tucked into a crisscross of yellow ribbon on a gray fabric pin board. Another photo, framed on the desk, showed a family of five, smiling on the edge of what I guessed was the Grand Canyon. They all looked so happy.

"Is this them?" I asked.

"Yeah," Keats said.

"How recent?"

"Not important," he told me, and pointed at the Faraday bag on the floor by the bed. That meant Gwen's phone had already been physically fingerprinted and sequestered. Now it was time for the geek squad, a.k.a. me. All things considered, I was grateful for the distraction and listened carefully as Agent Keats went over my instructions.

"I want to know who she's been in contact with, what she's deleted, what someone else might have deleted—everything," Keats told me. "Specifically, I'm looking for texts or images that are romantic or sexual."

I stuck my hands through the mesh sleeves that would give me access to the phone inside.

"What is it, do you know?" I asked. "iPhone? Android?"

"iPhone 11," he said. "It was powered up when we got here."

That told me where the port would be and what kind of cable I'd need to run a copy of the whole thing without altering any files. I dropped a connector cable into the bag, ran it through the exit port, and plugged it into the field kit I'd brought from the office.

One thing I'll say for the FBI: they've got the best toys.

"Soon as you finish that, I want you in the mobile unit outside. Any other devices we find, we'll bring to you. But this phone is your priority."

"What's the hurry on the phone?" I asked. I assumed it had

something to do with the fact that Gwen Petty had died so differently than the rest of her family.

Instead of an answer, though, Keats only gave me a tight smile. "Listen, Angela. I know this is new for you, and I'm going to do my best to help you through," he said. "Part of that is knowing your role and sticking to it. These questions are only wasting time, and from an investigative standpoint, the clock is *always* ticking. Got it?"

I got it, all right. I really did. This wasn't about me, and I didn't need Keats treating me with kid gloves, either. If anything, I appreciated that he didn't.

I'd deal with the inhumanly sad thing that had happened here on my own time. Right now, the best thing I could do for Gwen Petty—and for that whole family—was to tighten my focus and IT the shit out of this assignment.

IF ANYONE HAD told me five months earlier that I'd be collecting evidence at this hideous scene, I never would have believed them. But five months earlier, almost to the day, was when it all got set in motion.

The day I was kicked out of MIT.

There we were—me, my mom, and my two little sisters, packing me out of the graduate apartments in Ashdown House on Albany Street, where I was no longer a registered student, and therefore no longer welcome.

"Is this yours?" Mom asked, holding up a ratty old MIT crew T-shirt.

"No," I said. "Leave it."

I jammed shoes into a box alongside an algorithm design textbook, the world's ugliest teddy bear, and a huge tangle of miscellaneous cables. I'm not the most organized person under the best of circumstances, much less as I was hurrying to get out from under the dark cloud that MIT—not to mention my mother—had hung over my head. I wanted to get away from there ASAP. I'd get myself organized when I unpacked later, at home.

"I don't understand, Angela," Mom said. "We've gone over it five times and I *still* don't know what happened here. How is that even possible?"

"Because Angela's being *evasive*," my youngest sister, Hannah, chimed in while I kept my head down and kept on stuffing things randomly into boxes.

"Good word," Mom said to Hannah, but with her eyes still on me. "And a good observation, too."

My other sister, Sylvie, was too busy trying on my roommate's perfume to get involved. Hannah was more like me, sticking her nose in whenever things got tense.

Mom pressed on. "What exactly did the disciplinary board charge you with? Can you at least tell me that much? I mean, seriously, sweetheart. What's with the cloak-and-dagger act?"

"Please don't worry about it," I said. "It's going to be fine."

"How can you be so calm? You got kicked out of MIT halfway through your first year, for God's sake."

I was actually only two months into a graduate master's program in Computation for Design and Optimization. But I thought it better not to point that out. The less we talked about it, the sooner I'd be out of there.

Then again, my mother doesn't tolerate being ignored any better than I do. I had to say *something*.

"I don't think this program was right for me," I told her.

"That's bull crap," Hannah blurted out. "You said this program was *made* for you."

"Yeah, exactly," I said. "As in, I could teach this stuff."

That part was true. I'm not an egotist, but I'm not afraid of facts, either.

The facts were that I'd been one of the three youngest people admitted to the Boston Mensa chapter when I was four years old. I'd graduated high school with a 4.5 GPA, and I'd sailed through my undergrad years at Carnegie Mellon. I hadn't been retested for IQ since I was twelve, but the number back then was 180 on the nose. That doesn't make me a better person, but it's not something I try to hide, either.

"So you get yourself thrown out?" Mom said. "This is the solution?"

I just looked at her. She knew it was more complicated than that, even if I wasn't sharing the particulars. I hated leaving Mom so far out of the loop. It was just that the alternative—going into all the gory details of my academic demise—was an even more embarrassing prospect. Maybe I could come a little cleaner after the smoke had been clear for a few days. But in the meantime, I was all about making the quickest possible exit.

And before I had to manufacture anything else to fill that increasingly uncomfortable silence, the door to the hall banged open. My suite mate, A.A. Wang, was standing there now, heaving for breath like she'd sprinted the length of MIT's famous Infinite Corridor.

"I just heard," she said. "What the f..." She trailed off with a flick of her eyes in Sylvie and Hannah's direction. "Hi, girls. Hi, Mrs. Hoot."

"A.A., thank God you're here," Mom said. "Could you please shed some light? My charming daughter seems to be suffering from some kind of selective amnesia."

"She doesn't know any more than you do," I lied. "Leave A.A. alone."

A.A.'s birth name is Melanie, but she's a gigantic Winnie-the-Pooh fan, which is also to say an A.A. Milne fan. She took the name for her own in second grade, and it just stuck. My sisters absolutely idolized her, from the tips of her tattooed eyeliner to the toes of her fabulous shoe collection. Truth be told, I idolized her a little myself.

"Why are you just standing in the hall?" Sylvie asked.

Which is when I got the signal that A.A. had been not so subtly sending my way.

"Mom?" I said. "Can you and the girls take these last boxes down? I'll bring my bike and meet you at the car."

Mom begrudgingly accepted the box I held out, but her eyes were still on A.A. "She tells you *anything*, you call me," she said.

"Yes, ma'am," A.A. answered. She and my mother were practically friends on their own, for better or worse. I loved them both to pieces. Just not always in the same room at the same time, when they could gang up on me.

"See you downstairs, *Lisa*," I tried, and hip-checked her toward the door.

"A mother cares," Mom said. "That's all I'm saying."

A.A. said her own good-byes then, but the smile she gave the girls never quite reached her eyes. She just waited until Mom, Sylvie, and Hannah had cleared out, then closed the door and turned to face me again.

Here it came.

"What the hell, Angela?" she said. "You just shot your own career in the head."

"I'll be fine," I said.

"And it's all my fault," A.A. went on.

"Wrong again," I said. "Nobody did this but me. And that asshole deserved everything he got. I regret nothing."

She looked hurt.

"You know what I mean," I said. "I'm going to miss the hell out of you, but I'll only be a few minutes away."

A.A. didn't answer. I guess I wasn't the only one who could

wield a strategic silence, because I was feeling guiltier by the second.

"Has he texted you?" I asked.

"Only about eighteen times," she said.

"And?"

"I didn't answer," she said.

"Good," I said. "Knowing him, it'll only take another thirty-two tries before he gets it."

"He's really pissed, you know," she said. "He had to replace his whole hard drive."

I could tell A.A. was fighting between tears and laughter at that point, but her face darkened when she met my eyes again. I stared back, waiting for the inquisition, part two.

"What's wrong with you, Angela?" she said. "Real question."

"Where should I start?" I asked, but A.A. didn't even crack a smile. "Nothing's wrong," I said. "I'm fine."

"No. You're not, and don't try to tell me you are," she shot back. "You're crazy like a rooster in a cage, and I don't get it."

A.A. knew me well. Sometimes too well. It's the cost of a real friendship. The whole thing was like a giant paradox, because everything really was fine, and everything really was a complete mess, all at the same time.

"I'll be fine," I insisted. "Just not today. Okay?"

"Angela—" she said before I kissed her. Not on the cheek. On the mouth, just to shut her up. It was either that or we were both going to start crying, and one of the many things A.A. and I shared was a complete distaste for cheap drama. So I kept things moving instead.

"I'll talk to you soon," I said. Then I grabbed my bike off the wall and wheeled it out the door.

"Hey!" she called after me. "You left your crew shirt."

"Keep it," I said just before the door swung shut behind me.

CHAPTER 5

THAT VERY EVENING, I was summoned to Eve Abajian's town house for what I could only assume would be a world-class dressing down. Eve was the person I most dreaded talking to about the MIT "situation," even worse than telling my parents. I didn't know how she'd already heard about it, but Eve always had a lot of ears to the ground.

"What in the blue hell, Angela?" she said over the intercom at her front door.

"I brought food!" I answered. Eve and I shared a certain obsession with the fried chicken and ginger waffles from Myers and Chang, not far from her place in South Boston. It was like bringing a water pistol to a gunfight, but it was all I had.

When I didn't get any answer, or even a buzz-in, I beeped myself through with the keypad and headed inside to face the music. I knew this had to happen, sooner or later. Emphasis on the *sooner*. Eve Abajian was not one to be kept waiting.

Eve was also the one who got me into MIT in the first place. I'd met her when I was sixteen, at the summer robotics program there, where she taught coding and applied theory as a volunteer instructor. Ever since, she'd been a mentor to me, steering me toward Carnegie Mellon and then putting in a strongest-possible word with the graduate admissions committee back at MIT after that.

In other words, everything Eve had spent the last six years helping me accomplish had just gotten rerouted straight down the toilet. I wasn't looking forward to this conversation.

As I came up and into the town house's main living space on the second floor, I saw that Eve was parked behind her four-screen array. I could barely see her for all the equipment, which was just as well. Even the sound of her keyboarding was angry.

I paused there, not really sure how to proceed. When the silence stretched on for an uncomfortably long time and I still wasn't sure what to say, I took the food into the kitchen and started plating it up. Maybe I could still ply Eve with a little sweet and salty deliciousness.

"Do you want to hear my side, or just yell at me first?" I called out from the safety of the galley kitchen.

"You know you could have had your pick of jobs in two years?" Eve said. "With a fat paycheck, too."

"Yeah, doing incident response for some Fortune 500 company," I said. "Making sure the employees at GE stay off the porn during the workday. No, thank you."

"Excuse me, but you don't get to be the smartest one in the room. Not tonight," she said. She still wouldn't even look at me when I glanced out toward her workspace. Another silence settled over us, and I was starting to feel genuinely guilty now.

But then, when Eve deigned to speak again, the conversation took an unexpected turn. In the best possible way.

"Lay off the garlic sauce with dinner," she said.

"Excuse me?" I said. We were both complete devotees of that garlicky concoction. "Why would I ever do that?"

"Because you have an interview tomorrow morning at eight thirty, and nobody wants to smell garlic at that hour," Eve said.

My mind spun, processing this new information, or at least trying to. Eve was one of the few people on the planet who always managed to stay a step or two ahead of me.

"What are you talking about?" I asked, loading two plates with a little of everything, one of them minus the sauce. "Where am I interviewing?"

As I carried the plates out to the living room, she sat back in her black Aeron chair and really met my eyes for the first time.

"At my office," she said.

"Your office?" I asked. "As in the Boston field office of the FBI?"

It was a dumb question, and she didn't bother to answer it.

"You'll be meeting Assistant Special Agent in Charge Billy Keats, and I'm not sure who else. But you need to be ready."

"Are you kidding?" I asked. Dumb question number two. It was just such a surprise. "I mean... wow. I mean..."

I didn't know what to say. It was a little early for any happy dances, but this was amazing news.

"What's the job?" I asked.

"It's not a job. It's an internship," she said.

"Paid?" I asked.

"Don't push it, but yes," Eve answered. "It's supposed to be reserved for active students, so you're welcome for that, too."

"Will I be working with you?" I asked. This was getting better by the second.

"I'm only there a few more weeks before Guatemala. Then I go out on maternity," she said.

Eve was waiting on the birth of a little girl in Guatemala City, through an international adoption agency out of Phoenix. Within the month, she was going to be a first-time mom. I guess when she didn't meet Mr. Right On Time, she did what people like us always do: she hacked a solution.

It seemed safe enough to approach the rest of the way now. I finally put a plate of chicken and waffles in front of her and sat with my own in one of the guest chairs.

"Why are you doing this for me?" I asked.

"I'm not doing it *for* you," she said. "This is to make sure that ridiculous brain of yours gets put to good use in the world. And I don't mean making lattes at Starbucks."

I smiled around a bite of waffle. Eve's praise was like gold: valuable and rare. She's not the touchy-feely, hug-it-out type, but neither am I. It was embarrassing, how much I wanted to be exactly like her.

"Thank you, Eve," I said. "Really."

"You can thank me by not screwing it up," she said. "This is your last favor, and probably one more than you deserve."

"So, you're saying I have to *settle* for a spot at the FBI?" I asked, still grinning in spite of myself.

"I'm *saying* I got you in the door," she told me. "But you're starting somewhere back of square one. Disciplinary action at MIT doesn't exactly bolster your application."

"I've got this," I said.

She didn't contradict me, and I looked down at my food just to keep from showing her how freaking excited I was already. I think I still owed her a little back payment of contrition, but that could come later.

"What exactly am I going to be doing, anyway?" I asked.

Eve went back to her keyboarding.

"Probably just basic penetration testing to start," she said. "But mark my words, Angela. You play your cards right at the Bureau, and things could get very interesting for someone like you, very fast."

CHAPTER 6

WITHIN AN HOUR of arriving at the scene of the Petty murders, I was holed up in the Mobile Forensic Laboratory, or the M-LAB, parked on the curb. It's just a big white van on the outside, but inside it's a state-of-the-art facility.

I was still getting used to the whole "Angela Hoot at the FBI" role. Part of me was waiting for one of the "real" grown-ups to open the van door and shoo me out of there. But in the meantime, I'd get down to work.

I started with a basic search, looking at incoming and outgoing calls, texts, and saved images on my copy of Gwen Petty's phone. I also checked her contact list, bookmarks, and surfing history, but it didn't turn up anything relevant.

The next step was a full physical extraction of any hidden, deleted, or corrupted files on the operating system. That was going to take a significantly longer time than the first pass, but it was also an automated process, which meant I could start multitasking my way through this.

Once I got that scan going, I set aside the phone and did a

basic social media analysis on Gwen. That's where I could really start to get an idea of who she was. Or at least what kind of tracks she'd left behind.

The email associated with her phone turned up active accounts on Snapchat, Instagram, Facebook, Kik, and Pinterest. Besides the usual selfies, I saw a lot of the same friends in her photos—on the bus to a field hockey game, on the beach at the Cape, dressed up for prom. There was no boyfriend, as far as I could tell, except for a guy who showed up in a spate of tagged photos from the previous summer, a kid named Drew Pintone. I stared at his picture for a long time. Could this ordinary-looking kid be the monster we were looking for? It seemed pretty unlikely. Then again, so did everything that had happened in the Petty home that night. I wrote the boy's name down for Keats, in any case, and pressed on.

It was a shitty feeling, going through all of Gwen's stuff like this. I understood the necessity, but what teenage girl wants her private life pried open for the world to see? I couldn't change what had happened. In fact, I reminded myself over and over, I was at least helping to do something about it. But still, I felt racked with guilt and finally let myself cry for a few minutes. Right up until Keats came out to check on me.

"What have we got so far?" he asked. I had my back to him at first and made a quick swipe at my face before I turned around. If he noticed my red eyes, he didn't say so.

I gave Keats a quick lowdown and explained that it was going to be several hours before I'd have a full finished scan of Gwen's phone. I also told him about Drew Pintone, just in case.

"Yeah, we know about that kid," Keats said. "He's a nonstarter, been living in Michigan since September. What we're actually looking for is an adult male. Someone at least in his twenties, if not older."

"Does that mean you have a suspect?" I asked.

"Don't worry about that," he said.

But my brain was already spinning around this new piece of information. There had to be a reason Keats knew something about who he was looking for. And in fact, I realized, it was probably what had brought the FBI—federal authorities—to this crime scene in the first place.

"This isn't the first case, is it?" I asked.

I couldn't tell if Keats was annoyed, impressed, or both. But he nodded.

"Binghamton, Albany, and now here," he said.

Even as the words came out of his mouth, the gravity of the situation registered in my gut. This meant more murders. More dead families. And maybe more to come, too.

"Angela?" Keats's voice pulled me back, and I looked up again. "Eve said she thought you could handle this. It's your call, but you should tell me now if you can't."

Out of respect for the Petty family, I didn't give a knee-jerk "*I'm* fine" in response. I really did think about it and took my time answering.

"I can do this," I said. "Also, I want to."

"Good," he said, and turned to leave.

"Did you say Eve recommended me?" I asked before he could slip out of the mobile unit. I'd suspected Eve had put in a good word after my interview, but it was nice to get the confirmation.

"Don't let your head get too big," Keats said. "She also told me you had a checkered history at MIT." I could tell he was trying to lighten things up by getting a rise out of me. I appreciated it.

"And you still trust me?" I asked, half joking.

"I trust Eve," he said in all seriousness, and I could tell the moment of levity had passed.

In other words, I was still proving myself here. Not that I minded. I was just glad to know where I stood.

It was time to get back to work.

CHAPTER 7

BY THE END of the day, I'd finished everything there was to do at the Petty home in Lincoln and leapfrogged back to my little gray cubicle in the field office downtown. There was still a mountain of work to do, given all the electronics they'd pulled out of the Petty home, and I threw myself into it. Day stretched into night. And night stretched into late night.

I wasn't naive about the work they did at the FBI. But even so, I felt like I was staring into some unknowably dark abyss. What sort of monster killed entire families?

The whole thing made me want to call my mom, like I was a homesick college freshman all over again. It was probably just as well that it was one in the morning by then. So instead I called A.A., who I knew had Red Bull running through her veins.

Sure enough, she answered on the first ring.

"What's up, Piglet?"

"Hey, Pooh Bear," I said.

She was always Pooh, and I was whoever else, depending on her mood, or mine. Piglet for general bestie status, Eeyore when

I was being cynical, Owl when I was smart—that kind of thing. It was embarrassingly juvenile, but it was just between us.

"I'm still at the office," I said.

"Damn, Angela, I can't believe it. You sure landed on your feet. How's it going over at the Fun Bun Institute?"

"It's fine," I said.

"Just fine?"

I didn't want to talk about work. I didn't want to talk about me at all. The whole point of this call was to get out of my head for a few minutes. Or at least to try.

"How are you doing?" I asked. "Did Darren finally drop off the face of the earth?"

"Not exactly," she said. "He showed up drunk in the lobby the other night, with all kinds of blah-blah-blah about how he's changed."

"Right," I said. "Because he's so evolved. Please tell me you called security."

"He's harmless," she said.

"Harmless? He posted naked-ass pictures of you after you broke up with him!" I sputtered.

"And you took care of that," she said. "You're my little fairy godhacker."

"I just gave him the rope. He hung himself," I said. "Seriously, any MIT student who opens a supposed hot-wings coupon from an unknown source doesn't deserve to set foot on that campus."

The "coupon" I sent Darren had been a little home-brewed bit of malware for his laptop. It installed a keystroke logger and then broadcast his entire online life to the MIT student body and faculty—every message, every email, every disgusting little porn site he ever visited.

In a creative flourish just for myself, I'd named the program Sorry/Not Sorry. Not that he'd ever figure that out.

A.A. and I were both laughing now. It felt good to slip back into my old life for a few minutes.

"He still hates your guts, you know," she told me.

"And he still hasn't learned his lesson," I said.

He really hadn't, apparently. Not if he was still coming around drunk, after everything else that had gone down. So while A.A. and I kept on talking, I got online and sent Darren a little more rope.

His laptop wouldn't be vulnerable anymore, but any hacker worth her salt knows the value of a good backup. In this case, it was Darren's beloved Android. I'd parked a little of my handiwork on there months earlier, one morning while he was in the bathroom using up all our hot water. Then I'd just left it dormant, waiting for the right rainy day.

All it took was a quick update order and I was done. Now, the next time he turned on his phone, it was going to be frozen with a message emblazoned across the lock screen: "Darren Wendt is a boil on the ass of humanity." And it was going to stay that way, even when he took it to the Verizon store to get his unfixable phone fixed.

Sorry, Darren.

Not sorry.

Maybe I overreacted. Maybe it was some kind of displaced anger after everything I'd been through that day, and after what had happened to Gwen Petty's family.

But here's the thing about all that: I didn't care. Some people just don't know when to quit. Which is maybe the one thing in the world that Darren Wendt and I had in common.

CHAPTER 8

ABOUT AN HOUR after my call with A.A., I got a notification that my full scan on Gwen Petty's phone was finally done. What I had in front of me now was a list of hundreds of recovered files. But when I organized them by type, one thing jumped out. That's when the red flags started popping. I didn't need to cry anymore—I was on fire with this thing.

I was looking at a grouping of thirty-one encrypted items with a three-letter extension I'd never seen before: .glp. A quick google confirmed what I already suspected: that there was no such file type. And then it hit me.

I texted Keats right away. What is Gwen Petty's middle name?

Hang on, he came right back. And then, Louisa. Why?

Gwendolyn Louisa Petty. GLP. That was why.

Uploading files right now, I answered.

I hopped onto my terminal and posted all thirty-one to the case agent review network, flagged for Keats. He'd get a text about it in seconds, and if he was near a secure computer, he could have a look.

One thing had become clear by now. This killer either was or was working with someone who had high-level coding experience, enough to engineer their own unique file type. And to name it after their victim, too.

I couldn't help getting a little excited about the possibilities here. Already, I felt some kind of attachment to Gwen Petty. It wasn't like I knew her, but she wasn't a stranger to me anymore, either. And with any luck, I'd just taken one tiny step toward finding the sick son of a bitch who had killed her and her family. I hoped so, anyway.

When my phone rang a second later, I jumped.

"Angela Hoot."

"What the hell am I looking at?" Keats asked on the other end. My guess was he'd skipped past the file names and had a bunch of encrypted gibberish on the screen in front of him. So I explained about the file extension and got a long silence in return.

"Can you decrypt these?" he finally asked.

"Not yet," I said. "But if it's a unique file type and Gwen opened them, then there has to be a corresponding application to do that. I just haven't found it yet."

"Haven't you been all over that phone already?" he asked.

"Yes and no. I've never seen anything like this," I said. "I need to go back and strip it down, file by file."

"All right," he said. "Log out for now and we can pick this up tomorrow."

I looked at the clock. Two thirty. It already was tomorrow. "I'm just going to do one more pass on this thing—"

"Go home, Hoot," he told me. "I'll see you in the morning."

I got a click after that instead of a good-bye. Just as well, I thought. I wasn't going to say no to Keats. He was my superior, after all. But I didn't have any intention of going home, either. How do you go home when you're on fire?

Answer: You don't.

CHAPTER 9

"ANGELA, WAKE UP."

Nothing made any sense at first. For a second, I thought I was back in my apartment at MIT with A.A. But it wasn't a woman's voice I was hearing. It was Billy Keats.

"Angela!"

I lifted my head and felt the keyboard peel away from my cheek.

"What time is it?" I asked.

"Seven thirty," Keats said. "I told you to go home five hours ago."

I sat up fully now, trying to tongue the nasty taste out of my mouth. Embarrassingly, fried rice from a spilled container was spread across my desk.

"Shit!" I clumsily scooped the rice back into the container with my hand, spilling some of it onto the floor while I tried to shake the last of the cobwebs out of my head.

Keats didn't even try to hide his laugh. "You know, you don't have to work so hard to impress me," he said.

"I'm not," I said. "This is just me."

"Well, whoever you are, good get on those file extensions last night. I went back and checked the previous cases. There's nothing like this on any of them."

What was he saying? My face flushed at the thought that I'd jumped the gun and seen something that wasn't there.

"So, it's just a coincidence with Gwen Petty's initials?" I asked.

"No. More like the opposite," Keats said. "I think whoever's doing this is getting better at it. That's not good news, but it's good to know, anyway."

In other words, those .glp files really were a custom job—an upgrade to whatever digital trap this killer might have set for his previous victims. Which also raised the even more troubling question: where was all of this headed next?

I was awake now, for sure. *Wide* awake.

"I just need a minute," I said. "I'll hit the bathroom sink and be right back."

"Good-bye, Angela," Keats said. He started walking backward toward his own office and pointed me to the exit. "Believe it or not, the FBI will still be up and running when you get back. I'll see you in eight hours."

"Four," I said. "I already had half a night's sleep right here."

"Fine." He threw up his hands in surrender. "But don't come back dragging."

"I won't," I said. "Some of us just don't need as much sleep as you old guys."

"Shut up and go home," he said, but he smiled, too.

Keats never let anyone forget that he was one of only two agents in the Northeast to make ASAC before they were thirty. So it was fun to take him down a notch or two about his age.

I didn't mean to flirt, exactly. Or at least there was no endgame in mind. It was more like office-banter-as-smoke-screen, to help me avoid being completely intimidated. It's not like I was gearing up to ask him out or anything like that. I didn't even know if that was allowed.

But I will say this much. If Billy "Not the Poet" Keats had looked at me with those pale-blue Paul Newman eyes of his that morning and asked if I had dinner plans for Friday night, I knew exactly what my answer would have been.

I DIDN'T NEED rest. What I needed was some off-grid time.

They say Einstein came up with his theory of relativity while riding a bike. And I say if it's good enough for the father of modern physics, it's good enough for me.

That's why I keep my Giant Talon locked in the back of my car. The more thinking I need to do, the more I want to get out and hit the trail, which is surprisingly easy to do in Boston. It's only ten miles from downtown to Blue Hills Reservation. I'd been known to squeeze in a ride in one hour—much less than the four hours for which Keats had barred me from the office.

By eight thirty that morning, I had a venti dark roast in me, half a pack of wintergreen Life Savers saving my breath, and a deserted parking lot at the Blue Hills trailhead. That meant I'd have the place to myself. I pulled my bike out of the back of the car, jumped on, and headed into the woods.

By the time I was pumping my way up the first leg of Tucker Hill Path, everything I'd learned in the last twenty-four hours had started clamoring for attention in my mind all over again.

It wasn't easy to shake off what I'd seen up to now, starting with the crime scene I'd witnessed. They certainly don't set you up for that kind of thing at MIT.

Still, I knew I had a choice. I could wallow in the sadness and the grotesquerie or I could focus on solutions, and when I thought of it that way, it was a complete no-brainer.

I settled into an easy pedaling cadence and tried to focus.

Keats said he was looking for an older male, but I didn't see why this couldn't have been two people, or even more, operating together. Hackers work in unofficial dark net communities all the time. They're competitive, too, with one another, but also with themselves. It's always about doing better than, doing more than, reaching further than they did the last time around.

They just don't usually kill people.

So what was I missing here? Where was that app on Gwen Petty's phone? And how the hell did these assholes hide it so well? I had no idea, but one thing was for sure. I wasn't going to roll over on this. It was my first real job and the stakes couldn't have been higher.

Besides, like I said, hackers tend to be more than a little competitive, whether they're wearing black hats or white. There was no way I'd be letting this thing get the best of me.

I shot straight through the next juncture and into an uphill climb. The ground was steadily rising in front of me, and the sweat was building at the small of my back. I could feel the slope in my quads and glutes with the kind of burn I love to hate. There was a lot more hill to go, but it would be worth it when I was flying down the other side.

As I worked it just a little harder, another question presented itself in my mind, out of nowhere. Was I *meant* to find those .glp files? Anyone capable of engineering something like that could have easily initiated a remote wipe on Gwen's phone. But they hadn't. They left the files in place. Not only that, but whoever put them there knew that someone like me—someone smart enough to admire their handiwork—was going to find this stuff. Maybe they were just showing off at that point.

Yeah, well, mission accomplished, douchebag. I'm impressed. And I can't wait to see you crash and burn.

I'd done two circuits of the outer loops on either side of Houghton's Pond by now. So I headed in a new direction, up the Breakneck Ledge path, the closest thing they have to a black diamond out there.

My glutes were toast and my calves felt like rods, but I barely noticed anymore. And I didn't slow down, either. I was weirdly pumped, all things considered. Physical exhaustion aside, my mind was lit up like a pinball machine as I flew up and over the crest of that ridge just a little too fast. By the time I even realized my back tire was sliding out from under me, it was too late.

I turned hard into the slope, trying to regain control of the bike. My front tire hit a thick root that I hadn't seen coming, and it stopped me cold. The bike flipped straight forward. I went over the handlebars as it did and came down hard on both palms while my ride rolled right over me. My body kept going and I slid a few more yards on my stomach before I finally came to a clumsy stop against an ash tree on the hillside. It hurt, but probably looked worse than it was.

Still, that seemed as good a time as any to head back. I had a bloody shin from where my pedal had sheared off a layer of skin, and a fine sheen of dirt and sweat was covering me pretty much everywhere else. If I wanted to show up at work looking like a human being, I was going to need more than a bathroom sink now.

The good news was, I still had plenty of time to kill. More

than I'd need for getting cleaned up. If I played it right, I could grab a shower, make some progress on the questions flying around my mind, all in one stop, and still be back at my desk the minute my four-hour banishment was over.

What can I say? I'm nothing if not efficient.

CHAPTER 11

I PARKED OUTSIDE Eve's place on East Broadway and let myself in with the keypad. Eve's place was only a few miles from the office, while my own apartment was way out in Somerville, which was as much as I could afford after MIT. Mom and Dad had barely gone through the motions of inviting me to move back home. They knew I'd never go for it.

Eve was in the nursery when I came in, rocking Marlena to sleep in the hand-painted chair my parents had given her as a baby gift.

"How's it going?" I whispered.

"Still waiting for the hard part," Eve whispered back. She'd been deliriously happy about the whole motherhood thing since the day she'd come home from Guatemala. I'd already begun to wonder if she was ever coming back to work. But I couldn't imagine Eve *not* working, and I don't know if she could, either. It's like she has code running through her veins instead of blood.

Marlena was adorable, of course, but as for me and babies?

Not so much. I was looking forward to bonding with her as soon as she was ready to talk about space camp, or gaming platforms, or the infinite pleasures of solid food. In the meantime, I made myself generally scarce when it was time for holding her for a while, or feeding her, or God forbid changing her.

So I grabbed a quick shower in the guest bath. Borrowing a fresh shirt, I threw on my previous day's suit and found Eve at her big glass desk with the baby monitor next to her.

"I got a peek at your .glp files," she said, waggling a phone I didn't recognize. "Come take a look at this."

Who else but Eve kept a supply of iPhone and Android burners at home, much less with access to FBI case files? She'd already loaded a copy of Gwen Petty's operating system onto an actual handset.

"What am I looking at?" I said while she swiped from one screen to the next, back and forth, back and forth.

"Look at the lower right corner," Eve said, and swiped again, left, right, left, right. "You see that tiny refraction when I change the screen?"

"No," I said.

"Here." She gave me the phone, and I tried it myself. That's when I finally saw it, just a slight ripple, like that corner of the phone's wallpaper went watery as I swiped in and out.

"Wait, what?" I said. "No way."

"I think so," she said.

It was an invisible button, or at least it seemed to be. I put my finger on that spot and held it there, waiting to see if anything would happen. And then sure enough, after about five seconds, the screen opened up into an app I'd never seen before.

The interface itself wasn't fancy, or even particularly well designed. It looked like a simple chat program, as far as I could tell. There were icons to access the camera; the keyboard, which was rudimentary compared to most current standards; and a Send button. That was it. The amazing part was how well it had hidden itself, not just on the phone's screen but in the operating system.

"I don't get it," I said. "Where are they keeping the files for this?"

"We'll find out," Eve said. "But sometimes, Angela, you've got to look up from the files. It's not always about the code."

A little wave of anger passed over me. Frankly, I wasn't used to being outsmarted.

"Should I even be on here?" I asked. It was a little late for that question, but Eve shook her head.

"It's fine. That handset's cloaked. You can't even go online," she said. "And I'll wipe it as soon as we're done."

That was easy enough for her to say. She was Eve Abajian, as in *the* Eve Abajian, FBI superhero. I was still just Angela Hoot, lowly intern. My security clearance couldn't even touch Eve's.

Not that I was going to say no to any of this. If Eve was comfortable sharing it with me, that's all I needed to know.

I looked down at the phone screen again. There was no chat history, or even a way to access one that I could tell.

"What about the .glp files?" I asked.

"Try refreshing," she said, and hit two keys on her keyboard. "Now."

I closed and reopened the app. When I did, it was suddenly populated with thirty-one new messages.

"Just like that?" I asked.

"Yeah, but if it's this easy, it means they wanted you to find them," Eve said, echoing my own thought. "Don't ever forget that. It's a completely different premise. They could have squirreled these away much more deeply if they'd wanted to."

"They're putting on some kind of show," I said.

"Exactly," she said.

The problem was, everything had been scrubbed clean. There were no date stamps, no metadata to trace back the files, and certainly no forensic watermarking. All we had to go on was what we could see.

The files turned out to be a combination of images and text. The images were clear enough. There were no faces, but a lot of body parts. Some of them were coy—an open blouse, an unbuttoned pair of jeans—but it got more explicit from there.

The rest were text fragments, from what seemed to be an ongoing conversation. Or a seduction, I guess. It was horrifying to read through, knowing what was waiting for Gwen Petty at the end of it all.

The texts were also arranged in what seemed like a random order and chopped up into pieces. There was no way to know what *wasn't* there, or how much of the conversation we were missing. Any number of other files could have been overwritten since they were deleted, in which case we'd never get them back.

Or maybe they'd been deliberately left off by the killer, excising anything that might reveal more than he wanted us to know. I had no idea yet how much control the app's administrator had over the content, or even the devices that people used to access it.

All we could do for now was work with what we had. So while Eve called Keats to catch him up, I printed everything out in hard copy and spread it across her dining room table. Then we started moving the pieces around, trying to guess at an order, make connections, and hopefully start to pull this whole puzzle together.

Please tell me you don't actually watch that crap.

It's a good show.

Yeah—on MARS.

It's a good show EVERYWHERE.

Goodbye.
Nice knowing you.

Very funny

Do YOU think you're pretty?

Honestly, I don't know.

I know I'm not ugly but...

I bet you're beautiful.

What about you?
Do you think you're good looking?

Can I tell you the truth?

Of course.

Then yeah. I think I'm good looking.
Can I send you a pic?

Is your name really Beth?

No... ☺ Is your name really Rob?

No. Do you want to know my real name?

Not yet

That's ok. Besides, BETH IS WAY HOT.

Thanks, so is Rob.
Hope you don't mind
It's just good to be careful.

Your parents would be so proud.

Shut up.

I'm serious.

Keep shutting up.

☺

Where were we?

You were asking me to unbutton my shirt.
Next question?

Tell me something I don't know about you.

That's easy.
You don't know anything about me.

I know you call yourself Beth.
I know your personality is f-ing hot.
I know you were adventurous enough to find me here.

I also make really good burritos.

Okay then.
That's just about everything, isn't it? ☺

I'm also not wearing any underwear right now

I stand corrected.

Hold on.
I better lock my door before we go any farther here.

Good idea
You don't want your brothers walking in on this, haha.

??
How do you know I have brothers?

You told me.

I did?

Did you get the pic?

Yeah, and . . . !!!!
Is that really you?

Your turn.
Show me something I haven't seen before.

You are so GREEDY!

What's your point?

Okay fine.

Nice!!

Do you even know how beautiful you are?

You can't even see my face.

I don't need to.

You're sweet

You too

I really want to meet you sometime

Go on. What else?

I'm going to take my time.

I'm going to make you wait.

I'm going to make you take your time, too.

Do you want me to touch myself now?

Yes.

Good, bc I already am.

Do you think about me when you . . . you know?

By yourself?

Are you kidding? Every time.

Does this help?

Save it for later.

RU kidding??? NOT saving for later.

God, you're so f-ing hot. No lie.

Can I see your face?

Pls????

First I want you to get hard.

And then?

Show me.

And then?

We'll see.

Me too! I love that stuff. Can't get enough.

Now you're just saying that.

I'm not. Swear.

Have you been looking at my Snapchat?

How could I see your Snapchat?

I don't even know your name

Good point.

FWIW, I'm T.J.

Wow. Really?

For real.

Hi T.J. for real.

You don't have to tell me yours if you don't want.

It's okay
I'm Gwen.

I lay you down on your own bed
I ask you if I should keep going and you say yes
You feel me, grinding against your thigh as I kiss your neck

Wow
Don't stop.

I won't
This is only the beginning, Gwen
We have to meet
Sooner or later
Don't you think?

---

yes is a world
& in this world of

yes live
(skillfully curled)
all worlds

Did you just write that?

EE Cummings

Beautiful

Like you.
Say yes, Gwen.
Pls?

I can't.
Not tonight.

Please? Why not?

Parents here. So are my brothers.

I can be quiet.
Let me just come to your window.
One kiss and I'll go
Swear.

You don't even know where my window is

95 Geary Lane?

??????

It's called the internet.

You are so bad!

Is that a yes?

I don't know.

I'm coming over unless you say no
You still there?

Oh god
Are we really going to do this?

Ha. See you soon.
You won't regret it
xo

CHAPTER 13

"I HAVE TWO pieces of advice," Eve said as I was getting ready to leave. "When you're back to the office, I want you to take the credit for finding this app."

I shrugged on my jacket. "Won't they take me more seriously if I say it came from you?" I asked.

"Maybe at first," she said. "But it's still a boys' game at the Bureau, and it's time for you to start playing. We have to watch out for each other."

I was struck by the word *we*. Maybe I wasn't Eve's professional equal—not yet—but I was her colleague now. Which was amazing. It felt like just yesterday she had been walking little sixteen-year-old me through the very basics of robotics, and maybe five minutes ago she had been writing me a recommendation for grad school.

Now here I was working alongside her for the FBI. It hadn't stopped being surreal yet.

Even so, the idea of taking credit for something I didn't do sat on the wrong side of my gut. She was the one who discovered the app, not me.

"Isn't that just lying?" I asked.

"Oh, please." Eve shifted the baby from one hip to the other as we walked to the front door. "Would you have eventually found it on your own?"

"Of course," I said.

"Of course you would have," she said. "So take the damn credit and move on. There are a lot of ways you have to prioritize the bigger picture in this work, Angela. This is just one of them."

I knew she was probably right. I'd just have to wrap my mind around it. What a strange feeling, too. I'd been facing down all kinds of competition at MIT. But somehow, toggling that killer instinct over to the real, professional world was less instinctive for me than I would have thought.

Hello, adulting.

"You said there were two pieces of advice?" I said.

"Yeah," she said. "Now that you're really in this, you need to remember: don't ever let the work get personal."

That wasn't what I was expecting to hear. "Which part of the work do you mean?" I asked.

"All of it," she said. "The case. The murders. The lives that were stolen from people whose memory you're now in charge of protecting. It's very easy to feel like you're letting someone down if an investigation doesn't go the way it should. But you can't take that path. Don't even think about it. You'll burn out, faster than you can possibly imagine."

It was like every time I talked to Eve I got another new way of thinking about all this.

"Just for the record," I said. "What makes you think I'd take any of that personally?"

"Because I know you. I know how you get when someone you care about is attacked," she said, making a not so subtle jab about what had happened with A.A. "I also know that Gwen was the same age as your sister," she added.

That wasn't off base, either. Sylvie had crossed my mind about a hundred different ways since the night I'd stood in that room where Gwen Petty was asphyxiated. It was impossible not to imagine my own personal nightmare coming true after I'd seen it happen to someone else, firsthand. I shuddered at the echo of it all as it passed through my mind again.

Eve touched me on the shoulder, pulling me out of my thoughts. "This work will drag you down if you let it, Angela," she said. "Don't let it."

"Okay, but how?" I said. "All you ever hear is 'Suck it up,' but nobody ever tells you how to actually do that."

"You've got to look at your own stuff," she said. "Not that you'll hear this from any of the guys, but that's what makes us better at it. Take stock. Be ready for whatever's going to get the best of you *before* it takes you by surprise."

This wasn't just idle conversation, I knew. What happened to the Pettys and the two families before them could easily happen again. In fact, it probably would if the Bureau didn't work fast enough, or smart enough.

And that meant me, too, now.

"I'm handling it," I told her. She gave me a skeptical look. I gave back a little kiss on Marlena's cheek. *"Really,"* I said on my way out the door.

And I was. Barely.

But handling it all the same.

CHAPTER 14

THE NEXT MORNING, I went with Billy Keats to Lincoln-Sudbury High School, where Gwen Petty had been a student. I was a little surprised that he'd invited me, but maybe that meant I was doing a good job.

It didn't hurt that I'd taken Eve's advice. I wasn't crazy about claiming credit for that app, but I trusted her gut about how to play the game. And either way, it bought me some time alone in the car with Keats's undivided attention. As usual, I had an overabundance of questions.

"Can I just pose a theory to you, and you can tell me why it's wrong?" I asked.

"Sure," Keats said. He was nodding his head to an old Breaking Benjamin track on the stereo. You could tell he'd been a metalhead, once upon a time, but he sure cleaned up well.

"What if this isn't just one or two people, but some kind of network?" I said.

He gave it a beat and thought about it for a second, which I took as a good sign. It's amazing how many men in positions of power are threatened by smart women. I wouldn't have been shocked if he'd dismissed the theory out of hand—but he didn't.

"Go on," he said.

Even better. He wanted to know more.

"Well, here's the thing. Hackers work in collectives all the time," I said. "The price of admission is usually some kind of showboat move. Something to prove your skills. Maybe in this case, that means getting a new target to load the app on her phone. Or maybe even a murder."

"Sure," Keats said, a little more noncommittally now. "It's all on the table."

Fair enough, I thought. I hadn't proved anything.

"Does that mean you're looking for other cases like these?" I asked. "Because I was wondering if I might be able to get a look at those files—"

He stopped me with a flash of eye contact that read like a perimeter alert. Apparently, I was treading into questions above my pay grade—not about the case itself, but about how far into it I might be allowed.

"Okay, okay, I get it," I said, and went back to reading the file on my lap. There was plenty to absorb in there, anyway.

"For what it's worth, I'd be asking the same things," Keats told me. That was good to hear, but it didn't stop my mind from crawling with curiosity. What was there to know about these other families who had been killed? What kind of digital signature had—or hadn't—been left behind in those cases?

And meanwhile—

"One more question," I said. "Can I ask why you brought me along this morning?"

Billy reached over and flipped off the stereo. We were just pulling into the high school parking lot.

"You're closer to Gwen Petty's age than anyone else on this team," he told me. "Who knows? Maybe you'll see this place in a way that I wouldn't. But that's all you're coming to do. *Watch and listen.* Understand?"

"Aye, aye, captain," I said.

Basically, I was down with anything that kept me involved in this case. I'd give it my best shot, anyway. Keeping my eyes open was no problem.

As for keeping my mouth shut? Not exactly my strong suit.

CHAPTER 15

WALKING INTO THAT high school was like some kind of eerie flashback. Even the smell of floor cleaner mixed with cafeteria food took me back to those four awkward years I'd spent waiting to go to college.

We followed signs to the main office, where you could feel the quiet pall that had come over the place. Evidently, everyone was still in shock about the Petty murders.

A sense of not belonging settled over me as we passed through the halls. My own uncomfortable memories of high school started swirling in with the fresher images in my head from that horrendous quintuple homicide crime scene. I wasn't sure what to make of it all, but when I realized I'd slowed down enough to fall behind, I hurried to catch Keats and followed him into the main office.

The principal, Vic Oppel, was waiting for us when we came in. He was a strange bird right off the bat. Not suspicious, but not very generous with the eye contact, either. He looked at my shoes when we shook hands.

"I'd be happy to answer any questions," he told us. "But I'm sure our head guidance counselor will be more useful. She knew Gwen quite well."

He gestured us back out of the office and we started walking up the hall. I didn't see anyone going through the usual paces. There was nobody lingering around the bathrooms. No one sitting in the hall scribbling some last-minute assignment. No real signs of everyday high school life-as-usual—at all. It felt more like a funeral home, and something told me it wasn't just about the fact that Gwen Petty and her family had died. It was very much about the way in which it had happened.

Weirdly enough, the exception to that was Mr. Oppel himself. Whatever he might or might not have been feeling, he was self-contained on the outside, to say the least.

"Can you tell me a little about Gwen from your own perspective?" Keats asked. "Whatever you know about her."

"She was an excellent student," he answered. "Three point four grade point average. President of the math club. Band, orchestra, model UN. Quite popular, I'm told."

It was all dry facts, like he knew the gravity of the situation but the emotion of it was beyond him. I couldn't tell if he was just geeky-awkward, or maybe even a little bit on the spectrum. Either way, it made me like him more. I have a soft spot for geeks.

Oppel answered more of Keats's questions as he gave us a factoid-filled tour of Gwen's classrooms, eventually coming around to her locker, where we stopped to take things in.

A folding table in the hall was overflowing with flowers, stuffed animals, and sympathy cards. Two electric votives flickered softly. And the locker door itself was covered with little messages, all written in silver or gold Sharpie.

Love you, Gwennie.
Gone but never forgotten.
My heart is broken, xoxo.

"The response has been somewhat difficult to manage," Oppel said. "As you can see."

He may have been talking about the students' grief, but he could have just as well been talking about this roadblock of a memorial sitting in the hall. I thought it was beautiful, in its own way, and fought back the lump in my throat.

"It's quite something," Keats said in a husky voice. When I looked over, I was shocked to see tears rimming his eyes. He pinched them away with a swipe. "Sorry," he said.

"Don't be," I told him. If anything, I was relieved. It was the first indication I'd gotten so far that I wasn't the only one struggling with this case. It also told me that Gwen Petty's memory was in good hands with Billy. Even more than I'd realized. I had no doubt that he was excellent at his job, but this little glimpse of humanity only made him better, in my eyes. I thought about what Eve had said, about the way men worked differently from women at the Bureau, and I thought, *Well, yes and no.*

"The guidance office is just down here," Mr. Oppel said, pulling me out of my own thoughts. I started to follow, but Keats put himself in my way. He stared at me just long enough to lock in my attention.

"I've got this," he said. "Maybe you want to go grab a cup of coffee in the cafeteria or something."

He didn't owe me any explanation, and I didn't get one, but it pissed me off all the same. Just when I thought I was going to be sitting in on those interviews, I'd gotten shunted off to the side.

It reminded me of freshman year soccer, getting to suit up

for a varsity game and then spending the whole night on the bench. I understood. But still, the bench sucks.

"No problem," I said, staring back at Keats but keeping it professionally vanilla for Oppel's sake. "Just text me when you're done."

It wasn't until the two of them had disappeared around the corner that I even considered the alternative. Maybe Keats was trying to tell me something. Maybe *this* was the real watch-and-listen part, while he was off doing something else.

Or maybe that was just wishful thinking. I had no real way of knowing, so I went with the answer I preferred.

A second later, I turned around and headed off in the opposite direction to go exploring.

CHAPTER 16

I DIDN'T GET to shadow Keats the way I wanted, but I didn't leave that high school empty-handed, either.

After I'd picked up a truly bad cup of "coffee" from the cafeteria, I went back to Gwen's locker. A small group of girls had gathered there. They were holding hands, their heads down. It looked like some kind of prayer circle, but then one of them saw me and smiled through teary eyes.

"It's okay," she said, and let go of her neighbor's hand to make room for me.

On the other side of the circle, I recognized Kallie Sawyer. Kallie had been Gwen Petty's best friend, as far as I could tell from the social media analysis I'd done. A few of the other faces were familiar, too, but I couldn't remember the names. I'm better with numbers.

I took a hand on either side of me, fighting back the sense that I shouldn't be there. It was vaguely surreal, like taking a step deeper into Gwen's life without her permission.

As the others lowered their heads again, so did I.

"Dear Lord," Kallie said. "Please watch over our friend Gwen, and welcome her into your sweet embrace, forever and always, amen."

"Amen," I repeated with them, before everyone looked up again.

"Was she a friend of yours?" one of them asked.

I shook my head. "No. But I can tell she was really loved," I said, in all sincerity.

Kallie started to speak, then stopped to choke back tears, and tried again. "She was the best," she said.

And now it was me, reining in my own tears. The whole thing was beyond heartbreaking. I'd never had to face anything remotely like this in high school.

"I haven't seen you before," one of the girls said. "Do you go to school here?"

"Oh," I said. That one I wasn't expecting. I've always looked younger than I am, but it hadn't even occurred to me that someone might think I was a student. My mind scrambled for the right thing to say.

"No, I just wanted to pay my respects" came out.

It wasn't a lie, and it wasn't the full truth, either, but the one thing I couldn't bring myself to do was walk away. Not just yet. I felt like I owed it to Gwen to push myself, even now. If that meant asking a few more questions than I might have otherwise, so be it.

"Do you know if they have any idea who did this?" I asked. I felt like I was on a tightrope here, somewhere between doing the right and wrong things.

"I know who *I* think did it," one girl said. Two of the others shot her a look, but she kept talking. "It was that scumbag from Precious Moments."

"Precious Moments?" I asked. No turning back now.

Kallie's expression flashed from sadness to something darker. "It's this photography studio," she answered. "There's this super skeezy guy who took Gwen's senior picture. Pietro something." The girl on my left shuddered. "She said he was really gross about the whole thing."

"He even had a camera in the changing room," the shudderer said.

"That's just a rumor," another said.

"Well, I believe it."

"I'll bet you anything it was him," the first girl said, and nobody spoke up to disagree.

"Did anyone tell the police about him?" I asked.

"Yeah, but it's like they don't even care," another girl said. "They're not even looking into it."

I doubted that was true. If I'd learned nothing else so far, it was that the people behind these investigations cared about doing thorough work. But I also remembered what it felt like to not be taken seriously by adults.

"Supposedly, the FBI is going to be interviewing some of us, too," Kallie added.

"Well, make sure you mention it to them," I said.

I had all kinds of other questions, but my own common sense was finally knocking on the door. It was time to go before I'd dug myself a hole too deep to get out of.

"Anyway, I'm really sorry about your friend," I said, and stepped back.

Kallie seemed to look at me with clear eyes for the first time. "Don't take this the wrong way," she said, "but who *are* you?"

I just wanted to keep from upsetting them more than they already were. So I gave the only answer I could before I got out of there and left them alone.

"I'm Angela," I said.

CHAPTER 17

BACK IN THE car, I downloaded with Keats about my conversation with the girls, and especially about the Precious Moments photographer they'd mentioned. In return, Keats told me exactly nothing about his interview, or even who else he'd spoken with. Such is life at the bottom of the FBI food chain.

Although even then, there's an argument that I was already coming up fast at the Bureau, and that all my silent annoyance was just so much whining. Fair enough. But I wasn't stopping there.

I spent the rest of the drive asking Keats about himself instead—where he grew up (Potomac), what his family was like (close-knit, Catholic), how he'd landed at Quantico (recruited straight out of Georgetown). He was more forthcoming about all that, but I could tell something was still bothering him. I just wasn't sure it had anything to do with the case itself.

When we got back to the office, he pulled his Explorer right up to the curb on Cambridge Street and left it running.

"You coming in?" I asked.

"I'm going to park in the lot and catch up with you," he said.

"I think I can manage the walk," I said. "I'll even buy you a coffee at the Public Market."

"Go on ahead," he said, drumming the steering wheel without looking at me. Which is when I realized what was going on.

"You know, we're allowed to ride in the same elevator," I said. "We do work together. And we're both adults."

"Exactly," he said. "So why open up any questions about it?"

I didn't know if he realized how much of his own hand he was showing when he said that. It's amazing how often men don't.

"Are you afraid something might actually happen between us if you let it?" I asked, straight up. It didn't seem worth being indirect or passive about this anymore.

Billy Keats gave me an incredulous look and a tiny, sexy smile.

"Is there any question you *won't* ask?" he said.

"Sure," I said.

"Like what?"

"Like I'd tell you."

Finally, he clicked on his flashers and turned sideways to face me on the seat. It gave me a little flutter in my chest that I loved and hated at the same time.

"Listen. There's obviously some kind of a"—he moved his hands back and forth between us—"*thing* going on here. I'm not going to deny that."

At least he wasn't playing pretend with me. Extra points for that.

"Basically, that gives me two options," he went on. "I can ignore it, and we go about our business. Or I can get you reassigned out of the office."

"Then I guess you have to ignore it," I said. "Because I'm not going anywhere."

That internship at the Bureau was either going to be my ticket to the future or the last good opportunity I ever got. There was no way I'd be walking away from it willingly. Not to mention how attached I'd become to the case itself, and everything I felt like I owed Gwen Petty. And her family. And those poor, devastated girls at the school.

"So then we're in agreement," Keats said.

"Absolutely," I said. "Except for the part about why we can't ride the same elevator."

"You really don't know when to say die, do you?" he asked.

"Not usually," I said.

"God help me, I kind of like that about you," Keats said.

Good answer, I thought, but that was going to have to be enough for now. So I headed inside alone and rode the elevator to the sixth floor with a big dumb smile on my face. Whatever line I'd crossed in the car just then, I still got to keep my internship. I got to keep working this case. And I even got to keep the dirty little movies that kept running through my head, all about things that would probably never happen with Keats but were fun to think about anyway.

Not bad.

CHAPTER 18

MY SECTION OF the field office was called the CART—the Computer Analysis Response Team. It's like a cluttered hybrid of a regular office and a lab. We had workbenches and computer arrays for eight people spread around the space. We also had floor-to-ceiling windows with a killer view of Boston Harbor. As work environments go, you could do a lot worse.

To get inside, I had to pass an armed security station by the elevators, a locked door in reception, and then a card reader on the door to the CART itself. It's one of the few places in the building where open storage of evidence is allowed. That cut both ways. There was the pain in the ass of extra security, and then there was the fact that I had full access to the app from Gwen's phone and could tear down copies of it as much as I liked.

While my former classmates at MIT were mounting demonstration projects and simulations to impress their professors, I was interpreting code for the FBI. All other emotions aside, I'd be lying if I said I wasn't also feeling just a wee bit cocky.

Once I was back at my bench, the first thing I did was send another copy of the app from my workstation to a burner phone I'd checked out of the lab. When the app loaded on the burner, I could see the same chat program I'd seen on Gwen's iPhone. The difference this time was that I could monitor the conversation from both sides and see what the app sent back.

I started with the phone and sent out a simple text.

Hello.

It showed up immediately on my administrator's screen, and I typed back a quick reply.

Testing, testing.

Not exactly Dostoyevsky, but that didn't matter. Within seconds, I got a new pop-up window on my admin screen. The only thing in it was a single thumbnail image in the upper left corner. It looked like a white blur, so I clicked it open to full size for a better look. But even then, I wasn't sure what I was seeing.

Before I could figure it out, another thumbnail appeared next to the first. I enlarged that one, too, and got a picture of myself this time. It was taken from below, practically looking up my nostrils.

When I glanced down at the phone in my hand, the camera was essentially pointed right at me. Before that, it had been pointed at the ceiling. And when I looked up, I saw the glare of a fluorescent fixture over my head. That explained the two photos, anyway. But not whatever the hell was going on.

I stood up now and aimed the burner's camera out of the office window toward the water. After a few seconds, sure enough, another thumbnail showed up. This time, it was a shot of Boston Harbor through the streaky glass of our work space.

"Holy shit," I let out.

Jonas, the other intern, popped up from the next bench. "What is it?" he asked. In the CART, expressions like "Holy shit" usually mean one of two things: something bad has happened, or something very cool has happened.

Or in this case, both.

"Go get Zack," I said. "Right now."

Zack Ciomek was the lead investigator in the CART, and this was something he was going to need to see.

While I waited, I put the phone facedown to keep the camera lens dark for the moment. Then I swiveled to search the app's code on another one of my screens, where it didn't take me long to confirm what I suspected. They'd put a command string right there in the main source code, programming the app to take a photo on a default of every ten seconds.

My heart was going considerably faster than that by now. I knew a hell of a lot more than I had ten minutes earlier, but still nothing about where this was taking us, exactly.

Suddenly, there were voices everywhere. The room had started to fill up. Word had obviously spread fast. I stood up to make room for Zack as he slid into my chair.

"What do we have?" he asked.

"It's taking photos and sending them back without logging them on the phone itself," I said. "Which means the user never knows it's happening."

"What else?" he asked, and pointed at my screen. "What are these thumbnails?"

"I'm not a hundred percent sure," I said, "but maybe..."

I picked up the phone again and held it out in front of me. Then I did a quick lap around the room. By the time I came full circle, we had a dozen new thumbnails on the screen. That was a hell of a lot more than one every ten seconds.

"I think it's mapping the space," I said. I was 99 percent sure, anyway. "Some kind of geolocation function is telling it when the camera's on the move. If it can track in three dimensions, it knows which parts of the room it's seen and which need filling in."

"And when to start taking pics faster because there's more to see," Jonas said behind me.

"Exactly," I said.

"Holy . . . shit."

It wasn't over, either. Another window had just opened on the same screen, with no prompting from us. So far it just looked like one large, blurred image, but it also seemed to be resolving itself into focus. A thin, striped "thinking" bar cycled along the bottom edge as the pixels arranged and rearranged themselves.

"Is that compiling in 3-D?" Zack asked, his voice rising. It wasn't really a question. That's exactly what it was doing, and we all knew it now.

"This isn't good," one of the other investigators said.

"Someone call Billy Keats!" Zack yelled over his shoulder.

Already, a recognizable image of the CART was on the screen, with a small navigation tool in the corner. Zack used my mouse to pan back and forth, showing a 360 representation of the office around us, except for a few grayed-out blocks of space the camera had missed.

The implication hit me like bile in my stomach. This meant that someone, somewhere, had done the same thing to Gwen Petty's bedroom, if not her whole house.

And the thing was, we'd only begun to crack this open. So what else was this app capable of? Or for that matter, how far was our mystery hacker going to get before we reached the bottom of the rabbit hole?

CHAPTER 19

IMMEDIATELY, THE SPECIAL agent in charge of the Boston field office, Audrey Gruss, called a full meeting in the big bull pen just outside the CART.

They had two rows of monitors set up at long tables, with screens on three walls showing crime scene photos, regional maps, screen caps from the app, and CNN on mute.

Keats and his other case agents were there. Also analysts from every department, including my team, physical forensics, and medical. Eve even conferenced in by video. She didn't waste any time throwing me a bone, either.

"Angela, what else can this thing do?" Eve asked from her screen.

We'd already gotten a briefing from Zack, and now a few dozen pairs of eyes turned to look at me in the back of the room. I probably should have been nervous, but there was too much else to think about. Not to mention how badly Eve would roast me later if I didn't take advantage of the opening she'd just created. So I jumped right in.

"Basically, it's a Swiss Army knife of surveillance tools," I said. "It has geolocation-driven imaging and direct listening for sure, all running in the background without the user knowing it. The app doesn't even have to be open, once the operating system is infected."

It was strange to see all these seasoned analysts and agents scribbling notes in direct response to what I was telling them. On the inside, my impostor syndrome was raging, but on the outside, I kept it cool. I wanted these people to at least *think* I felt like I belonged there, even if that idea was still a work in progress for me.

"So basically," Zack added, "whoever sends this app out has uninterrupted access to any user's phone, once it's loaded. The only barrier is about whether or not the user accepts the invitation to install the app in the first place."

"Nobody does that anymore, do they?" Gruss asked. "Who downloads unknown attachments like that?"

I thought about Darren Wendt and almost smiled.

"You'd be surprised, Audrey," Keats answered. "It's the same kind of spear phishing that got some amateur hacker into the CIA chief's personal email account a few years back."

"Or the shutdown of those Ukrainian power grids," someone else chimed in. "Remember that?"

"Anyway, moving on," Gruss said with a note of justifiable impatience in her voice. She was the top brass in Boston. At the end of the day, this was on her. "Anything else to add?"

"The app also names itself for the given target," I said, jumping back in. "When I opened the copy I sent myself, the files had already self-converted to an *A H* file format."

"*A H?*" Gruss asked.

"For Angela Hoot," Keats said, and ticked his head in my direction. Gruss looked over like she was memorizing my face. I'm not sure how much I'd been on her radar before that.

"And there's no way to trace it back to the sender?" she asked, still on me.

"I'm sorry, no," I said, and immediately saw Eve wince on her screen. *Don't apologize if it's not your fault.* It was one of her favorite pieces of advice.

"But we're working on it," I added quickly. "The problem is, with cloud-based computing, there *are* no rules about relative locations. They can route this through any server in the world if they have access to it."

I wasn't telling them anything they didn't already know, but it seemed worth emphasizing while I had the chance.

And just like that, the meeting moved on without me. My head was spinning through everything I'd reported. Hopefully, I'd made a good impression, not that it mattered in anyone else's bigger picture. The real mandate here was to get a handle on this quixotic piece of coding, ASAP. I forced myself to stay focused on the conversation at hand, while various members of the team threw out different theories.

"We have known victims in Boston, Binghamton, and Albany, yes?" Gruss asked the room. "What's the radius here? Tristate? New England?"

"Hard to say," Keats answered. "It goes back to what Angela was telling us. At this point, the pool of potential targets is as large as the internet itself. They can send this app to anyone they want."

"That's the second time one of you has said 'they,'" Gruss pointed out. "Where's that coming from?"

Keats's eyes flitted over me before he answered. "This could be some kind of collective as opposed to a lone-wolf operation," he said. "We've been considering the possibility. They still need feet on the ground for the actual murders, but it's unclear where and how it's coordinated. Just that it *is* coordinated. All of which points to some kind of team approach."

SAC Gruss ran a hand across her mouth. There was no one in the room to be mad at, but you could tell she was pissed as hell.

"And that all means that the next targets, the people we need to make sure don't wind up dead, could be—"

"Yeah." Keats was right there with her. "Beijing, Cleveland, or two doors down," he said. "This could happen literally anywhere, at any time."

CHAPTER 20

I TOOK A short dinner break and walked out toward the harbor to clear my head. One of the perks of our office's location was easy access to the wide-open space of Boston Harbor. If I can't get out on my bike, just being near the water is the next best thing for me.

On my way, I grabbed a veggie burger from Kinsale's and then called A.A. while I wolfed it down on the go.

"Owl!" she answered.

"Hey, Pooh," I said. "Tell me a joke or something. I need it."

"I can hear it in your voice," she said. "Take a breath and unclench, will you? Tell me what happened."

"I wish I could," I said.

"Have people died?" she asked.

"Yeah."

"Does it have anything to do with that family who was killed in Lincoln?"

"I can't say."

It was driving me crazy, keeping all this from her. A.A. was the one person I knew outside of the Bureau who could appreciate the scope of this sick puzzle. And it wasn't like I thought she'd spill any details if I told her. It was more about sticking to the code of ethics I'd signed up for the minute I took the Bureau internship—much less gotten involved in a case like this one. Just like you never know which details will become relevant, you also never know which casual slip of the lip could be fatal to an investigation. For the time, anyway, I was going to walk a razor-straight line through the Bureau's confidentiality policy.

I think A.A. knew it, too, just from the way she shifted the subject.

"What about Agent Blue Eyes?" A.A. asked. "How's he treating you?"

"Like an employee," I said. "Nothing's going to happen there. My little crush is too much of a cliché to be taken seriously."

"Why do I think that means exactly the opposite?" she said.

It was a fair question. But the truth was, I had no idea if my feelings for Billy were real or just another part of playing the game. Like maybe winning over Agent Keats was more about winning than it was about Agent Keats, for me.

None of which seemed worth untangling right now. I felt beyond useless out there on the street while everything that really mattered was happening back at the office. What I needed was to get back to work.

"I guess I just wanted to say hi," I said. Already, I'd done a U-turn and started walking fast, back through Quincy Market. "But I've got to go."

"Don't you even want to *ask* about Darren?" A.A. said then.

That got my attention. I hated even hearing his name, almost as much as I hated what this probably meant.

"*Please* don't tell me you slept with him," I said as I waited for a crosswalk sign to change.

"Oh, God, no," she said.

"Good."

"I told him he had to prove himself capable of adult behavior first, and I meant it," she said. "If I'm satisfied by Friday, we'll get a beer. That's how I left it with him."

A.A.'s no pushover. If she said she meant it, then she did. She'd probably give that jerk a little hell in the meantime, I thought, and maybe even enjoy doing it.

But still, why was she bothering? Darren Wendt was the definition of a futile pursuit. Thinking he was going to change was like waiting for a pig to clean up its own pen. And it wasn't like she'd ever raved about the sex, either. Honestly, I had no idea what kept that doofus on A.A.'s radar.

"Don't be mad," she said.

"I'm not," I told her, going for something like sincerity. "This is the new me. The one who doesn't take things so personally anymore."

"When did you ever take this personally?"

"Apparently, I take everything personally," I said.

"Oh, please," A.A. said. "Did you get that from Eve?"

"I love that you know that," I said. "But listen, I really do have to go." The light had changed now, and the closer I got to the office, the less I could think about anything else. It was time to get back to work. Past time.

"Text me later," she said. "I don't think I can take the new you all at once. I'm going to need you to yell at me at least a little bit about Darren."

"That I can do," I said.

"And Angela?" she said. "Be careful, okay? Don't do anything stupid I wouldn't do."

"No promises," I said just before I hung up and headed back into the belly of the beast.

WHEN I GOT to my desk again, Zack Ciomek asked me to compile a full report of everything I'd done with the app so far. Record keeping is important, and it all funnels into the intelligence reports that are disseminated to the various key players in any given case. I knew that.

But it was still paperwork. Basically, being asked to compile a report is the FBI's version of "Go clean your room."

"Welcome to the suck," Ciomek said. "Shouldn't take you more than a couple days to finish."

I wasn't off the case, but so many new people were involved now that my role had gotten watered down. Way down.

The good news was, my hands are like lightning on the keyboard, and if I'm being honest, my brain fires faster than most. By lunch the next day, I'd posted my report and was sitting there in the CART without nearly enough to do. Nobody was around, or if they were, nobody was pulling me into any meetings.

So I turned my attention to something else.

One thing I hadn't been able to get out of my head was this

photographer I'd heard about from Gwen's friends. I had no idea if anyone had taken that tip and run with it. I just knew that I had to do something, for my own peace of mind. Anything to rule this guy in or out. It felt like keeping a promise to those girls, even if it wasn't one I'd made out loud.

I started with a basic online search, and it was quickly apparent that this scum bucket, Pietro Angeletti, had a whole lot more stink on him than I ever expected to find so quickly.

With the resources we had in the CART, it took only a few minutes to find his Precious Moments franchise in Hingham and, more importantly, to see that he had a small but distinct criminal record.

Angeletti had been convicted twice on domestic violence charges. The first was four years earlier, against his own sister, in Michigan. More recently, there was an arrest and an overnight in jail after a fight with his girlfriend in Dedham. None of it was a slam dunk, but it sure didn't make the guy look *less* suspicious.

From there, it seemed like the next logical step was to go get a firsthand take on this dude and see what else it might tell me. So I called Angeletti's studio and made an appointment for the next evening after work. I didn't even consider identifying myself as FBI. Just the opposite, actually. I used a fake name, Amy Smith, and said this was for my high school senior portrait. I was just slightly alarmed at how easily the lie slid out of me.

Maybe I was getting a little obsessed. It wouldn't have been the first time, or the second. Hell, at MIT, obsessive thinking is the kind of thing they give you As for. And I was too curious to stop now.

But of course, we all know what they say about curiosity, right? Just call me Angela the cat.

CHAPTER 22

PIETRO ANGELETTI'S STUDIO was a storefront in a crappy strip mall in Hingham. The window was etched with PRECIOUS MOMENTS and he had a row of faded school portraits hung in frames across the bottom of the glass. The whole place felt just about as sketchy from the outside as I might have imagined.

An electric bell chimed when I went in.

"Be right there," a male voice called from the back.

"Take your time," I answered while I scanned around, looking for a phone, laptop, or anything with an internet connection. I didn't have a plan, exactly. Just to do what I'd been doing in the field all along: watching and listening.

As I was glancing through one of the brochures by the door, I heard the click of a shutter. I looked up and saw someone, presumably Angeletti, standing by the partition wall that divided the front from the studio in the back.

"Amy, right?" he asked, lowering the SLR camera he'd been pointing my way.

"That's me," I said.

"I always like to start off with a few candids," he said. "I hope you don't mind."

The surprise was how hot he was—nothing like the porn-stache-wearing letch I'd been expecting. He was at least six one, with a cultivated shadow of a beard and the kind of shoulders you can't help noticing.

It made sense, I realized, if he was seducing pretty girls. Which was still just a big *if*, of course. I was out on a limb here and I knew it.

"You said this was a senior portrait?" he asked, coming over to shake my hand. "I would have guessed you were older than that. You don't look like a high school girl."

"I get that a lot," I said.

The irony was, he didn't even know he was right. It was just cheesy flattery to try to make me feel special. I'd been here less than a minute and Pietro was living right up to his own creepy reputation.

"Come on back," he said, thumbing over his shoulder. The partition behind him was just a flimsy wall with no doors, so I didn't mind following him to the studio area. I wanted to get a full look around. And besides, I didn't come completely unprepared.

In the back, he had the usual collection of umbrella lights and a posing area with a collection of backdrops you could pull down from the ceiling. Off to the side was a desk on which I could see a laptop sitting open. Next to that, he had what looked like a Samsung phone. Those were the things I really wanted to get to.

"Did you bring a change of clothes?" he asked. "Most girls like some options."

"Oh, I didn't want to do the portrait today," I said. "I just wanted to ask some questions, and maybe see some of your work." I pointed to the laptop on the desk. "Do you have any kind of website or online gallery I can look at?"

"Well, the thing is, you asked for a portrait," he told me. "I already booked an hour of studio time, so you might want to just go ahead and do it today."

"I don't think so," I said. "I'm just here for the consult. I'm not ready to do the rest."

He stopped and screwed up his face like he was considering something, even though I'm pretty sure he knew exactly what he was about to say.

"I don't think you understand," he told me. "I already cleared the hour, and the rate is a hundred and forty-five. We can take the pictures or not, but I'm going to need to be paid either way."

So he was a sleaze *and* a crook, I realized. Amazing. But was he also a killer? I was starting to get more creeped out than I wanted to be. In fact, I was starting to wonder what I'd been thinking, coming here alone like this. The mistake of it all was becoming real clear, real fast.

"I'm sorry for the misunderstanding," I said. "But you didn't say anything about that on the phone. So, I'm just going to go and not waste any more of your time."

"Hang on," he said. Already his tone had softened, but he was also moving around me to block the way. "Listen, I'm not unreasonable. I'm sure we can work something out."

My throat tightened. I wasn't 100 percent sure that this had risen to any kind of emergency yet, but I did know that I wanted to get out of there ASAP.

"Excuse me," I said. I tried to step past, but he matched my move, keeping himself in the way.

"I'll take a kiss instead," he said. I think the look on his face was meant to be playful. "Then we'll call it even."

"Did you really just say that?" I asked. I was pissed for sure, but terrified now, too. And working hard not to show it.

"Come on," he said, pushing in closer. "That's a pretty good deal for a hundred and forty-five bucks. You might even like it. Win-win, right?"

When he ran a finger down my arm, I thought I was going to puke.

"Get the hell out of my way," I said and tried to push past him, but it was like pushing into a brick wall.

Everything changed fast—too fast. With another big step, he plowed me right into the bathroom door. His hips ground into me. Two strong hands were on my arms. His breath smelled like cherry candy, and my scream got swallowed up with his mouth on mine.

What had I done? What the hell had I done?

IT WAS A claustrophobic nightmare. His grip kept my arms pinned at my sides, and even though it couldn't have been more than a few seconds, it seemed to go on forever.

"I'll pay you," I got out. "Okay? Just get off me—"

"Don't worry about that," he said. "God, you're beautiful. You know that?"

"Just let me pay you and I'll go," I said.

"I'd rather have another kiss," he said as I wormed a hand into my jacket pocket. My fingers closed around the small metal canister in there, but I still didn't have the leeway to pull it out.

I started to scream again, and he pressed his disgusting mouth into mine—for maybe half a second. That's how long it took me to wrench my arm free. I flipped the cap with my thumb, pulled the can out of my pocket, and hit him in the eyes with a full shot of bear spray. I'd been carrying the stuff around for a long time and always hoped I'd never have to use it. Just like any insurance policy.

He screamed and staggered back two steps, but then lurched at me, swinging wildly. Before I could avoid it, the back of his hand caught me in the nose. I felt a warm gush of blood on my lip even as I pushed him away. This time, he fell onto his own shitty couch and went down hard, still roaring.

"Jesus! What did you just do to me?" he yelled. His eyes were squeezed shut and streaming tears, from the mix of pepper and whatever else was in there. The backs of his hands were running like windshield wipers, back and forth, over his face, like that was going to do anything. And was I enjoying his pain? Yeah, I was. Just a little.

Maybe more than a little.

"Is this how you do it?" I yelled back at him. "Preying on girls like some kind of animal? You're done, asshole! Do you hear me? *Done!*"

"I'm going to make you *so* sorry," he screamed, and even then, it sent a sharp tingle down my spine. All I could imagine was Gwen, and all I could feel was anger. Lots and lots of anger.

"You can't even see me, you piece of shit!" I yelled. "Stay back unless you want more of the same."

That stopped him, at least for the moment. He really couldn't see anything, I realized. Which meant this was my chance to take a real look around. I should have run, but I turned back toward the desk instead. If I was lucky, I could at least take a quick look and check his hard drive. And I probably would have, too, if someone hadn't come in just then. I heard the electric chime first, and then a voice calling out from the front.

A very familiar voice.

"Hello?" Billy Keats called out. "Anyone here?"

CHAPTER 24

IT WAS JUST as well that Billy came in when he did. If not, I probably would have broken at least a couple of laws: searching Pietro Angeletti's laptop and phone without his permission.

Still, I wasn't out of trouble yet. When Keats came into the studio to find me standing there with a bloody face and Angeletti moaning on the floor, his expression was as blank as I'd ever seen. He looked like he'd just walked into some kind of bizarre dream—which is about how I felt.

"Angela? What the hell? Are you okay?"

"I'm... um..."

I didn't know what I was. I hadn't seen myself yet, but I could see the blood on my shirt. My nose was throbbing and my heart hadn't slowed down yet. I had to fight back the tears, too.

"*What the hell is going on in here?*" Angeletti spluttered out. He was still half blind, and the slits of his eyes were bloodred.

"Sir, calm down," Keats said, holding both hands out in front of him. He glanced from Angeletti back to me again.

"Go ahead," I said. "I'm okay."

"*Calm down?*" Angeletti yelled back. "Who the hell *are* you people?"

"I'm Agent William Keats. I'm with the FBI—"

"Are you kidding me?" Angeletti kept yelling, even as he continued to try to wipe the pain out of his streaming eyes. It looked pretty bad. Almost enough to make me care, but not quite.

"What's wrong with him?" Keats asked me.

I held up the can to show him. It was clear that Billy had about a hundred questions now, but all of that was going to have to wait. Just as well. I needed a little time to recover, not to mention figure out how I was going to explain myself for this one.

"We'll get some water for your eyes," Keats said, and shot me another look. I went into the bathroom and threw some water on my face, then soaked a handful of paper towels for Angeletti. I could hear him raving the whole time, not having any of it.

"I'm going to sue your asses so bad you aren't going to have a pot to piss in. You hear me? This is federal now, and I intend to take it as far as I can!"

"One thing at a time," Keats said placatingly as I came back out. "Let's get you over to the sink first." He had Angeletti halfway to his feet already.

"Get your damn hands off me!"

"I'm telling you, sir, you need to calm down! Just let me—"

That's when Angeletti took a swing. His eyes were obviously still no good, because the punch only glanced off Keats's jaw. Still, it was enough to get him a full roundhouse bitch slap in return. Keats's open palm literally knocked Angeletti down to his knees.

"I told you to calm down!" Keats said. "Now just stay there and don't move."

That seemed to be the peak of it all. Angeletti's shoulders slumped, and his groans had winnowed down to a soft whimper. He didn't try to get up again.

Meanwhile, I was standing there with a wad of wet paper towels in my hand, just starting to realize how close I'd come to a real disaster. *Who knew what Angeletti might have done?* I thought—just before it all came up and out of me. Literally. My gut heaved, and I turned back toward the bathroom, *almost* fast enough to get to the toilet. I ended up puking all over Pietro Angeletti's studio floor instead.

Sorry, Pietro.

Not sorry.

CHAPTER 25

AFTER THAT, ANGELETTI was arrested and taken in without incident. As for Billy, he wouldn't even talk to me until we were outside on the sidewalk, getting ready to leave. I could tell the ball was in my court.

"I'm sorry I disappointed you," I said.

"You didn't disappoint me. You pissed me off," he said. "If this guy's dirty, you just set any federal prosecution back by a goddamn mile."

"I never told him I was FBI," I said. It was déjà vu, with me grasping at straws all over again. Except this time instead of Mom, or Eve, or the disciplinary board at MIT, I was pleading my case to a federal agent. I'm not sure that counts as coming up in the world, but the comparison wasn't lost on me.

"Do you know what could have happened to you?" Keats asked, but then he held up a hand to stop me. "Sorry. Never mind. I know you know, but Jesus, Angela. You're lucky I showed up when I did."

I wanted to say, *Well, kind of.* The truth was, I'd taken care of Angeletti by the time Keats had gotten there, but that didn't seem worth pointing out just then. Especially considering the fact that I might have made things even worse if Billy hadn't shown up when he did. Part of me still wished I'd had the chance to get a look at Angeletti's phone and hard drive, but mostly I knew it was best that I hadn't.

"Why were you here, anyway?" I asked.

"Angeletti's name came up with Gwen Petty's friends, more than once," he said. "He's been on my list."

"Does that mean he's a suspect?" I tried, but all it got me was another one of Keats's tight-lipped glares. Not that I needed a verbal confirmation. Obviously, Angeletti was *some* kind of suspect.

"Let me have your address," Billy said. "I'll follow you home and make sure you get there okay. Unless you'd rather go to your parents'."

"My parents?" I said.

"You've just been through a lot. I'm not sure you should be alone tonight," he said.

At any other time I would have jumped on that double entendre.

"I'm fine," I told him. "I don't need anyone to hold my hand. And you don't have to follow me all the way out to Somerville, either. I can make that drive in my sleep."

"I wasn't asking," he said, and gestured at my dirty Subaru with the bike still in the back.

So I made like a good little intern, didn't push it any further, and drove home with Keats riding my ass the whole way. He even waited in his car at the curb outside my building until I'd found a parking space and walked back over.

"You sure you're okay?" he asked from his car. "I can give you the number of someone to talk to, if you want."

"I appreciate it, Billy. I really do," I said. "But I'm just going to open a bottle of wine and Netflix it until Monday morning. Go worry about someone else, okay?"

He gave me one more skeptical look after that, and finally drove off without another word.

As soon as he was gone, I ran upstairs. Then I took off every stitch of clothing I'd been wearing that day and threw it right in the trash. Then I took the world's longest shower, packed a bag, and headed back out again. Straight to my parents' house.

But Billy Keats didn't need to know about that.

CHAPTER 26

I GOT TO the house in Belmont just in time for dinner. I never needed a reason or an invitation. Everyone was always glad to see me, so it was a relief not to have to explain myself. All I really wanted was something like a normal evening after the day I'd just had.

Dinner was Dad's lemon orzo chicken with Mom's roasted broccoli—perfect comfort food. Tucking in with my parents and sisters, I finally started to unwind.

But that also cuts both ways, and just like that, my guard was down again. I'd taken only a few bites before I could feel the tears starting to burn my eyes. I tried to focus on the conversation, but I couldn't stop thinking about Pietro Angeletti. The way he'd pressed me up against that bathroom door. Those greedy hands. That sickeningly sweet breath.

While my parents and sisters chattered on, I thought about Gwen Petty, too. How she'd walked into the same trap, and much worse after that, with nobody there to help her.

Not to mention the other girls in this case. And their families. It was overwhelming.

Before I could stop myself, I dropped my fork and started sobbing.

"Angela?" Mom said. "My God, what is it?"

Both of my sisters were wide-eyed. Everyone had stopped eating and all eyes were on me, of course.

"I'm okay," I blubbered like an idiot.

"It doesn't look that way to me," Dad said. I tried to wave him off, but he came and put his arms around me anyway.

"I'm just working through some stress," I said, punting on the specifics so I wouldn't have to show too many of my cards. "It's been kind of intense at work lately."

"Kind of?" Hannah asked quietly.

"Angela, Angela..." Mom reached over and stroked my hand across the table. "You take on too much. You always have. It's like anytime you've got a mountain to climb, there's nothing else you can see."

Mom's an English prof at BU, with a specialty in myths and fairy tales. For her, everything is a mountain to climb or a dragon to slay. But it's from Mom that I get my sense of right and wrong in the world. You can learn a lot from fairy tales. And nobody gets to "happily ever after" without a few scars.

"I knew something was wrong," Mom said. "Especially since...well..."

"Since what?" I asked.

"It's nothing," she said. "A.A. might have mentioned that you seemed a little stressed out lately. More than usual, I mean."

"Did she call you?" I asked, genuinely surprised.

"Three times," Sylvie chimed in. I glared over at my other sister and got a shrug in return. "What? She's *your* friend."

It wasn't unlike A.A. to have her own conversations with my

mom, but at a minimum, I would have thought she'd give me a heads-up about it.

"The point is," Mom said, "I'm not crazy for being concerned."

"The point is, A.A. is a drama queen," I told her.

"She loves you," Dad said, still holding on to me. "We all do."

I leaned my head into the crook of his arm and took a deep breath.

"Can I just stay here tonight?" I asked.

It sounded weak. Not that anyone was begrudging me a night in my old bed. But this wasn't the person I wanted to become—someone who ran home after every crisis. I was better than that. Stronger, too. I worked at the FBI, for God's sake!

Which was kind of the point. Coding is one thing. A murder investigation is something else. They don't give classes in human suffering at MIT.

This was exactly what Eve had warned me about. The work was going to bring me down if I let it, she'd said. So now, more than ever, I had to make sure I didn't let it.

Somehow.

CHAPTER 27

WHEN I GOT to the office on Monday morning, I was told in no uncertain terms that I'd be sticking close to my desk for the foreseeable future. No surprise there.

Keats did throw me a bone, though. He asked Zack Ciomek to let me scan all of Angeletti's seized media from the photography studio. That included his laptop, cell, and a separate external drive where Angeletti stored everything from the two cameras they found hidden in his dressing room.

So it was confirmed now. This guy was exactly the serial predator Gwen Petty's friends had suspected. But was he also Gwen's killer?

As it turned out, no.

It didn't take more than a quick look through Angeletti's social media to determine that he'd been in the Bahamas on the night of the Petty murders. That was backed up with the Bureau's check on travel manifests for the United flights that Angeletti had booked and with security footage from the hotel where he'd stayed.

That sleazebag was going to jail, for sure. Just not on a murder charge.

All of which meant a couple of things for me. I was off the hook for any interference I might have caused in a federal investigation. But I was also back on the outside of this case, looking in. As soon as Angeletti was cleared of the killings, the Bureau handed all physical and digital evidence over to the local police.

Keats didn't stop there, either. I think I really had pissed him off, and I wasn't quite sure what to do with that, professionally or personally. I felt awkward around Billy now, even if I wasn't 100 percent sorry. At least I'd managed to make good on my promise to Gwen Petty's friends and bring down that scumbag, regardless of anything else.

Meanwhile, it wasn't like Keats was going out of his way to make me uncomfortable, but he was most definitely reining me in. My copy of the app was deleted from my workstation, along with everything I'd uploaded from Gwen's various devices. By the end of the week, I was back to entry-level threat assessment and penetration testing. It was like I'd never been attached to the case at all.

I understood where Keats was coming from, but that didn't mean I could just forget about it. If anything, my detour through Angeletti's hellish little studio had me more resolved than ever. I guess I'm stubborn that way. Or obsessive, depending on who you ask.

There wasn't much I could accomplish from the Bureau field office. But lucky for me, I just happened to know someone else with a vested interest in this case. Someone who might be feeling a little cooped up herself and might appreciate a conversation that had nothing to do with midnight feedings or diaper rash.

So as soon as I could get away from the office that evening, I headed over to Eve's for some unofficial consulting. I didn't know what I expected from her, exactly, but the alternative was to do nothing at all.

And that just wasn't an option.

AN HOUR LATER, we were sitting at Eve's dining room table, slurping down bowls of pho from Bon Me while I bitched about my day.

"Okay," she said once she could get a word in edgewise. "Let me ask you this. If it were your case, what would you be doing?"

I liked the question. It was exactly what I'd been asking myself all day.

"I'd tear down that app from scratch, one subroutine at a time," I said. "There's got to be some kind of vulnerable function in there. Some way to swim upstream back to whoever's sending it out."

Eve smiled down at Marlena, cooing and gurgling in her little tabletop bassinet.

"Black hat hacking the black hats," she said. "I like it. But don't be too sure of yourself. They know what they're doing."

"It's moot, anyway," I said. "Keats took away all my toys. I can't even look at the app anymore, much less run it. I should be asking what *you'd* do."

"I'd be doing the same thing, starting with a full audit on the source code," she said. Then she glanced across the room at her workstation and back to me again with a canary-eating look on her face.

"In fact," she said, "maybe I already am."

That's when it hit me, like a Mack truck with a big DUH on the license plate.

"You still have the app on your system, don't you?" I asked.

Eve smiled again. "I thought that's why you were here," she said.

"It is *now,*" I said.

All of a sudden, I wasn't the least bit hungry. If anything, I was aggravated with myself for missing something so obvious. I hate making mistakes, and I really hate when they're unforced errors. It was like I'd just lost an hour I couldn't get back.

That said, there was nothing stopping me now. When I walked over to Eve's desk, I saw that she already had a web vulnerability scanner up and running. That was a good start, but I needed to put my eyeballs directly on that app's code.

"You were just waiting for me to figure it out, weren't you?" I said.

Eve shrugged. "Once a mentor, always a mentor, I guess."

I pulled her desk chair halfway out. "Do you mind?"

When she didn't stop me, I took a seat in front of the best-equipped array I'd ever known outside an actual lab. I reached for the mouse, but she got there first and laid a hand over it.

"This is a coding practicum, okay? A *lab.* Not an investigation," she said. "For the record, you have no authorization from me to conduct any official Bureau business."

"Got it," I said. My fingers were itching. I couldn't wait to get started.

"I can't be looking over your shoulder every minute, either," she went on. "I'm not going to be accountable for what you choose to do when I'm upstairs with the baby. Agreed?"

"Of course," I said.

"Good," she said, and stepped back. "Now if you need anything, I'll be upstairs with the baby."

I tried not to smile.

A second later, she disappeared with Marlena and left me alone at the helm, fingers already flying.

I SPENT THE next several hours pounding double espressos from Eve's fancy Belgian machine and breaking the app's source code into manageable chunks. This audit was going to take days, if not weeks. I'd only been a fraction of the way through it when Keats took the app off my system, and God only knew what kind of updates had been implemented since then.

At around two, my eyes were starting to cross. I'd written code for twenty-four hours straight before, but this kind of analysis was a more intense discipline. Looking for vulnerabilities in a program isn't just about finding something unusual in the code. A lot of times it's about noticing what might not be there, which is another whole kind of insight and nearly impossible to process with a tired brain. Not that I was kicking off for the rest of the night, but I did have to pace myself. So I took a break. I stole some dulce de leche Häagen-Dazs out of Eve's freezer and gave A.A. a quick call to catch up on things.

"Hey," she answered just after the first ring.

"Hey, Pooh," I said. "I hear you've been having some unauthorized communication with my mother. Care to comment?"

I thought she'd laugh, or get a little defensive, or something. But instead, there was just a long silence.

"Hello?" I said.

Then finally she said, "I can't talk right now."

"What's wrong with your voice?" I asked. "Do you have a cold?"

"I'm not alone," she whispered.

"Ohh!"

For a second, I was happy. At least one of us was getting laid again.

But that's when I heard a depressingly familiar snore in the background. It was the same half pig, half buzz saw drone that had kept me awake through the thin walls of Ashdown House on way too many nights before.

Darren.

"Seriously?" I said. "You know there are three hundred thousand men in the city of Boston alone, right? Not just one."

"I know, I know," she said. "It kind of just happened, somewhere after the tequila shooters at Lolita. Can we talk about it later?"

"Sure," I said. "Or not. Whatever."

"Are you all right?" she asked. "I can go in the other room."

My mind was racing with all kinds of things, but nothing I wanted to say out loud. For starters, Darren was a piece of gutter scum, and A.A.'s taste for him truly baffled me. But more than that, if I was being honest, I felt betrayed. Just not in a way that I could see putting out there on the table for discussion. Not right now, anyway. Maybe never.

"I'm fine," I told her. "I should have texted. I'll catch you later, okay? Have a good night."

"Angela?" she said.

I pretended not to hear her. A.A. was free to make all the stupid, horny mistakes she wanted. God knows I'd made a few of my own. But that didn't mean I had to sit there chatting away while that human error she called an ex-boyfriend slept in the bed next to her. Thanks, but no thanks.

As soon as I hung up, I got a text from her.

Don't be mad. Please?

I'm not mad, I wrote back.

I didn't intend to say anything else. It was more like my thumbs had little minds of their own and just kept going.

But you deserve better and you know it, I wrote.

Then I turned my phone all the way off and got back to work.

CHAPTER 30

OVER THE NEXT several days, my life fell into a pattern. I'd leave for the office in the morning and stay until a reasonable hour. Then I'd clock out and pick up some dinner on the way to Eve's. I knew what she liked: anything Pan-Asian or Mexican, veg-and-protein salads, veggie pizza. It was all like the grown-up version of the junk I ate in college. Once a computer jockey, always a jockey, I guess.

I also knew she had enough sensitive information under her roof that she didn't much care for delivery guys coming to the door. Part of showing up for work with Eve was about knowing the rules and not giving her any reason to think I might be compromising her security. It was a small price to pay for getting access to a system as cutting-edge as hers was.

After dinner, I'd park myself at her desk and work as long as I could on the app, usually all night. Eventually, my static analysis—reading code—gave way to dynamic analysis, which is basically putting the program into action. That's where I could really put the app through its paces. I'd send myself modified copies and then track what it did in real time, always looking for some clue about how to trace this thing back to its original source.

As long as I kept it inside Eve's network, there was no way of being detected, which was key. It wasn't just Keats I needed to hide this little project from. It was also whoever else might be watching, given the chance.

For that matter, it was entirely possible that my work was redundant to whatever Keats's team was doing. In fact, I'd have been shocked if they weren't breaking down and analyzing this app in the same way as me. But the thing was, I didn't get to know. Ever since Keats had dropped me from the investigation, I was completely in the dark about what he or anyone else over there was up to.

So I was more than a little surprised when all of that changed again, about a week later.

It was early on a Tuesday morning. I was just wrapping up another marathon session when I got a call from Keats out of the blue.

"Where are you?" he asked.

"I'm at Eve's," I said. "I was just about to leave for the office. Why?"

"We've got a bead on something at Boston Latin School," he said. "I'm heading over there now."

I could hear in his voice that this wasn't just any lead. Something specific had happened. I could only hope nobody had died.

"The truth is, you were a big help at the last high school," Keats went on. "I want you to ride along, just in case we can use you."

"Seriously?" I said. "I thought I was in time-out, or whatever."

"See, one of the cool things about this job is that I don't have to explain myself to you," he said. Even now, he was a little adorable. I couldn't help noticing. "Can you be at Beacon and Arlington in fifteen minutes? I'll pick you up."

I checked the clock. It was five after eight. The city was going to be packed with rush hour traffic, but I knew how to hack this one, too.

"Do you have room for a bike in the back of your car?"

"Yeah, why?" Keats asked.

"Then I'll be there in ten," I told him, and hung up on my way out the door.

CHAPTER 31

EVERYTHING WAS MOVING fast now. Including me.

I barely checked the lights as I flew up Fourth Street out of South Boston. Sure enough, the roads were clogged and I was passing traffic at a good clip. It had been 8:06 when I hung up with Keats. I wanted to be in sight of him by 8:16, if only to start the day by kicking a little ass. It's not unusual in Boston to hit maybe twenty miles an hour on my bike, but for a couple of straightaways, anyway, I was definitely north of that number.

My mind was flying, too. I had a million questions about this new incident and how it fit into the larger picture. Considering where we were headed, this had to be something about a prospective victim. A high school girl like Gwen Petty.

God willing, this one was still alive.

Once I passed under I-93, I took a right on Tremont, where everything opened up with wider streets and fewer buildings.

I put my head down and pedaled into the wind, while my thoughts churned just as hard.

I wasn't going to tell Billy about how I'd been spending my nights. Not until I had something constructive to share. I didn't want to lie to him, but I didn't want to say too much without a good reason, either. Not until all that moonlighting actually led to something worth sharing—

"Watch where you're going, asshole!" someone screamed to the tune of their own car horn. I wasn't sure if they were yelling at me or someone else, but I *had* just swerved onto Charles Street at the last second. The city's been working toward more bike lanes for years now, without much progress. The motto of the road in Boston might as well be God Bless and Good Luck. I dodged another right-hooking truck, went around his left side, and kept going.

From there, it was a straight shot to the Public Garden, where Keats was picking me up. I ignored the burn in my legs and powered on. It was the fastest I'd ever biked in the city. And if I was being honest, part of that was about making sure Billy couldn't give me shit for anything when I got there. This was my chance to be taken seriously again, and I wanted everything to go perfectly.

Then again, I always do.

By the time I was flying through the park, it felt like all the joggers, walkers, and other traffic were moving in slow motion around me. I goosed a yellow light to catch a left onto Beacon and saw Keats just up ahead, parked illegally on the opposite side. His flashers were on and his hatch was already up.

I checked over my shoulder, crossed both lanes in a fast diagonal, and hopped off my bike at a run.

"What time is it?" I asked.

"Eight sixteen," he said. "You're late."

"I'm exactly on time," I said. I hoisted the bike into the back of the car and he slammed the hatch.

"If I'm waiting, you're late," he told me, with just a hint of sarcasm. Then we jumped in on either side and Keats accelerated away from the curb, heading west.

No slowing down now.

"THERE'S A FILE on the seat," Billy told me. "Take a look and tell me what you see."

It was an ordinary manila folder with a red strip reading CLASSIFIED across the subject tab. Even there, I knew I was in new territory. Nobody had handed me a classified anything since I started at the Bureau, much less a case file like this one. I could feel myself getting drawn more and more deeply into this case, even as we hurried toward that high school. It may or may not have been an actual turning point for me, professionally, but it sure felt that way. Some part of me didn't even want to open that folder—didn't want to know about another victim, another murder, another piece of darkness, just waiting to seep into my brain.

At the same time, some other part of me was beyond anxious to know exactly what was about to happen and, for that matter, what had happened to put this new twist into motion.

So it was with something like the definition of mixed feelings that I flipped open the file and started reading.

A laser-printed school picture of a teenage girl was clipped to the top of the packet inside. She was white, with dirty-looking dreads set off by two big ladybug barrettes.

"Nigella Wilbur," Keats said. I flipped past the school pic and to the report that lay underneath. "She's been using the app for just over a week. We found all that"—he stabbed with one finger at whatever was inside the file—"forty-five minutes ago."

"Please tell me she's still alive," I said.

Keats's mouth constricted into a tight line. I guess that was the question of the hour. It was like a lateral move for my nerves. Nothing had been confirmed or denied yet, but there were still plenty of possibilities for a worst-case scenario here.

Or rather, *another* worst-case scenario.

My hands were shaking by the time I started flipping through the rest of the material in that file. I told myself it was because I'd been biking without gloves, but that wasn't it. I could see that the next several pages were a transcript of text messages and conversation fragments, just like the ones I'd found for Gwen Petty.

Behind those pages were printouts of several images, presumably camera snaps sent back and forth between Nigella Wilbur and whoever this person was coming after her.

The pictures themselves were all over the map, from innocently playful and flirty sorts of poses all the way up to stuff that was explicitly hard-core. They were the kind of images that could get a man arrested, assuming Nigella Wilbur was as young as she looked. My heart was already breaking for her, just knowing the kind of trap this girl had wandered into.

I took a deep breath, clenched my fists against the shaking, and started to read.

What's up?

Meeeee
I just smoked some skunky weeeeeed

Congratulations.

For what?

Sounds like fun.

Oh
yeah it is

Are you alone?

Hangon
Now i am.

Where are you tonight?

Friends house
Where you?

I'm outside watching you through the window.

?!?!?!?!?

Haha. Just kidding.

Jeezus...
Scared me.

Don't be scared. I'm friendly.

I know
But weed makes me parnoid

In that case—I lied.
I really am watching you through the window.
Take your shirt off for me.

Very funy

I'll bet people say you're different all the time.

What do you mean?
Different??

Good different.
Awesome different.
But I'll bet not everybody thinks so.

Why you say that?

Just a hunch.

Well your right
But screw everybody

No...screw me. :P

You have a 1 track mind

Guys always think with their dix

You say that like it's a bad thing.

Don't put words in my mouth

Ha. Too easy.
I'm not even touching that

:-))

Can I see a pic?

If you're good

You don't think I've been good?

No.
I mean yes
You have

So?

Here

Nice!
More!

Like this?

MORE

Last one

(0) (0) !!!!
That's what I'm talking about

That's all you get for now

Here something for you.
Fair is fair.

Holy shit, dude!
Did you really just take that on the street???

Nobody saw
It's all good

I'll visit your ass in jail

:-)

Guess what?
I just bought a half ounce of the best green you'll ever smoke.

Awesome

And I share . . .

wow. Super subtle.
I see what you're doing.

You're supposed to see.
Let's get together. Pretty please?

Maybe

Does that mean probably? Or probably not?

It means maybe

Don't tease me.

You luv it

True.
I'm so into you it's not even funny.

I wasn't kidding on Tuesday. I really do want to meet you.
You ready for me?

Maybe tomorrow

Really?

Let me think about it, k?

Just say yes.

Tell me why i should

yes is a world
& in this world of yes lives,
skillfully curled,
all worlds

I don't even know what you just said

It's a poem.

Oh
I'm getting a F in English

I'll give you an F in whatever you want

day-um . . . !!

So is that a yes?

That's a probably
Got to go . . .
already late for skoooool
talk later?

CHAPTER 33

I LOOKED UP at Keats from the pages on my lap.

"The Cummings poem," I said. "It's the same one he sent Gwen Petty. 'Love Is a Place.'"

"Good memory," Keats said.

I didn't even bother asking how they'd found this, because I knew he wouldn't tell me. It had to be some kind of targeted SMS search, but that meant scanning an unfathomable mountain of raw data. Then again, I had no idea how deep the resources went on this thing. In terms of the FBI, I was the smallest possible cog in a machine that was bigger, and reached further, than I'd probably ever know in my entire career. For all I knew, they had some kind of mega team working this thing from every angle, and from any number of locations around the world.

That's one of the upsides of cyberforensics. A significant amount of the work can happen from just about anywhere. Though of course that cuts both ways. The bad guys are just as mobile as the good ones, and that makes them harder to find, if they know what they're doing.

So it was possible that the Bureau had found these text strings, like some kind of needle in a haystack, through sheer workforce numbers. But on the other hand, they may have just gotten astronomically lucky. It happens all the time. The number of high-achieving coders who take credit for their own good luck as if it were something they built from the ground up is . . . well, impossible to know. But it's a big number.

And speaking of teams, Keats had a local crew already on-site by the time we pulled up in front of Boston Latin. Half a dozen personnel were gathered outside. I recognized three agents from the field office, including Adam Obaje, who was just coming out through the school's main entrance.

We got out of the car and met them all halfway. Keats didn't stop me from joining in as we huddled there on the sidewalk.

"So?" he asked.

Obaje's expression was dark. "She was in homeroom but didn't show up for first period," he said.

"Goddamnit!"

"Ten minutes earlier and we would have had her. She's not answering her phone, either."

"I'm not losing this girl," Keats said. "I want at least one agent on every floor inside, right now. Parker, get some crime techs here, just in case, and I want cruisers on every corner, checking cars. What about the family?"

"Contacted," Obaje said. "Everyone's fine, and the mom's on her way here, but she's coming from Attleboro."

As far as I knew, all of the previous murders had gone down in private family homes. But clearly, Keats wasn't taking any chances.

"Where do you want me?" I asked.

"Take this." He handed me a radio on the fly. "I want you thinking like a high school girl. Where would she go?"

I started to answer, but he'd already turned to head inside. There was no time for chitchat with the intern. I was just an extra pair of eyes, at best, and a second later I was standing alone on the school steps. I wasn't even sure if I'd just gotten folded further into this thing or shut out of it.

But I did have some idea about where to look.

Based on what I'd read in the file, Nigella Wilbur didn't much like school, loved weed, and wasn't afraid of taking risks, either. That's what had gotten her onto our radar in the first place. Opening the app was a risk in and of itself, whether or not she knew it; but then on top of that, I had the distinct impression that a little bit of danger wasn't such a bad thing to Nigella.

When I was in high school, I was fairly straight and narrow, but I did know plenty of girls like her. And I knew a little something about how they operated. My first thought was that Nigella might have gone out for a little wake-and-bake to help her face the day. And to do that, she'd need to be outside.

It was just an educated guess, which was as much as I had to work with. I didn't actually expect to be right.

But as it turned out, I was.

CHAPTER 34

BOSTON LATIN SCHOOL has no campus to speak of. It's just one huge building in the middle of the city, with alleys and parking on either side. The Fens was only a few blocks away and a likely spot for stoners, given all the woods, paths, bridges, and other good hiding places over there. I figured I'd start with a quick lap around the school and work my way out from there, depending on what I saw, then maybe head to the park after that, if nobody found Nigella in the meantime.

I headed up the north alley first, scanning every nook and cranny along the way. From there, I moved down Palace Road behind the school and back up the other side. I was almost all the way around and had pretty much written this off when, sure enough and to my own surprise, I got a whiff of marijuana.

It didn't take long after that to hone in on Nigella's little smoking party. There were four of them, two boys and two girls, passing a vape pen around. Nigella was wearing a huge pair of sunglasses, but I recognized the blond dreads right away.

They had a pretty decent hideout, too. It was a three-walled alcove in the parking lot, meant to shield two dumpsters from view. Anyone inside the school wouldn't have been able to spot them. But from there in the alley, I had a clear sight line.

I stepped back and radioed Keats.

"This is Hoot," I said. "I found her. She's with some friends in the parking area on the south side of the building."

Some part of me felt bad for busting them. That's not what I was there for. But they definitely had a serious buzzkill headed their way.

"Keep an eye on her, but do not approach," Keats came back. "I'll be right out."

"Got it," I said, trying to sound calm. I'd been wishing to get thrown back into the pool, and now here I was, swimming alone in the deep end. I wasn't afraid of high schoolers, but by the same token, I hadn't been left to my own devices like this before. Not with the stakes as high as these were.

A second later, Nigella's group was on the move. One of the boys chirped open a RAV4 with his clicker and they headed toward it.

Shit. Shit. Shit.

"Keats, where are you?" I radioed.

"On our way," he said.

There was no time. And no way I was going to be the rookie who found and lost this person of interest before Keats could catch up to her.

"Nigella!" I called out before I could even consider it either way.

All four of the kids turned to look at me. The other girl let out a little half scream, followed by a nervous laugh. I had to remind myself that I was the grown-up here. It still wasn't intuitive for me.

"Hold up a second," I said, hurrying over.

Nigella lowered her shades to give me a raised eyebrow as I approached. "Do I know you?" she asked. Her lipstick was bright red, but her clothes were all downscale funk. Old army jacket, Rolling Stones tee, and hand-ripped leggings over oxblood combat boots.

"I'm Angela Hoot," I said, "and—"

"Hoot?" one of the boys said, and they all cracked up at once. Clearly, they'd had enough to smoke. Not that I hadn't been mocked for my last name pretty much all my life.

"Listen," I said. "I'm with the FBI—"

"Yeah. Sure you are," Nigella said. "Do you have some kind of badge or something?"

"I don't have my credentials on me," I said, which was embarrassingly true. I'd left everything in the car. "My supervisor will be here in a second—"

"Bridget? Get this on your phone, 'kay?" Nigella said, still eyeballing me.

"Annnd we're rolling," Bridget said, pointing her iPhone our way.

"You've got the wrong idea," I told them. "This is for your protection, Nigella."

"Sure," she sniped. "Because the cops are so good at 'protecting' people these days."

When she started to get in the car, my patience officially ran out. There were all kinds of feelings running through me now, but none of them stopped me from grabbing that car door and holding on to keep her from pulling it closed. I think it took Nigella by surprise. I'd kind of surprised myself, for that matter.

"What the hell?" she said. "I don't know who you think you are, but you need to step off—"

"Let me put this another way," I interrupted. I was on a

roll now, no stopping. "In about thirty seconds, you're going to have half a dozen federal agents out here, all of them wanting to speak with you. If *I* were stoned, I'd want to be ready for something like that."

"*Whut?*" one of the boys grunted out. The other one looked around nervously.

But Nigella stayed icy. "Who said anything about stoned?" she asked, meeting my gaze.

I didn't want any trouble here. Not the wrong kind, anyway, and I was this close to saying a thing or two I might have regretted. Lucky for me, I could just see Keats and a few others rounding the corner.

And I was starting to think that a little buzzkill was exactly what this girl needed.

CHAPTER 35

TO MAKE THINGS worse—much worse—Nigella Wilbur refused to let us examine her phone. Ironically, the school could (and did) take it away, but we weren't allowed to touch it without her permission, unless we could get a warrant or parental consent. And her mother was still a good half hour away.

Right now, the phone was sitting in a drawer in the principal's office, which was just as well. Given what we knew about the app's listening capabilities, we couldn't afford to interview Nigella anywhere near that thing. So we holed up with her in the detention room, appropriately enough.

"This is extreme bullshit," she said for the fourth time. "You can't intimidate me."

"We're not trying to intimidate you," Keats said. "We're trying to protect you."

I could tell he was straining for patience. The longer this conversation went on, the colder our trail was getting.

"We're also trying to protect whoever else might be at risk," Keats went on.

"By illegally tapping my phone?" Nigella asked.

"That's not what happened," Keats tried again. "If you'd just listen—"

"Save it," she said. "I'm not interested in enabling your right-wing NSA crap. This is exactly why people like me don't trust people like you. Don't you see that?"

Ironically, she had a grain of a point in all this. I had plenty of friends of my own whose trust of American law enforcement was at an all-time low, for reasons I could understand, if not agree with. But by the same token, a lot of that knee-jerk resistance was based on equal parts information and misinformation.

In any case, we seemed to be at a kind of standstill.

Billy took a beat. Then another. I could just see the gears turning in his mind and wondered if he was trying to use the silence to make Nigella uncomfortable. But as it turned out, it wasn't that at all.

"Angela," he said, "tell Nigella about your first night on this case, will you?"

"Excuse me?" I wasn't expecting him to pivot like that, but now they were both looking at me.

"Tell her what you saw in the house that night in Lincoln," Keats said. "All of it."

So far, he hadn't disclosed any details about the other murders. For a second, I was shocked that he'd go there. But then I realized where he was taking this—and why. Every minute counted right now, and he was pulling out all the stops.

I took another few beats to gather the memory of that night in my mind. The bodies. The dried blood. The smell.

Then I started talking.

"It was my first crime scene," I told her. "And the first dead bodies I'd ever seen, too."

Nigella stood up right away. Her chair tilted back and crashed onto the floor. "Are you kidding me with this? I don't have to listen to you!" she said.

"Yeah, you do," Keats said, righting the chair for her. "Sit down and shut up."

When she didn't move, Billy nodded at me to go on anyway. I had no idea if this was the right thing to do, but that wasn't my call. I just followed his lead.

"They found the father in the kitchen, shot through the chest," I said. "All the others had been killed in their rooms upstairs. There was a mom, two little boys, and a girl about your age."

Nigella had gone completely still now. It was either a show of defiance or fear. Sometimes it's hard to tell, but I was getting the impression that Billy knew exactly what he was doing. The more I went on with this, the more I felt like I was moving the needle in the right direction. At least this was a chance to use Gwen Petty's death to try to make sure the same thing didn't happen to someone else.

"She's the one who had been using this same app," I went on, talking about Gwen now. "I never actually saw her. I only saw the body bag they carried her out in."

"That was the third family in this case," Keats said. "We've been working as hard as we can to make sure there's not a fourth."

Nigella's eyes rolled up and to the side now, fighting tears. I didn't know if she cared about some nameless other family, but I did think she was finally doing the math on what she might have wandered into herself.

"It's just an app," she said softly.

"That's what you're supposed to think," I told her.

"I don't understand how it could be that dangerous . . ."

Suddenly, she seemed much younger. I wasn't going to

lecture her. We'd already rounded the corner we needed to get around.

"Nigella," I said. "Can we *please* get a look at your phone? I don't want this to happen to anyone else. And to tell you the truth, I don't want to face another night like that last one."

I had to stop there. My voice was thinning out and I was starting to choke on the lump in my own throat. I hadn't even realized the last part until I'd said it out loud. As much as I couldn't let go of this case, I was also terrified of what else I was going to have to see along the way.

My body felt hollow, like I'd just let go of something I could never get back. And the look on Nigella's face told me she was feeling something similar. The first real tears were rolling down her cheeks.

"Fine," she said. "You can do what you need to. But I'd better get my phone back when you're done."

Keats was on his feet now. This was good news, but we had to move fast.

"Believe me," he told her on our way out the door. "You don't want that one anymore."

CHAPTER 36

BEFORE WE PICKED up the phone from the principal's office, Keats briefed me quietly in the hall.

"I want to make contact with this guy right away," he said. "And I want you to be the one to do it. As Nigella."

"Are you serious?" I asked. It was a stupid question, mostly just a knee-jerk bit of nerves. Obviously, Keats was serious, even if it did mean putting both of us out on a limb here. So I quickly added, "I mean, yeah, of course. If you want me to, I'm down."

The idea of it scared the hell out of me, but it didn't take long to see where Billy was coming from. I was more qualified to do this than anyone else on hand, just in terms of my age, my experience, and the way my mind worked. It was the same reason he'd brought me along in the first place.

He didn't want to change locations, either. If we moved Nigella's phone away from school property, the app she'd downloaded would track our movements and send that information right back to whoever was on the other end. So we stayed put.

A few minutes later, I was carefully placing the phone into a borrowed backpack to blind the camera. Then I carried it down the hall to the same room where we'd interviewed Nigella. Keats closed the door from the outside and watched through the glass while I silently got to work. We couldn't afford to be seen, heard, or detected here.

I took the phone and carefully laid it flat on the table in front of me. The only thing the camera would see from that angle was ceiling tiles.

Then I opened the app and typed in my first message, going for Nigella's "voice" as best I could. I'd read through her texts that morning. It was all the research I had time for.

Heyyyy! You still there?

For several long minutes, nothing happened. I kept looking at Keats, and he stared back encouragingly, keeping to his side of the glass until finally a little *swoosh* sound told me a new message had come through.

I looked down without leaning into the camera's range and read what was there.

Hey sexy.

This was it. Whether it was coming from a killer, or someone who hired killers, or even just one cog in a much bigger machine, it was our first direct contact of any kind. Talk about going from zero to sixty in one shot. My adrenaline was uncomfortably high, but I knew what I had to do. I carefully keyboarded in a reply, making sure I stayed out of the camera's way.

Can't stand this place!! I said. I'm ditching. you still wanna meet?

He came back at me almost immediately.

For real? Hell yeah.

I gave Keats a thumbs-up to let him know it was progressing.

Awsome... where? I asked.

I'll come to you, he said. What school?

Boston Latin, I answered.

I was just kidding, he said. I know what school you go to.

you do? I asked.

Sure. I know a lot about you, he said. And then, Like for instance, I know this isn't you.

Right on top of that, a photo came through. It was a snapshot of the school, taken from across the street. When I pinched it open to enlarge it, I realized what I was seeing. It showed Nigella standing on the sidewalk out front, along with me, Keats, and several other agents, just after we'd found her.

My mouth literally dropped open. I heard a soft tap on the glass and looked up at Keats's confused expression. Then I heard one more *swoosh* sound.

When I looked down, I saw that another text had come in.

You people are seriously underestimating me. Fuck off.

CHAPTER 37

THEY FOUND THE corresponding phone in a trash can just up the street from Boston Latin. It was just a cheap burner, the kind of thing anyone can pick up at a convenience store or a Best Buy, use anonymously, and then ditch without any danger of getting tracked down.

Even so, it felt like a taunt as much as anything. My guess was that we were meant to find the phone, as a little reminder of how closely we'd been observed all morning and how little we could do with that information. Keats couldn't even put out an APB, since we had no idea who we were looking for. The whole team worked for several hours, combing the neighborhood, but it was a lost cause.

When Keats and I headed back to the field office, it was just after six o'clock. Neither of us had eaten a thing since breakfast, so we picked up some sandwiches on the way. We got as far as the parking lot before we broke down and decided to eat them right there in the car. I guess Billy was as starving as I was.

"You really rolled with it today," he told me. "How are you doing?"

"I'm fine," I said.

"You know, you say that a lot," he told me. "And the more you do, the less I tend to believe it. I saw you get pretty emotional back there, during the interview with Nigella. I'm sorry if I put you in a tough position—"

"You didn't," I said, mostly because I didn't want him to think so. However tough my position might have been, it was nothing compared to the bigger picture here.

But Billy wasn't buying it. "Come on, Angela. It's just us," he said. "Don't bullshit me."

I nodded and stalled with a long draw on my iced coffee.

"Yeah, okay," I said. "You're right. It wasn't easy. And maybe I'm not made of the kind of nails I'd like to be. But hey, I'm still here, right? And I'm still ready for more."

Everything I'd just said was true. This thing was kicking my ass, but that's not the same as wishing it weren't happening. It was more like the opposite. I didn't want to give Billy a single reason to stop bringing me in on this case.

He took his own time responding and smiled at me over the Coke can he was sipping from. Then he sat back and stared just long enough to give my pulse a little uptick.

"What?" I said.

"I'm just going to go ahead and say it," he told me. "You're impressive. You really are. I know you've got this massive IQ, but you're tough, too, in your own way. You're going to be great at this, if you want to be."

"Does that mean I'm not yet?" I asked half seriously.

"Well," he said with another smile, "you did almost lose Nigella Wilbur in the parking lot. But other than that—"

I don't know what he was planning on saying, but he never got there. I'd already leaned across the seat and planted my lips on his.

There was no plan for it. No premeditation. It just *happened*, as A.A. might have said. And sweet Jesus, the man's lips were as soft as those blue eyes of his. Once I started I didn't want to stop.

Billy didn't pull away and he didn't lean in. He just let me kiss him, which was its own kind of mixed message.

"What was that?" he asked when I sat back.

"Um . . . a kiss?" I answered.

Sometimes I like to do things just because I'm not supposed to. Or maybe there was more to it than that. Either way, I wasn't in the mood for apologizing.

"All right, well, that conversation's going to have to wait," he said. "I've got a lot of people expecting to hear from me at the shift meeting."

"Understood," I said, and we got out of the car. I wasn't sure I needed to talk about that kiss, anyway. Not on top of everything else. But it was moot for the moment. What I really needed to do was get out of his hair, let him get to his meeting, and be on my way.

Or at least so I thought. My bike was still in the back of his car, but when I went around to get it, he was already heading toward the office.

"Hey!" I said, and he turned around.

"What are you doing?" he asked.

"I need my bike," I said. "I'm going to take it to Eve's and drive home from there."

"So you're *not* coming to the shift meeting?" he asked.

"Oh," I said, too numb to be surprised anymore. "Yeah. I'm definitely coming."

"Let's go, then," he said. "What are you waiting for?"

Answer: Not a damn thing, now.

CHAPTER 38

THE NERVE CENTER for this case—as well as my office—had been moved down to the fifth floor to accommodate a larger team. When I got there, people were milling around, taking seats, and getting ready for whatever came next. I got lost in the shuffle and took a seat on the side of the room where I could see everything. Just as well. I literally didn't know my place here.

Audrey Gruss was seated near the front, and Zack Ciomek from the CART was on hand, too, along with most of the expected players, plus a dozen or more unfamiliar faces. There were also six screens with alternating live feeds from various field offices around the Northeast. I saw Albany, New Haven, New York, Newark, and Philly all represented, along with whoever else might have been looping in by conference call. This operation had bulked up considerably since the last meeting I'd been allowed into.

Keats got things started with a full briefing of the day, including some credit thrown my way, which I appreciated. Then he handed the meeting over to Zack.

"For those of you who haven't seen this, let me give you a current snapshot of the app's penetration," Zack said.

He used his laptop to pull up a map of the US on several screens around the room. Then he toggled in to show just the Northeast. It was overlaid with swaths of green in different shades, from darker to lighter. The biggest dark patch emanated from Boston, with several others concentrated around various population centers.

"Darker green indicates a denser saturation," Zack said. "Lighter green down to white means less, or none at all. In total, we're estimating that the app has landed on approximately 12,300,000 devices around the Northeast. Primarily cell phones. That's as of thirty minutes ago."

"I'm sorry, did you say twelve million?" someone asked. It was the same question I had. That number seemed unfathomable, considering the relatively short amount of time the app had been in play.

Zack nodded. "That's right. Twelve point three million and growing fast. This morning, the number was eleven point nine mil."

He tapped out a command on his laptop and the screen displays jumped to a similar graphic but with smaller clusters of every shade on the map.

"Here's a simulation of what we've seen over the course of the last week," he said. Then he hit another key to set the program into motion.

A time sequencer ran across the bottom of the screen while the clusters darkened and grew over the course of a seven-day period. It was like watching a biological virus spreading out of control.

"How are you doing this?" I asked. I didn't know if I was supposed to be inserting myself, but I couldn't help it.

Zack eye-checked Keats before he answered. "One of our DC analysts found a way in," he said. "Not by following the app directly to individual users, but with a surrogate marker at the ISP level that allows us to see where it's landing."

"So you can't tell who's opening it, versus leaving it dormant on their systems?" someone from Philly asked.

"That's right," Zack said. "That's one of the limitations. Anything more specific than that is coming through Keats's team, which you already heard about."

Keats picked it up from there.

"Obviously, they're casting a very wide net in the name of picking up just a few victims," he said. "If there's good news, that's it. And all of those incidents have been consolidated in the Northeast."

"For now," Gruss interjected.

"Yes," Keats said. "For now. But if they find a way to activate the app without permission from individual users, then we're going to have a whole new shitstorm on our hands."

We sure will, I thought.

To the tune of twelve million and counting.

CHAPTER 39

WORD FILTERED PAST my desk the next morning that another incident had been linked to Keats's investigation. Authorities in Portland, Maine, were reporting a missing girl who had either run away or been taken from her bedroom overnight.

The girl's name was Reese Anne Sapporo. A series of suspicious texts found on her phone had been uniquely formatted with an .ras file extension. It was like the app's signature move, using the victim's initials that way.

But the disappearance? That was something new.

I got my first details from Zack when he told me I'd be traveling with the case.

"You'll be there overnight, at least," he told me. "You can expense back a few things—"

"Not a problem," I said. I had an unopened toothbrush and some deodorant in my desk. I'd improvise around the rest.

"Keats wants two from the CART," Zack told me. "I'm sending you and Candace. She'll be point of contact for the lab and you'll assist."

Candace Yamaguchi was a senior ITS-FE, also known as an Information Technology Specialist–Forensic Examiner, basically one step up from me. I saw her pulling together a field kit at the back of the lab and went to help.

"How much do you know?" I asked.

"Not a lot," she said, "but we just got this. It was sent directly to Reese Sapporo's phone about thirty minutes ago."

Candace navigated to an image file on her tablet and turned it around to show me. "I guess the parents saw this before the police did. As if this bastard wasn't already cruel enough."

What I saw was a picture of a girl, presumably Reese Sapporo, in the open trunk of a car. Her wrists and mouth were duct-taped, and her eyes were wide and wild.

Even after everything else I'd seen, that photo sucked the air right out of me. But I knew I had to make a choice. I could get emotional right now, or I could get ready to go. Not both. So I grabbed a second field case and focused on the checklist of things we'd need for this trip.

Camera, tool kit, gloves, blue tape, wire cutters, evidence tags...

Twenty minutes later, we were in a van with Keats and the rest of our six-person team, heading to the helipad at Boston Harbor. One of the Bureau's black Bell helicopters was waiting when we got there, and by eleven, we were lifting off for the forty-five-minute flight to Portland.

It was a surreal feeling, watching the city fall away beneath that chopper—my biggest reminder yet that I was running with the big guns now. Which also meant no wiggle room. If the FBI couldn't get this done, who could?

Tiny mistakes were the difference between life and death here. I was going to need to do everything I could to hold up my little corner of this investigation. And no matter what else happened now, I just hoped we were moving on this fast enough to make sure that Reese Anne Sapporo made it back home alive.

That is, assuming we weren't already too late.

CHAPTER 40

WHEN WE LANDED in Portland, two reps from the Cumberland County Sheriff's Office met us with cars at the airport. The reps were fairly cool and neutral about the whole thing. It was hard to gauge if we were a welcome resource or some kind of law enforcement interlopers to these people. That seemed to be the norm in the cop shows and movies I'd seen, but then again, I was on a pretty steep learning curve these days. It was all about where those stories left off and reality picked up.

From the airfield, we drove to the Deering neighborhood, where the Sapporos lived. I rode with Keats, Adam Obaje, and a Detective Friebold, who briefed us on what they had so far.

There were no indications of a forced entry, or a struggle of any kind, at the Sapporos' house, Friebold said. Other than a single window left unlatched in the girl's room, the whole place had been left undisturbed.

"We're guessing Reese let this creep in but didn't leave willingly. Might have been drugged," Friebold told us. "If only because her phone was left behind. You don't see a lot of fifteen-year-olds doing that, you know?"

I'd been thinking the same thing. Especially not when it came to fifteen-year-olds who were phone-oriented enough to fall into an app like this one.

Friebold went on. "As soon as that photo came in this morning, we reclassified the case from missing persons to an abduction," he said. "But there's been no word since. No demands. Nothing. Her poor folks are out of their minds."

An Amber Alert had gone out, and police were already speaking with Reese's friends, teachers, and neighbors. They were also covering all major transportation hubs, but it was impossible to know how many hours' head start the kidnapper might have had. I tried not to imagine it too much from Reese's perspective, how freaked out and terrified she would have been. But at the same time, I tried not to push it away, either. I could feel myself sharpening my analytic skills, even if that lingering dread in my gut was the same as ever.

"What are the chances she's still alive?" I asked Keats. "Statistically speaking."

"Statistically? Ten percent, maybe," he said. "But there's nothing typical about this."

I wasn't completely sure what Keats meant by that, but something told me to cut off the rookie questions at that point and just focus on the briefing we'd had.

When we reached the house, Keats met with Mr. and Mrs. Sapporo while Candace put in a call to the family's ISP to start tracking down whatever we could get on every device in that house. I shut myself up in Reese's bedroom and got busy with her Samsung Galaxy phone. It had already been fingerprinted and left as it had been found, on the unmade bed.

Knowing what we did about the app, my instructions were

to work silently, avoiding any possible eavesdropping through the phone. I sequestered it in a Faraday bag, cabled it to my laptop, and started running a copy right away.

Once that was going, I turned my attention to Reese Sapporo herself.

Besides the bed, everything about her room was crazy tidy. The only things on the white painted desk were a gooseneck lamp and a rose gold MacBook Air laptop. Her books were organized by color, and the clothes in her closet looked like they'd never been worn.

A quick check on her social media showed me a heavyset, plain girl. She didn't seem to have a ton of friends, and her postings tended to be on the geeky side. I saw several *Game of Thrones* references, and lots of generic memes with vaguely inspirational or funny little sayings.

> Even the smallest person can change the course of the future.
> Is it Friday yet?
> If you love something, set it free. If it comes back, that means nobody wanted it. Set it free again.

Not that there was anything wrong with all that. From what I could see, Reese was the same kind of girl I'd been at fifteen. Which is also to say, nothing like the other known targets: Gwen Petty, the pretty, popular one, and Nigella Wilbur, the aggressive wild child.

Something told me that Reese was drawn into these online conversations as much by loneliness and insecurity as Gwen had been by vanity and Nigella by raging hormones.

The question was, what did they have in common? Certainly they were all risk-takers, whether or not they knew it. Loading that app onto their phones was like hanging a COME AND GET ME sign on the front door.

Now one of those girls was dead. One was still alive. And one was missing.

But what did this guy plan on doing with Reese Sapporo?

Or even worse—had he already done it?

CHAPTER 41

AS SOON AS I had a secure copy of Reese's phone on my system, I used it to open the app and see what had been left behind.

The most recent item was the photo of Reese from that morning, bound up and wide-eyed with fear in the trunk of that anonymous car. I skipped over it as quickly as I could, but not before it had burned another little hole in my psyche. It was hard to think about and even harder to look at.

After that, I found a long string of texts and conversation fragments going back almost five months. He'd taken his time with Reese. Something told me he'd had to. Even here, the only responses she offered to his long texts were nothing more than shy little bursts, heavy on the stickers, hashtags, and emoticons.

At least, that's what we were allowed to see. There was never any knowing what the app's administrator was editing out—or adding in—for purposes of his own.

In any case, as I read through what was there, it was easy to see shades of the same guy from before. His sentences were full and well punctuated. His language was mature for a teen, but not quite adult, either. And while I didn't see the Cummings poem this time, there *was* one verse of old-fashioned poetry. I had to google it to find out it was Percy Bysshe Shelley's "Love's Philosophy."

The fountains mingle with the river
And the rivers with the ocean,
The winds of heaven mix for ever
With a sweet emotion;
Nothing in the world is single;
All things by a law divine
In one spirit meet and mingle.
Why not I with thine?

He was wooing his target this time, as opposed to seducing her. The character who came across, through this line of communication, seemed like a young and naive person, just like Reese herself, and much less overtly like some lothario trying to get into a girl's pants. That's the version I'd seen in his communication with Nigella Wilbur, and to an extent with Gwen Petty, too.

There were no selfies this time, either. No nude pics or anything overtly sexual at all. Basically, he had turned himself into the kind of person Reese Sapporo would respond to. And he'd told her exactly what she wanted to hear, as she wandered further and further into his trap. I hated seeing these strings in retrospect, where it all seemed so clear, even if it hadn't been to the victim at the time. But reading them over now felt a little like watching the crime play out through soundproof glass, while Reese flew like a moth toward that flame.

He'd even called himself JonSnow2 on-screen. It was a

reference to the best-looking guy from *Game of Thrones*, who also happened to make regular appearances on Reese's Instagram.

For that matter, it wasn't hard to imagine my own fifteen-year-old self responding to some of this. The secret boyfriend. The kindness he showered on her. The attention he paid. Even the little moments of self-deprecation. It all added up.

And it was all lies.

CHAPTER 42

Let me tell you what I imagine when I think of you. I imagine a girl who has no idea how beautiful she is. I may not know what you look like, but I do know you're beautiful. I hope that doesn't make you uncomfortable. It's just the truth.

I know you're just saying that, but thanks #dontstop ☺

Would you ever want to meet in person? I'd like to be friends if that's okay with you.

Totally want to be friends!
Let me think about the rest. I'm kinda shy...

Actually, the truth is I want to be more than that, but not if it scares you off... I'm not even sure if I should be honest about this stuff or just shut up...

#behonest

You want to hear something embarrassing? Sometimes I pretend you're my girlfriend. How lame is that? I can't help it.

That's not lame. It's sweet.
I pretend the same thing sometimes
(And now I'm REALLY blushing... ☺)

The truth is, I've never had a real girlfriend. I don't even have that many regular friends. I don't know why. I just don't really fit in at my school. It's kind of depressing, to be honest.

I can relate
<3 <3 <3
hugz

I'm just going to say it. You're fricking adorable.

No... you are
You really are. I mean it.

Guess who's getting his license on Monday? That would be me!!!

#iwish
#jelly

If you ever want to meet, I can go anywhere you want now. McDonalds? Your school? Hell, I'll meet you at the police station if that makes you feel safer . . . :-). Seriously, it doesn't matter where, and it doesn't have to be a "date" or anything. I just want to meet you. For real!

You are soooo sweet
Can I think about it?
I want to. I'm just shy (obviously . . .)

Don't let me screw this up by coming on too hard, okay? We can just keep talking if that's what you want.

No prob
Def keep talking
Tx!

I do have one request. If you're going to dump me, don't just disappear, okay? I'd hate if we stopped talking, but I'd hate it even more if you didn't at least say goodbye.

I would never do that to you
I'm 100% serious

You don't have to worry about that.
I'm not going anywhere.

You've done so much for me, way more than you know. Thanks for listening.

#youtoo
#anytime
#meanit

Hey. Do you like surprises?

Depends. What kind?

I have a good one for you.

????

You're going to have to be patient. But I promise it will be worth it.

I can wait
No I can't
Hahaha...
Tell me more

CHAPTER 43

A FEW HOURS later, I spotted Keats out the window in the Sapporos' backyard. He was just standing there by himself, staring into the woods behind the house. So I went outside to check on him.

"Billy?" I said. "Everything okay?"

"Just gathering my thoughts," he said without turning around. "Problem is, I have too many of them."

"I'm familiar with the feeling," I said. I was trying to keep it light, but I don't know if he even heard me.

"The thing is, I can't tell if we're getting little glimpses of who we're chasing here, or if it's just a nonstop stream of fabricated bullshit," he said.

"It's the same thing with the texts," I told him. "He can be anyone he wants online, and these girls are paying the price."

Keats nodded silently, then kept going.

"I mean, are we in the endgame here? Or is this all leading up to some kind of larger target?"

"What do you mean? What kind of target?" I asked. I was curious, but I could tell he needed to talk it out, too.

"Take your pick," he said. "The way this app's spreading, it could be anything. Utilities. Air traffic. Banking. There's nothing that's not networked anymore. And the longer this goes on, the harder it's getting not to blame myself."

"For what?" I asked, but Billy just shrugged. I assumed he meant the murders, and now this abduction.

I'd seen him worked up before. I even saw tears in his eyes at Gwen Petty's high school. But I'd never seen Keats question himself like this. His whole stance was tight, with arms crossed and shoulders hunched.

"Well, I know what my mom would say," I told him.

He looked almost amused at that, like he figured I was about to lay some kind of motherly folk wisdom on him. Which I basically was.

"She'd say you're taking on too much. It's like you're climbing a mountain and all you can think about is the mountain itself."

"As opposed to what?" he asked.

"As opposed to putting one foot in front of the other," I said. It sounded lame even before I was done saying it, and I wished I'd kept my mouth shut. But now that I'd started, I kept going.

I pointed back at the house and lowered my voice. "Maybe you can't save this girl," I said. "I don't know. But I'm guessing there are two parents in there who need you to think you can. I'd start with that."

Billy didn't respond, other than to take a deep breath and let it out. His eyes were still on the woods, like maybe the answers were out there somewhere.

"Hey, Keats?"

Someone had just called from the house. We both turned and I saw Obaje standing in the back door, holding up a phone.

"We've got Audrey Gruss on the line?" he said, and Billy turned to go inside. A second later, he was gone.

I knew he'd pull through this, one way or another, but it was hard to watch him struggle. And my little two-cent offering didn't seem to be worth much more than just that.

Maybe I should have quoted Winston Churchill instead of my mother, I thought. Churchill was the one who said, "If you're going through hell, keep going."

Because that's exactly what Billy needed to do. And really, there wasn't any other choice.

CHAPTER 44

KEATS CUT THE team in half at the end of the day. He sent two people back to Boston and put Obaje on a commercial flight to DC, to go meet with the Bureau's Special Crimes Division. The rest of us checked into a Ramada and kept on working.

By midnight, I was holed up in my room, running scans through my laptop, with Jimmy Fallon on mute while I texted A.A. and picked at a chicken salad from the Chili's next door. Nothing like a little late-night multitasking.

How it goes, Piglet?

Kicking my ass to be honest.

I miss you. MIT's not the same . . . :-(

You too, Pooh. We have to hang when I'm back.

YES

You need to get a bike so we can hit some trails

Hello? I don't DO bike, remember?

You'd love it

Sorry, can't hear you . . . going into a tunnel . . .

:-)

Just then, another message popped in. This one was from Keats.

You up? he asked.

I'm always up, I sent back. What do you need?

Right away, a soft knock came at my door.

Of course, I thought. Billy never stopped working, either. I walked over and looked at him through the peephole.

I assumed this had something to do with work, but I'd have been lying if I said it was the only thing that crossed my mind just then. What can I say? It's not like Billy Keats's good looks had an off switch.

Be right there, I texted. I'm all the way on the other side of this ENORMOUS ROOM.

I watched him read it and smile. Then I opened the door.

"What's up? Did something happen?" I asked. "I can be ready to go in just a sec—"

"Nah," Billy said. "Nothing like that. I just never got a chance to thank you."

"For what?" I asked. I honestly didn't know.

"For this afternoon," he said. "It's been a rough one, obviously. I don't like to make a habit of losing my shit. But I really appreciated what you said."

I was almost embarrassed. Billy had done so much for me, and this seemed like the tiniest possible thing in comparison.

"Don't worry about it," I said. "I'm glad if it helped. I felt kind of corny, if you want to know the truth."

"Oh, it was corny, all right," he said with the same kind of soft sarcasm he always gave me when he was busting my chops. "Still, it helped. And um . . . just . . . thanks," he added.

"You're welcome," I said. I was genuinely glad to know that I hadn't been a total goofball with him, and even more, that I'd been able to help on that level. For that matter, my own mother had a tendency to be corny and insightful at the same time. That must be where I got it.

Meanwhile, Billy was still standing there.

"So, anyway..." he said.

He pressed his lips into a tight smile and looked at the ground. I thought there was more coming, but the silence just kind of hung between us.

That's when I realized the subject had just changed—or was about to—and that maybe I wasn't the only one having "thoughts" just then. Maybe, just maybe, Billy Keats had come to my room with more than one thing in mind.

It had been a while since I'd been with anyone. Too long, if I'm telling the truth. And it wasn't like I'd gone out looking for him. Not this time, anyway. He'd come to me.

It was cute, actually, watching him stand there in my doorway now, shifting on his feet and trying to come up with the right thing to say. Or maybe he was trying not to say it, for all I knew.

So I went ahead and did it for him.

"Do you want to come in?" I asked, stepping back to open the door a little wider.

I was wearing a cheap hoodie I'd bought on the fly that afternoon. It had a big red lobster on the front and didn't exactly scream *Take me now,* but Keats didn't seem to mind.

He smiled again. Then he stepped inside, took the hoodie's zipper between two fingers, and pulled me closer.

"Yeah, I do," he answered, shutting the door behind him. "I really do."

SO, YEAH. THAT HAPPENED.

It wasn't the night I was expecting to have. I'm guessing that Keats would have said the same thing, up to a point. But no regrets. I needed that, even if it did mean getting about two hours' sleep, max.

When Keats's phone rang at around dawn, I thought it was my own and jerked up in bed to answer.

That's also when I remembered I wasn't alone. Or wearing anything.

"Yeah?" Keats said into his phone.

I lay back and pulled the sheet up to my shoulders. It suddenly felt a lot weirder to be naked than it had when I'd fallen asleep, all cozy and satisfied.

But there wasn't much time for feeling awkward, anyway.

"*What?*" Keats said. He sat up on the edge of the bed. "Wait, wait, wait, wait. How many—"

"What is it?" I asked, but he ignored me. He shouldered the

phone, stood up, pulling on a pair of white boxers, and went into the bathroom.

"What time was she found?" I heard him say. And then, "How much?" Then, "Well, give me a range."

I was up now, too, heart pounding as I reached around for whichever clothes were closest at hand. The clock said five twenty, and it sounded like Reese Sapporo had been found.

But what did that mean? Found how? Alive?

"Yeah, yeah, okay," Keats said over the sound of running water. "Text me the location. We'll be there as soon as we can."

A second later, he came back into the room, moving with a purpose.

"Sorry about this," he said.

"Don't be stupid," I said. "What's going on? Did they find her?"

"Yeah. She was dropped out of a car, blindfolded, in a parking garage at the Portland airport," he said. "Maybe half an hour ago."

Thank God. With the Nigella Wilbur case, I'd been hugely relieved to find her alive. This was like more of the same, but on steroids. If I was being honest, I really hadn't been expecting Reese Sapporo to make it back from whatever had happened to her. I wasn't sure if Keats had been thinking the same thing, but a palpable sense of relief rushed through me.

"They just... let her go?" I asked. "Unharmed?"

"That's right," he said, yanking on his pants. His jaw was set tight against whatever else he wasn't saying. Something more had obviously happened, but Keats tended to clam up whenever he took a hit.

"Come on, Billy. Spit it out or tell me to stop asking questions," I said. "What's going on? Am I allowed to know?"

He grabbed his shoes off the floor and sat on the edge of the bed.

"Another family was attacked last night," he said. "Three dead, including a nineteen-year-old girl with the same app loaded on her phone."

Even now, after everything else that had happened, I couldn't believe it. Any sense of reprieve from the Reese Sapporo case had just been snatched away and replaced with this, like tripling down on the stakes in a blink. Three more people had just died.

"*No,*" was all I managed to say.

"There's a fourth victim who survived," Keats went on. "An older brother home from college they probably weren't expecting to be there. The kid was shot in the throat and left for dead. He's in surgery now, but ought to be out by the time we get there."

"Where are we going?" I asked.

I was throwing things into my bag as fast as I could. Keats was ready to leave. He pocketed his phone and put a hand on the doorknob.

"Mass General," he said. In other words, we were headed back to Boston. "That's the other kick in the nuts. This family lived in Harbor Towers condos off Atlantic Avenue."

And the hits just kept on coming.

"You mean—?"

"Yeah," Keats said. "While we were chasing our tails up here, they were taking out their next targets five goddamn blocks from our office."

CHAPTER 46

OUR CHOPPER LANDED on the roof of Massachusetts General Hospital at nine thirty that morning, and we went straight to the ICU.

Keats was the only one allowed in, so I waited with another agent, Carl Baillette, in the nearest chairs. There was still plenty I could get done with my laptop.

And plenty to think about, too. This latest move wasn't about spreading us thin. The FBI had more than enough resources to cover as many crime scenes as these slippery sons of bitches could throw at us.

No. It was about flexing their muscles and showing off.

I'm no criminologist, but I know hackers. They're driven by three things: ego, money, and notoriety, which is really just more ego. This was all about toying with us and controlling our moves. And so far, they were succeeding.

Emphasis on *they*. If there had been any lingering doubts about this as some kind of solo operation, those were gone. We now knew that the Nicholson family had been attacked in Boston within the same hour that Reese Sapporo was dropped off at the airport garage in Portland. And nobody was calling it a coincidence. This had been a carefully orchestrated sequence of events.

At a minimum, there were two perpetrators involved here, if not more. And they were clearly upping their game. Fast.

As for where it might be headed next, I could only guess.

A few minutes after Keats had gone in to do his interview with the one surviving member of the Nicholson family, he was back again. I looked up from where I was sitting and saw him motioning me over through the glass doors of the ICU.

"I need your help," he said, handing me some kind of visitor's pass to clip on. "The kid's name is Justin Nicholson. He's cogent, but he can't speak. You're going to help him do that. I just need you to sit and hold his hand. Okay?"

"Absolutely," I said. My head was swimming, but there was no question. Of course I could do this. I'd have to. And I was glad Billy had come to trust me this much—not just because I wanted to be involved, but because I wanted to give him as much support as I possibly could.

I followed Keats through the ICU doors, into the antiseptic smell of the unit, and down to the last bed on the hall. That's where I saw Justin Nicholson for the first time. He seemed to be asleep, but when we came in, his eyes fluttered open.

He was a huge guy, linebacker big, and took up most of the bed. There was a tracheostomy tube in his throat, and I could see a yellow-and-rust-colored stain on the gauze around the entry point. From there, a ribbed white hose ran to a respirator, which was helping him breathe.

"Justin, this is Angela," Keats said. "She's going to assist with these questions."

Right away, Justin seemed agitated. He looked at me wide-eyed and opened his mouth, but nothing came out. I went to the side of the bed and put my hand on his.

"Don't try to talk," I said. Two tears ran down the sides of his face and I wiped them away with a tissue. It was heartbreaking to see him so devastated, and to think about everything he'd just lost. For all I knew, I reminded him of his sister, who hadn't been much younger than me. Instead of asking any of the million questions coursing through my mind, I tried to keep it professional and let Keats take the lead.

Keats put himself at the foot of the bed where Justin could easily see him. I stayed where I was, focused on Justin, ready to do whatever I could for him.

"I'm just going to ask a few yes or no items," Keats told him. "You can squeeze Angela's hand once for yes, and do nothing if it's a no. Okay?"

I felt a tentative squeeze on my hand and nodded at Keats to keep going. This had to be quick. Justin was in no shape for a long interview.

"Justin, did you see the person who attacked you last night?" Keats asked.

I got another squeeze and gave Keats a fast nod.

"Did you see more than one person?" Keats asked.

There was no response. I shook my head for no.

"And the person you did see—was it a man?"

Yes.

"Anyone you recognized?"

No.

I could feel a kind of quickening in the air. This was progress—the closest thing we had to an eyewitness—even if it was too little, too late. Justin kept shifting his gaze from Keats to me and back again. I could tell he wanted to say something. It must have been incredibly frustrating.

Then he mouthed my name—*Angela.*

"That's right," I said, and moved a little farther down the bed so he could see me more easily. But nothing I did seemed to calm him down. Not that I expected it to. He'd just lost his entire world.

"One more question," Keats assured him. "Did this man say anything to you, Justin?"

Yes.

He pulled his hand out of mine then and brought both of his own together in some kind of gesture.

"What is it?" Keats asked.

Justin was insistent, motioning as emphatically as he could, which wasn't much. He pointed with his right index finger and moved it back and forth across the other palm.

"Do you want to write something?" I asked. He tried to nod and winced from the pain.

"Stay still," Keats said. "We've got you."

Keats pulled a pen out of his jacket pocket. I managed to find a small legal pad in my bag. I put both of them into Justin's hands. He was shaking and dropped the pen, then waited for me to put it back in his grasp.

"Take your time," Keats told him. "Tell us what this guy said, and then we're going to let you get some rest."

Justin was clearly struggling to get something down. The pen scratched and shook across the page, forming three barely readable words. When he finally stopped and dropped the pad, Keats came around to see what it said.

I'd already read it. I wasn't even sure if I could believe what I was seeing. But I did know one thing now. They never meant for Justin Nicholson to die. He was their messenger.

And right there, in a faint wavering scrawl, was his message from the killer.

Tell Angela hello.

CHAPTER 47

OUR DAY ENDED with a 6:00 p.m. shift meeting at the field office.

This time around, everyone knew who I was, partly because I'd been around the block a few times by now. But mostly, it was because of the way my name had been so suddenly introduced into the mix of this case. Word about Justin's message to me from the killers had obviously reached the field office ahead of this meeting. And judging from the looks I kept getting around the room, I think they were expecting me to be more freaked out than I felt.

But the truth was, we'd already been targeted by these people. They'd taken our picture. They'd sent us running up to Maine, where I had no doubt they'd kept an eye on us.

And now this. It smacked of bully tactics, going after the perceived weak link—the young female intern. It was predictable, and in a strange way, I was losing respect for whoever was behind it. Up to now, they'd shown some real chops with the app in a way that I couldn't help admiring. But this move almost felt like a cheap shot in comparison.

On the other hand, I'm not stupid, and I'm not suicidal. So I didn't say a word when Keats insisted on a security detail for me. Starting that night, I was going to have my very own conjoined twin, courtesy of the FBI. It didn't thrill me, but it was better than moving home and, God forbid, letting my parents know what had happened.

Meanwhile, at the meeting, we heard from all corners of the investigation, starting with Keats's report on the last thirty-six hours.

Word from Reese Sapporo was that she'd been lured out of her room at two in the morning, attacked, and then drugged in the dark woods behind her house. She'd told the authorities in Portland that she remembered feeling a sharp stab under her arm before passing out. Then she remembered waking up in the trunk of a car. That was it.

She never saw anyone's face, including whoever took her picture. That person, she'd said, was wearing a ski mask. Probably because he knew he'd be letting her go.

She wasn't sure, either, if it had been a lone assailant or if there had been more than one of them. It was all hazy in her memory, and there hadn't been much to see in the dark.

"We'll be following up with Justin Nicholson as soon as his medical team lets us back in," Keats reported. "Not sure how much of a description we're going to get from him, though. It was dark in that house, and his memory of the whole thing is sketchy at best."

"Where are we on the larger picture?" one of the DC contacts asked from a screen on the wall. "Any new word on who's doing this, or why?"

I was pretty sure I saw a twinge in Billy's eye just then. He'd been calm and pulled together the whole time, but this was his sore spot. He looked over to SAC Gruss, and she took it from there.

"Obviously, they're well organized, with some amount of infrastructure, and certainly a high degree of technical acumen," she said. "Not to mention funding. Beyond that, it could be some kind of snuff network, or a hacker collective, or of course a terrorist cell, domestic or international."

"So you think there's some kind of larger objective here?" the DC agent followed up. "That maybe all this movement is just some kind of opening salvo?"

Keats answered that one. "We don't know," he said. "But it does seem like a lot of trouble to go to, just to find people to kill."

You could feel the edge in the room. Nobody was comfortable with how little we had so far.

"Whatever they are, they're up to fifteen million unduplicated copies now," Zack Ciomek chimed in. "Which, again, points to some kind of larger-scale operation."

I wanted to speak up in the worst way. I wasn't as ready as most in the room to dismiss the idea that these attacks might be taken at face value. Everything they'd done so far was unprecedented in hacker circles, but by the same token, it was just a bigger version of what you might expect from people like that.

There's no hacker on the planet who wouldn't want to see his work duplicated on fifteen million devices. It could have easily been its own objective, just to see how far they could take it. In my mind, it all felt like giant egos run amok. The attention seeking. The showy programming. Even the murders.

But I didn't have anything more than my gut instinct and an aborted grad school education to back me up on that one.

Presumably, Keats and Gruss were privy to all kinds of data I hadn't seen.

And if nothing else, I'd already gotten far more attention that day than I wanted. So I kept my thoughts to myself.

For the time being, anyway.

"HEY, ANGELA, WAIT UP!"

I put my hand on the elevator button. Keats nodded at the two security guards as he passed, got on with me, then waited for the doors to close.

"You okay?" he asked once we were heading down.

"I'm fine," I said. "I'm not going to let this throw me."

"Maybe you should," he said. "You know. Worry a little more?"

"Where have I heard that before?" I asked. "Oh, right. Everywhere."

"Angela—"

"It's not like they didn't already know who we were," I told Billy and kept going before he could cut me off. "Besides, I'm meeting my new boyfriend, George, right down here in the lobby."

George Yates was the retired agent who had the dubious pleasure of being my first security officer. He was going to be with me through the night.

"What about you?" I asked. "Are *you* okay?"

The elevator hit the ground floor and we stepped out into the lobby. I saw George outside by his car and held up a finger to let him know I'd be right there.

"We never got a chance to talk," Billy said. "After last night, I mean."

"I know."

I think he was expecting me to be on pins and needles about it, which was sweet, in a way. But not really necessary.

"Last night was incredible," I said. "*You* were incredible. Just what I needed. But I know the deal here, Billy. I know all the reasons why it was a mistake, and I know that none of them are personal."

Billy never would have used that word—*mistake*. In his own way, he was a gentleman. But he didn't contradict me, either.

"I'm not sure what to say to that," he said.

"It's fine," I told him. "Besides, who knows? Maybe we'll get to make the same mistake again sometime."

"No, no, no," he said. "Don't take this the wrong way, but that can't happen again."

"We'll see," I said, partly because that's what I thought. But also because Billy was fun to mess with. It was like coming full circle, back to Office Flirtation 2.0. "I'd better get moving. My guy's waiting."

It could have been uncomfortable. Maybe it even should have been. But it just wasn't. Billy seemed to vibe with me about it, too, and my joke glanced off him without any tension.

Which of course only made him hotter. Dammit.

When we got outside, Billy stopped to say hi to George and catch up a little, before he said good night to both of us. Then as he turned away to head back inside, I hit him with a parting shot, just for fun.

"Hey, Agent Keats?" I called out.

Billy stopped and turned. "Yeah?"

"You were a *beast* last night," I said. "I've never seen anyone work a case so hard. Or so long. Go get some sleep, because you deserve it."

Billy shook his head at me but kept a poker face.

"Thank you, *Intern Hoot,*" he said, giving back a little better than I expected before he moved off into the night. I guess I wasn't the only one who could roll with the punches.

And good thing, too. Because I was about to get hit with a big one before that day was over.

"WHERE ARE WE heading?" George asked.

"Eventually out to Somerville," I said. "But I need to make a couple of stops across the river, if you don't mind."

"Your call," he said. "I'm on the clock until seven a.m. Doesn't matter to me where I spend it."

On our way to Cambridge, I got an earful about George's kidneys, his Dobermans, and his ex-wife, whose remarriage was saving him a bundle. He seemed to mistake me for one of his lodge buddies, but I couldn't really complain. I wouldn't want to play babysitter, either.

In any case, while George chattered away, he didn't seem to mind, or even notice, that I was texting with A.A. at the same time.

You around? I asked.

I can be, she came back right away.

Coming to hang with you if that's ok? Can't stay too long.

Excellent. Pick up a bottle?

I can do that.

The truth was, I'd come out of that shift meeting thinking about five people: my mother, my father, my sisters, and A.A.

I'd already gone over every internet-connected device in my parents' house and given them all the old "Surf safe" lecture. Twice for my sisters. But now I wanted to check A.A.'s phone. If there were fifteen million copies of this thing, what were the chances one of them had landed with her?

I asked George to stop at the Starbucks on Mass Ave and ran in for two venti dark roasts plus two double espresso shots. After that, I picked up a pint of Jameson at the liquor store to go with the coffee. A.A. and I called it Irish Ritalin. It was just the right combination to put an edge on and take it off at the same time.

When we got to Ashdown House, George pulled up and parked illegally right in front.

"Do you have to come in with me?" I asked.

"Take this," he said, and handed me a radio. "It's got a GPS on it and a dedicated channel. I'll be right here if you need me. And don't go anywhere else."

"Fair enough," I said. "I'll be an hour, tops."

"No problemo."

I appreciated the personal space, whether or not he was supposed to give it to me. And I was psyched to get a little time with my bestie, too. The night was going about 90 percent better than I would have thought, considering the ridiculous day I'd had.

So I was disappointed, to say the least, when I saw Darren Wendt coming down the building's main stairs. It looked like he was just leaving as I was coming inside. Maybe that was why A.A. sent me on a drinks run, I thought—to buy herself a little time with the Cro-Magnon creep himself.

Just not enough of it, apparently.

"Hoot!" Darren said before I could pretend not to see him. "As I live and sneeze."

"Darren. What an unpleasant surprise," I said. "Why are you still coming here, anyway? I thought you liked your women dumb."

"Yeah, well..." He looked around, playing it up like some bad actor. "It's MIT. There are no dumb girls here."

"Plenty of assholes, though," I said.

I meant it, but he just laughed. He was obviously in a good mood and I hated to think about why.

"All right, then. Good talk. Gotta go," I said, and kept on moving.

"You know she's never going to be your girlfriend, right?" he called after me, loud enough for anyone to hear.

I shouldn't have stopped. The best MO with guys like him is always some combination of "Ignore" and "Keep walking." But there was just something about Darren that demanded constant shutting down.

"So now you're the only one who can hang out with her?" I said, against my own better judgment.

"Get over it, Hoot! You lost!" he yelled. People were starting to stare. "And the pathetic thing is, you don't even know how obvious you are."

Then he stepped back, reached out with one hand, and dropped an invisible mic. Just when I thought he couldn't hit the douchiness any harder, he did.

"Hey, Darren," I called back, also loud enough for anyone to hear. "How are those small balls working out for you?" It wasn't an empty insult. I knew from A.A. that it was true, and I waited just long enough to watch Darren's face fall before I turned and headed up the stairs.

I didn't stop this time, either. At least, not until I was standing outside A.A.'s door. That's when I noticed how hard my heart was beating. There was a hollow thump in my chest, like someone was chasing after me. And it wasn't from climbing stairs.

It was what Darren had said, I realized.

She's never going to be your girlfriend.

Something about it had stuck to me. And the reason why was just starting to light up my brain.

Was it possible? Could Darren Wendt have seen something about me that I hadn't even seen myself? I was usually immune to his comments, but this one had gotten under my skin, and I couldn't just shake it off. Which was humiliating.

But also—strangely enough—interesting.

No. Exciting.

Energizing.

Or maybe just plain . . . true.

CHAPTER 50

A.A. TOOK ONE look at me and called it as soon as I was through the door.

"What's up?" she asked. "You look weird."

I set the drinks down and cracked open the Jameson. Then I took a first shot from the bottle before I poured another into each of our coffees.

Whatever was going on inside me, it was all moving too fast. I couldn't completely deny what Darren had said. But my attraction to Billy Keats was just as undeniable. Unless I was fooling myself about one thing or the other.

Oh, man. My head was going in circles.

All I knew for sure was that I didn't want to say a word about Darren. If I was going to talk about this at all, it had to be on my own terms, not his.

And not right now.

"It's been a day," I said.

"And a half, I guess," she said, watching me take another swig of whiskey. It burned its way down my throat and started settling with that warm, comforting feeling in my gut. I didn't want to get drunk. Not right now, anyway. I just needed to slow down my system a little and change the subject—back to the real reason I'd come.

"Hey, so anyway," I said. "If I asked to look inside your phone, no questions, would you let me?"

She gave me a squint and I just stared back. She knew me well enough to know that I'd be asking for a good reason. And then sure enough, A.A. smirked, took her phone off the desk, and handed it over.

"Still weird, but okay," she said. "And how flexible are we on the no-questions policy?"

"Drink your Ritalin," I said.

I trusted A.A., of course. Hundred percent. But I was determined to maintain the case confidentiality that was required of me at the Bureau, no matter what.

Without another word, I cabled her phone to my laptop and took a look around inside. First, I checked for any files with an .aaw extension, or .mw, accounting for her birth name. There were none. Then I searched for email attachments containing executable programs. And that's where I found it.

As it turned out, A.A. was one of the fifteen million people with a copy of this insidious thing sitting right there on her device. I wasn't shocked, considering that the app's epicenter was Boston. But still, it sucked to see it here, so close to home.

From what I could tell, the original email was four days old. A.A. had trashed it right away, of course. She knew better than to open an attachment as fishy as that. I permanently deleted it from her trash anyway, just to be safe. Then I handed back the phone.

"Did I pass?" she said.

"Close enough," I told her, and gulped my doctored coffee.

It was everything I could do to keep from sharing at least a few key details with her. Not because I was afraid for her safety, but because I knew how badly she'd love geeking out on something like this.

"I don't mean to sound like a broken record," she said, "but are you sure nothing's wrong?"

She sat back on my old bed. I'd always kept it fairly tidy, but now it was littered with papers, books, and laundry. I looked over at her, lounging there with the hot coffee, and the crop top, and the sarcastic smile she never knew she was giving.

And that's the moment I realized Darren had been right. That asshole.

I'd never been one to keep secrets from A.A., and now I had two big ones weighing me down. The one about the app was a nonstarter, but as for this second, much more personal one, I knew I'd have to say something about it eventually. One way or another.

Just not now. Not yet. It was still too fresh. Or maybe more like raw.

So I ran in the opposite direction instead.

"I do have one little piece of news," I said. "Well, medium-sized to big, actually."

"Go on." She leaned back against the wall and sipped her drink. For the first time since I'd gotten to Ashdown House that evening, things felt a little bit like they used to.

"It's about Billy," I said.

A.A.'s spine straightened. "Agent Blue Eyes?" she asked.

"In the flesh," I said. "No pun intended."

"Ooh," she said. "I like the sound of that. Keep talking. I want to hear *everything*."

GEORGE AND I got to my place in Somerville a little after eleven o'clock. Before we went in, I surprised myself by asking him to set up in the living room, as opposed to staying out in his car. So maybe I was just a little on edge. I appreciated Billy looking out for me, even if I'd been ambivalent when he set up the security detail in the first place. Not that it was up to me, as it turned out.

"I was planning on coming in, anyway," George said. "It's one thing to let you have an hour with your friend back at MIT, but make no mistake, Angela. They wouldn't have set this up if it wasn't for a good reason."

I wondered what Keats had said to him about me. Certainly I had a cavalier reputation, but I wouldn't want George to think I took this for granted, either. I guess it was a fine line.

"Okay, then," I said, getting out of the car. "*Mi casa, su casa,* and all that."

"Don't know what that means, but I wouldn't say no to something to eat," George answered.

"Close enough."

As soon as we got inside, I pointed him to the fridge, told him to help himself to anything he liked, and went to dump my stuff in the bedroom. I'd barely dropped my case onto the bed when I heard a text dinging into my phone.

A.A., I thought. *Has to be.*

But in fact, it was from Eve.

Call me. Now if you can.

There was nothing casual about that. Eve never told me to call her, much less ASAP. And considering everything else going on, I knew this was some kind of serious business.

Maybe fifteen seconds later, I had her on the line.

"What's up?" I asked, sitting down on the bed, still in my jacket.

"I'm sending you a link," she said. "And FYI, it's not traceable back to me."

"What kind of link?" I asked.

"You'll know what to do," she said. "Just take the damn credit this time, will you?"

I had no idea why she was being so vague. I was about 70 percent curious and 30 percent concerned.

"Well, hang on, I'll open it while you're on the phone," I told her. I was already pulling out my laptop and flipping it open. "Did you send it to my work account or my Gmail?"

Eve didn't answer.

"Eve?"

When I looked down at my phone again, I saw that she'd hung up. I guess she was pretty serious about letting me take ownership of whatever this was. And now I was more intrigued than ever, given the cloak-and-dagger routine, which wasn't really like her.

When I got to the email a second later, the subject line said

SALT-AND-PEPPER SHRIMP. That was Eve's favorite dish from Myers and Chang—presumably to let me know that this was, in fact, from her. More cloak-and-dagger. What the hell?

The body of the email itself was empty, except for a read-only script file sent as a straightforward attachment from an address I didn't recognize. There was no signature, and no additional text, beyond the attachment itself.

I was tempted to call Eve back before I did anything else. Certainly, if this were anyone other than her, I'd never trust that random attachment. But Eve had clearly sent it this way, without comment, for whatever reasons of her own. So I kept going. I ran my finger over the track pad, navigated my pointer to the attachment, and clicked.

Immediately, the attached file disappeared from my screen. But I had a pretty good guess about where to look for it and took only a few seconds to find it in my root directory, where it had replanted itself.

Everything about this was outside of the usual protocols, but I wasn't going to stop now. So I rebooted the laptop to run the program. I should have been exhausted after the last twenty-four hours, but it was more like the opposite. As my laptop shut down and restarted, I felt like I'd just woken up and started a whole new workday.

When the screen finally came back on, I'd been directed to some kind of generic platform. It was nothing I'd seen before. If anything, it reminded me of the app we'd been chasing all this time. The design was simple, in three colors, with a rudimentary, almost intuitive interface.

A few clicks later, I realized I was looking at a database of some kind. The screen in front of me showed an empty form, with spaces for FIRSTNAME, LASTNAME, ADDRESS, PHONE, ISP, HOST, and NOTES. A few drop-down menus from the top ribbon showed me a dozen or more commands, all the usual kind you might expect from a rudimentary DB platform.

I stumbled around a little bit more and managed to run a sort based on one of those available fields, last name. That turned up just over twenty-one thousand records. I scrolled through several of them but didn't see any names, addresses, or anything, really, that I recognized.

Then a new idea hit me, and I ran a new search, this time for a specific last name: Petty.

What I got next was a single entry for Gwen Petty, the first victim I'd known about in this case. A little more looking turned up Nigella Wilbur and then Reese Sapporo as well. All of them were listed with correct street addresses, if my memory served me right. Which I was sure it did.

"Jesus Christ," I said. Something told me those twenty-one thousand records belonged to all of the people who had opened the app on their phone after receiving it, for whatever reason. And among those twenty-one thousand were the three known victims since I'd come on board. It was all pulling together.

"Everything okay in there?" George called from the living room, and I flinched. I'd actually forgotten he was out there.

"All good!" I called back. I wasn't ready to share this yet, and even when I did, it wouldn't be with George. First I needed to dig a little deeper.

And what I found next changed everything.

IT TOOK SEVERAL hours to weed through the database's code, but I finally hit the pay dirt I think that Eve expected me to find. It was a certificate thumbprint number, correlated to an anonymous user who had posted several updates through a server in Coba, Mexico.

Bingo.

Coba is a small town on the Yucatán Peninsula. It's mostly famous for its Mayan ruins, but in my world, Coba was infamous as the last known base of a cyberterrorist organization called the Free Net Collective, or FNC.

With Eve's implicit stamp of approval, I knew this was no coincidence.

Ironically, FNC's terrorist philosophy was based on two principles that I stood behind completely: the need for internet privacy and the importance of net neutrality in the marketplace.

Their means, though, were both criminal and violent. They

crashed servers, cleaned out cash accounts, and made physical attacks against any individual or organization they deemed hostile to their goals.

A year earlier, they'd disrupted internet service for over a million people on the East Coast after one ISP tried to introduce tiered pricing based on the internet content its customers were accessing.

Even worse, FNC had claimed responsibility for firebombing the home office of a Nevada congressman who had been leading the privacy deregulation charge in Washington. Two staffers and a housekeeper had been killed in that attack.

The rumors were that all of FNC's operations had been moved offshore, since a joint raid between US authorities and Mexico's Agencia Federal de Investigación had found the Coba facility empty. Most people I knew assumed FNC was working from a ship of some kind, or several linked vessels in the Gulf of Mexico, the Caribbean, or maybe even out on the Atlantic. The world was their haystack now, and they were one of its most notorious needles.

But none of that explained what these sexting murders had to do with FNC's mission. I just assumed from the evidence—from Eve—that some kind of further connection could be made here, if I dug deeply enough, or asked myself enough of the right questions.

What was the larger objective here? How did this invasive app at the heart of it all tie in? And for that matter, how was FNC coordinating with whoever was on the ground for them, stalking and executing these victims?

As usual, the questions were piling up faster than the answers. But one thing was clear: this case had just level-jumped to a matter of national security. Which put me in well over my head, but then again, nothing new there. If anything, I was getting used to feeling like I was drowning all the time. The trick was to just keep swimming.

So I did what I assumed Eve meant for me to do. I immediately called it all into Keats. It was only 5:00 a.m. when I left an emergency message on his secure line, but I heard back right away.

"Are you home?" he asked.

"Yeah. What do you want me to do?"

"Stay put. We're coming to you."

"*We?*" I asked.

"That's right. Get yourself ready. It's going to be... Well, just be ready," he said.

But he didn't say for what.

I FIGURED I could either take time to make coffee for Keats's team before they got to my place or I could keep learning as much as possible about all of this before someone told me to stop digging.

Guess which one I went with.

I texted A.A. first, but she didn't answer right away. So I called and woke her up.

"Speak," she said. Her voice was still thick with sleep, but at least I didn't hear any snoring in the background. Not that Darren was on my list of worries right now.

"I'll make it quick," I said. "What do you know about FNC?"

I figured that would wake her up, and it did.

"*The* FNC?" she said. "As in the Free Net Collective? Seriously?"

"How much do you think you could find out about their current operations, if you really had to?" I asked.

I wasn't going to break any confidentiality laws here, though I was definitely bending them a bit. I was on thin ice just by bringing this up, but nobody I knew outside the Bureau had deeper research skills than A.A. And nobody *inside* the FBI was going to share this kind of info with the cyber intern.

"That's some dark web shit," she said.

"I know."

"Not that I couldn't do it."

"I know," I said again. "That's why I'm calling."

I could hear A.A. moving around, probably pulling her laptop out from under the bed, where it usually slept.

"I've heard they use brute-force tools on some kind of massive scale. It's how they crippled that power grid in Texas last year," she said. "Why exactly are you asking, anyway?"

"Because I have a book report due in the morning," I told her. She knew full well that I couldn't give the real reason. And I knew full well that she'd be intrigued enough to keep going anyway.

"Fine. Just use me for my superior skills and then cast me aside," she said.

"I knew you'd understand."

That got a cute little growl out of her, but it was the last of the resistance.

"I'll see what I can find out," she said. "There's a mock terrorism task force in the Graduate Women's Group. I could probably pick a few brains over there, too, if you want."

"As long as nobody knows it's coming from me," I said.

"Duh," she said. "But Angela? I'd hate to think you were getting in over your head. Sometimes that kind of thing happens before you even realize it, and then it's too late. I mean, this *is* you we're talking about. You're staying safe, right?"

I looked out my bedroom door, from which I could see George reading a paper at my kitchen table with a Glock 19 holstered on his hip.

"Never been safer," I said. "Swear to God. Now go back to sleep. You can jump on this in the morning."

"Yeah, right," she said. "After everything you just told me? I'm wide awake."

Which was basically what I'd expected her to say. "Okay, then, in that case—"

"I'm on it, Piglet. Talk to you soon."

"Thanks, Pooh."

I knew I could count on her. No matter what.

CHAPTER 54

HALF AN HOUR later, I had four federal agents clomping around my apartment and asking questions. I was sure the downstairs neighbors were absolutely thrilled, at five thirty in the morning.

Keats relieved George for the last few hours of his shift. I'd see him again at the end of the day, with another agent assigned to me starting at 8:00 a.m.

That left me with Billy, Obaje, and two others, Miller and Gao, all hovering around my living room. I felt like I'd fallen into some kind of Russian spy novel, and not in a good way.

"I'm not going to go into too much detail," Keats said, cutting off most of my questions, "but how long have you been in possession of those database files?"

I looked at the clock. "It's been two hours and forty minutes," I said.

"Can you say for sure that nobody else has seen them?" he asked.

"Of course not," I said. "But I'm as sure as I can be, and I trust my source."

"Eve?" Billy asked.

"Well . . . yeah," I said. There was no question about obscuring anything at this point.

"Why didn't you call right away?" Gao asked me. Keats was the lead interviewer, but that hadn't stopped the other three from jumping in with questions of their own.

"Because I didn't know what I had. As soon as I did, I called," I said.

"What kind of keystroke log do you keep on your laptop?" Miller put in. He was taking written notes, too.

"I don't," I told him. It was never worth it to me to leave that kind of virtual trail as I worked. My own memory was good enough for that, and as for anyone else, it was none of their business. Or at least until now.

"What about—" Gao started to ask, but Miller jumped back in. They were practically falling over each other to get what they needed here.

"Hang on," Miller said. "What other connected devices do you keep in the apartment?"

"My phone," I said, pointing to where I'd set it on the coffee table. "And there's a tablet in the bedroom that I hardly ever use."

I started to get up but Obaje put out a hand. "Just tell me where," he said. "I'll get it."

"Jesus. Pile on much?" I said. "I'm not the terrorist. You guys know that, right?"

Billy lowered his chin and gave me a stare. "I understand this isn't any fun," he said. "But do you know what you're sitting on here?"

I saw his point immediately, and just as quickly as my temper had flared, I reined it back in. If anything, I was embarrassed for speaking out, considering the circumstances. I'd just introduced some highly sensitive information to the mix, with national security implications. There was no reason for the FBI to take my word on anything here. Just the opposite, if they wanted to do this right.

"Sorry," I said. "I guess I'm still catching up."

Billy's eyes softened long enough to signal something like "Hang in there" before he went on.

"It's going to be a long day," he said. "And there'll be more at the office later, starting with a polygraph. You just need to gut this out."

I took a deep breath. It's not like I couldn't separate work and pleasure, but it had been only about twenty-four hours since Billy and I had been doing something *very* different at that hotel in Maine. It was a lot of gears to shift.

"Let me ask you this," Billy said. "What do *you* make of it all?"

I appreciated the question. For whatever rookie complaining I'd been doing up to that point, it was also true that this was the kind of conversation I thought they'd come to have with me in the first place. I wanted to help, and in fact, I felt like I could, given the chance.

"I think the whole point was to write their own app from scratch," I said. "And I think they did it for some really specific reasons."

"Go on," Billy told me. The others sat back and seemed to take me in in a new way—probably based on the trust that Billy was showing me right now.

The relevant truth was, all kinds of jihadists, drug dealers, gangsters, and terrorists used basic commercial apps like Snapchat and WhatsApp to communicate with their people. But even the likes of ISIS had gotten burned when it turned out that those mainstream apps were ultimately less anonymous and more hackable than they'd seemed at first. It happens all the time. Every "perfect" app is just another *Titanic* waiting for someone to come along and punch a hole in its supposedly impenetrable hull.

"My guess is they went homegrown to control any vulnerability. Since they built this app themselves, they can update it anytime they please, and they can patch it indefinitely," I said. "The trade-off is that they had to start with an audience of zero users. But they've obviously made some headway." I pointed at the database open on my laptop. "There are over twenty thousand names in there, *with* contact info."

I saw Keats holding back a little smile. "Not that you've given it any thought," he said.

I shrugged. "It's what I do."

"Let's get Eve Abajian on the line," Keats said. Obaje took out his phone. I gave him the number to Eve's personal cell and he dialed.

"Voice mail," he said several seconds later.

"On the first ring?" I asked.

He shook his head no. He said it had rung four times first. That meant her phone was definitely on.

"Let me try from my cell," I said. "She'll pick up."

"I'll call," Keats said, taking my phone off the table before I could do it. Something told me I wasn't getting that phone back, either.

He put it on speaker and dialed. It rang four times again, went to voice mail, and I heard the usual spiel.

"You've reached Eve. Please leave a message or text me. Thanks. Ciao."

"Eve, it's Billy Keats calling from Angela's phone," he said. "Give me a call back if you get this, ASAP. We're on our way over to you. I assume you'll know what this is about. It's urgent, obviously."

It wasn't until Billy hung up that I started to worry. Marlena was always awake by now. Maybe Eve was giving her a bottle, but she never kept her phone out of reach. She would have seen those calls coming back-to-back and known something was up.

"We should go," I said. "Like, now."

"We're going," Keats said. Everyone was already packing up. "Miller, get BPD on the line and send a cruiser over there right away."

"On it."

I gritted my teeth as I threw on my shoes. I could only hope my imagination was getting the best of me. Because the alternative was too grim to think about.

All I knew for sure was that suddenly it felt like we couldn't get over to Eve's place fast enough.

BY THE TIME we pulled onto Eve's street, I was fighting panic. I've never been the worrying type, but it was creeping up my neck like a rash. When I saw the cruiser parked in front of her town house, I nearly jumped out of the moving car.

As soon as we came to a stop, I did jump out. I wasn't waiting for any invitations.

"She's not answering," one of the two cops said over his shoulder to Billy.

"I've got this!" I yelled, and pushed my way to the front. Maybe it wasn't appropriate "intern" behavior, but screw that. I needed to know if Eve was okay.

I put in the code for her front door, threw it open, and let them go ahead. The cops went first, along with Billy and Obaje. And because nobody said otherwise, I followed right behind.

The foyer was empty, with no indication of a break-in. But that didn't mean anything.

"Eve?" I called out. Billy was yelling for her, too, as we ran up to the second floor.

"All clear here," one of the cops was saying.

"What about the third floor?" I said. "The nursery and bedroom are up there."

"Wait here," Keats told me, and I sweated it out while they checked the other rooms. With every ticking second, I got a worse feeling about this. One cop stayed with me while Keats and Obaje hit the third floor, and the second officer stationed himself down by the open front door.

"I don't see her!" I heard Obaje say a minute later.

"Nothing over here!" Keats's voice came from somewhere farther away.

They were both on their way back down when I heard the cop at the front door.

"Excuse me, ma'am, you can't come in here."

And then, with a rush of relief, I heard Eve's voice right on top of that.

"Who in the blue hell are you, and what are you doing in my house?"

I hurried over to look down to where she was pushing her way past the cop through her own front door, folded-up stroller in one arm and Marlena in the other.

"Eve!" I said, and she gave me a steaming look. I knew right away how angry she'd be about whatever misunderstanding had just gone down. Coming into her place with strangers, much less uninvited, was beyond a cardinal sin in Eve's book. It was, quite literally, an affront to the way she made her living, much less her safety and her way of life.

"Make yourself useful," Eve told the cop, handing off the stroller before she headed up the stairs. "That goes in the back closet."

"Ma'am, are you all right?" the other cop asked as she reached us.

"No, I'm not," she said, glaring at Billy. "I took my daughter for an early-morning walk and *this* is what I come home to?"

"We got a call that there might be trouble," the officer told her, but Eve was clearly in no mood for listening.

"Will somebody show these gentlemen some ID and get them out of my house?" she said.

It was like the air had rushed out of me all at once. Thank God she was okay. Despite the false alarm, this was a good reminder to save the worrying for when there was actually something to worry about. The rest was just paranoia, and that's not a good color on me.

It didn't take long for Keats to thank the police and send them on their way. A second later, we were alone in her living room, where Billy and Eve threw eye darts at each other.

"What the hell, Eve?" Keats asked. "Why didn't you return my call?"

"What the hell, yourself?" she answered, bouncing Marlena on her shoulder. "There's nothing you need me for. I gave Angela everything I had, and she can source it back as well as I can."

"Don't condescend to her," Keats said. "This isn't the way to get Angela broken in, and you know it."

I had the sudden impression that it wasn't the first time they'd discussed me. And now here I was, literally in the middle of it. I appreciated Eve looking out for me the way she did, but the same could be said for Keats. I didn't want any unfair advantages here.

"And just so we're clear," Keats kept going, "how do we know all this communication with Angela isn't being tracked?"

"Because I'm good at what I do, Billy," Eve snapped back.

It was getting more uncomfortable by the second, but then Obaje jumped in and cut through it for us.

"Did I lose track of something?" he asked. "I thought we were here to discuss the case, not fight over Angela."

My face flushed, but he was right, and we all knew it. After that, we sat down at the dining room table for a quick, tense briefing.

It turned out Eve was entirely correct. She had nothing substantive to add that I hadn't already covered, and she'd sent everything there was to send. But at the same time, I totally understood where Billy was coming from. Just because Eve wanted to position me as the go-to person on this new development, that didn't mean she needed to ignore his urgent calls.

In any case, Obaje's point was the most important one. Our focus here needed to be on the case, not each other, and within half an hour, we were getting ready to head back out again, leaving for the office this time.

"You don't happen to have a burner I could use, do you?" I asked Eve. They'd sequestered all my devices, and I felt naked without at least a phone.

Eve gave me a *Silly question* look. Then she disappeared into her stash and came back with a new unit, still in the blister pack.

"It's not exactly state-of-the-art, but at least you'll be reachable," she said. "Pull the SIM card and incinerate it when you're done."

"Thanks for everything—" I started to say, but Keats was already bellowing from the car.

"Hoot! Let's go! This isn't summer camp!"

"Good luck," Eve said with an eye roll in his direction. A second later, I was running to catch up. It was only 7:00 a.m., but I felt like I'd already put in a full day.

"I don't suppose we can swing by Starbucks?" I asked as I fell into the backseat behind Keats and Obaje.

"Very funny," Keats muttered.

I wasn't joking. But I didn't ask again.

IT WAS NO picnic, taking that polygraph back at the office. I understood the need for it, but spending forty-five minutes answering the same question eighteen different ways—no, I was not, had never been, and had no plans to be connected to the Free Net Collective or any other known terrorist organization—wasn't how I wanted to use my time that morning. There was a boatload of work to be done. Now more than ever.

Finally, just as the polygrapher clicked off his machine and I thought I was good to go, his phone rang.

"Yes?" he answered. And then, "Okay, will do."

My eyes flicked up to the red light on the ceiling camera and I wondered who might be watching.

"You can unhook yourself," he told me. "Then wait here."

The Velcro on my arm cuff made a loud ripping noise as I tore it off. "Wait here for who?" I asked. "What happens now?"

"Not for me to say," he answered on his way out. A second later, I was alone.

After what felt like a long wait, I heard the metal door

click open behind me. When I turned and saw SAC Gruss standing there, my heart sank. Whatever the special agent in charge of our field office wanted with me, this didn't feel like a good sign.

I'd wandered pretty deeply into this case. Maybe more deeply than I should have. If I were taking bets, I would have said it was time to start looking for a new career.

"Quite a morning, huh?" Gruss asked as she pulled back the other chair and sat down.

"Yes, ma'am," I answered.

She looked like somebody's mother. I could imagine her at a PTA meeting pretty easily, although I also knew that Audrey Gruss had stared down some seriously intense casework on her way up, including a year in Mosul for the State Department and a key investigative role after 9/11. She was an interesting mix that way.

"Ma'am?" I said. "If it's okay to ask, am I in trouble here?"

"Not necessarily," she said.

I wasn't sure what to make of that, or even how to respond. But Gruss kept going.

"Your IQ is quite impressive," she said.

"I haven't been tested since I was twelve—"

"Your track record at MIT, however? Not so much," she said.

I was starting to realize that SAC Gruss had been watching me more closely than I thought. The question was, did she like what she saw?

"You've proven yourself to be an asset, Angela, but I'm honestly not sure what to make of you. I know you've been working closely with Eve Abajian," she said.

"That's right," I answered. There was no sense denying it, but no need to go into details that Gruss wasn't looking for, either.

"So let me ask you this," she went on. "Are you as smart as you seem?"

"Excuse me?" I said.

"This database you've turned up," she said. "Is that your work? Or Eve's?"

I thought about Eve's advice: *Take the damn credit.* And I thought about what felt right to me.

Then I split the difference.

"Eve found it and passed it on to me," I said. "But I'm the one who cracked it open. Most of that legwork was mine."

It was 90 percent true. Close enough. But Gruss was still just staring at me.

"If I may say so, ma'am," I tried again, "yes, I'm as smart as I seem."

Her eyes smiled, even if her mouth didn't move. Then, like the polygrapher before her, she simply nodded and stood up to leave.

"Is that all, ma'am?" I asked.

"That's it," she said. "Keep up the good work. You're free to go back to your desk."

I tried not to look as relieved as I felt. I guess this meant I'd passed their polygraph, anyway, not to mention Gruss's muster.

But I still felt like I was flying blind into a storm.

CHAPTER 57

WHEN I GOT upstairs, the office was on high alert. With the new possibility of involvement by a designated terrorist organization, everything had ratcheted up. Again.

Homeland Security and the Attorney General's office had been looped in. Emergency plans were already put into place, along with increased server surveillance along the entire Northeast Corridor. Nobody had seen a response like this since the Boston Marathon bombing.

I didn't know where Keats was anymore, but I spent the rest of the morning running theory and attack scenarios with Zack Ciomek and the rest of the CART team. It was gratifying and frustrating at the same time to hear that a lot of my own instincts paralleled what the higher-ups were thinking—but that they'd also already been tried or rejected.

"What about crashing the app?" I asked at one point. "We could flood it with server requests and at least cripple their operation for a while."

"We did try crashing it a few days ago," Ciomek told us.

"It bought about an hour of time, tops. My guess is they have cloud-based backups on everything they touch."

"Which means all they have to do is reload onto a new server and they're back in business," Candace added.

"With no data or integrity loss whatsoever," Ciomek said. "That's right."

This was exactly the double-edged sword of cloud-based computing. Measures to increase privacy standards for legal online activity also made it that much harder to pin down and quash illegal operations.

"If there's a silver lining," Ciomek told us, "it's that we at least have a conduit to these people."

"Online, anyway," I said.

"That's right," Ciomek concurred.

As for finding them out there in the real world, that was another prospect entirely. One that had dogged every resource the FBI had to throw at it so far. And something told me this was going to get a lot harder before it ever got easier.

If it got easier.

WITH EVERYTHING THERE was to do, I didn't expect to leave the CART, or even my desk, all day. So I was more than a little surprised when Keats pulled me away a few hours later.

"Meet me downstairs," he said on the phone. "We're heading to Mass General again. I've got a follow-up interview with Justin Nicholson."

"And you want me there?" I asked. "Not that I mind."

"I think he needs to see you're okay."

I knew that meeting me had spooked Justin pretty badly, right after my name had come up in the course of his attack. It had spooked me, too, but this poor kid was already grappling with the loss of his family. If there was anything I could do to help, I wanted to do it. In fact, there was a certain symmetry to the whole thing. Maybe he needed to see that I was okay, but I needed to check in on him, too.

Or at least I wanted to, given the opportunity.

When we got over to the hospital, we learned that Justin had been transferred to a private room. That was good news. He was sitting up now, breathing without a respirator, and had some limited mobility in his neck. He could croak out a few words, but we set him up with a laptop for the interview. I was next to him like before and read off his answers while Keats asked the questions.

Billy knew enough to use this time efficiently, and he got right to it.

"Justin, could you identify the man who shot you the other night, if you saw him again?" Keats asked.

IT WAS DARK IN THAT HALL. I'M NOT SURE. I DIDN'T SEE HIS FACE, Justin typed out, and I read it to Billy.

"What do you remember about him?" Billy asked. "Any physical traits? The way he held himself? Anything at all?"

HE WAS SHORT FOR A GUY, MAYBE ANGELA'S HEIGHT. AND HE HAD SOME KIND OF ACCENT.

"A foreign accent?" Keats asked. "Anything you recognized?"

MORE LIKE SOUTHERN, I THINK. AMERICAN.

His hands were working the keyboard pretty well, and his eyes were alert. He seemed more alive than before. My guess was that he needed to get this out, and it was helping him to tell his story. Sitting silently in that bed couldn't be good for his mental state. Not after everything he'd been through and everything he'd lost.

"You already mentioned that he gave you a message for Angela," Keats said. "Did he say anything else?"

NOT THAT I REMEMBER. EVERYTHING WENT BLACK AFTER THAT.

While Keats took down a few notes, Justin turned to me and typed out another line.

SORRY THIS HAPPENED ANGELA. SUCKS FOR YOU TOO.

Keats wasn't done, so I didn't say anything. I just waved a hand at Justin to say, *Don't worry about me. I'm fine.*

After another twenty minutes of back-and-forth, we had as much of a description as we were going to get. The suspect was well under six feet tall. He may have been white and may have been in his twenties, as far as Justin had been able to tell, but it was all uncertain. He'd seen no facial hair, scars, or tattoos, either. And no other distinguishing characteristics, beyond the accent.

It wasn't much, but it was more than we'd had.

"If there's anything you need, I want you to text me," I told him. I wrote the number for my new burner phone on a pad by the bed. "And I'm checking on you tomorrow either way, so you might as well ask for something. Otherwise, you'll just get some tacky teddy bear and a potted plant."

That got a weak smile. "Thank you," he croaked out in a hoarse whisper.

"No, thank *you,*" I said. "And save your voice. I'll see you tomorrow."

As we were walking to the elevators, Keats squeezed my shoulder.

"You're a good person," he said. "You know that?"

I shrugged it off. "Anyone would do what they could for this guy," I said.

"Some people, but not everyone," Billy told me. Given his years with the Bureau, I figured he would know.

Out on the street, my new phone gave an unfamiliar chime. I looked down and saw it was a text notification, with a message from Justin.

Chocolate shake tomorrow? he'd written.

Now it was my turn to smile.

You got it, I wrote back. See you then.

Something about that request, for a simple thing like ice cream, felt hopeful to me. I knew Justin had been permanently scarred. He'd probably never be the same again, but I could tell he wasn't giving up, either.

He was going to be okay. Maybe not soon, but eventually.

And that was the best news all day.

CHAPTER 59

GEORGE MET ME outside the office again that evening and drove me over to Eve's. Her place was way more comfortable than mine, but I doubted she was going to be okay with having him inside.

I bought dinner for all three of us, even if he did have to eat his in the car.

"I won't be more than a few hours," I told George. I hoped that was true. Working the electronic angles on this case was, for me, a very easy hole to fall into. But I was going to try to get us both back to Somerville before the middle of the night, if I could.

Meanwhile, I settled in at Eve's array and went to work on the app again, dissecting its code and looking for any new updates I could find.

Eve spent the night coming and going. She'd check on me, answer a few questions, and then disappear again. I could feel her holding back, probably for my own sake. I think what Billy said that morning had stuck to both of us. She couldn't prop me up forever. At some point, I was going to have to stand on my own, and we all knew it.

That said, I wasn't above leaning on my other friends for help. So as soon as Eve went to bed, I called and checked in with A.A.

"How's it going over there on the dark side of the moon?" I asked.

"Frustrating," she said. "But interesting."

"Go on."

"It's not hard to find people talking about FNC," she said. "The problem is knowing what to believe."

"Nothing new there," I said. The anonymity of the dark web definitely cuts both ways. Anyone can post whatever they like, which means you have to be on your toes about truth versus fiction and information versus misinformation.

Meanwhile, I may not have been able to discuss the specifics of the case with A.A., but as a general topic of conversation, this was fair game. In fact, A.A. and I had discussed the Free Net Collective several times in the past, mostly at MIT and long before I was at the FBI. Anyone with an interest in coding, hacking, and the dark web knew about FNC, at least in theory.

"For whatever it's worth," she went on, "most of the chatter is about everything they did before they went underground. Or out to sea. Or wherever the hell they are."

"So have you been able to find anything current at all?" I asked.

"Again, it's hard to say," she told me. "But there is one thing. I found this user who goes by Hermes online. Have you ever heard of him?"

"I don't think so," I said. "Hermes, as in the messenger of the gods?"

"And the god of transitions and boundaries," she said. "Yeah.

He's positioning himself as some kind of go-between with FNC. He says he can offer direct access for a hefty Bitcoin exchange, but only if you download his app first. Of course."

Just that word, *app,* burned right through the phone line into my ear. Was this the exact, full-circle moment I'd been hoping for?

"What kind of app?" I asked.

"Some kind of private chat platform," she said. "I only mention it because he's been just about everywhere I've looked. But likely as not, he's some pimple-faced fifteen-year-old in a basement in Teaneck, New Jersey. You know what I mean?"

"That sounds about right," I said, playing it off. On the inside, though, my mind was reeling.

Maybe this was a nonstarter, like A.A. said. Then again, maybe not. And there was just one way to find out.

"So where do I find this Hermes dude, anyway?" I asked.

CHAPTER 60

THE FIRST THING I did was launch Tor, which was the go-to software for anyone who wanted anonymous communication online. It was how most people accessed the dark net, whether they wanted to buy drugs, watch a bootleg movie, or just poke around the web without anyone looking over their shoulder.

I'd known about all this since I was ten years old and starting to find ways around the parental controls Mom and Dad had put on the computers at home. It was kind of cute, the way they thought they could keep an eye on me back then. But that was before people had started throwing words like *gifted*, *genius*, and *prodigy* my way.

Lucky for them, I've always been the kind of genius who wants to use her powers for good and not evil. Unless of course you cross me, and then all bets are off.

Once I was in, it didn't take long to find Hermes at all. A.A. was right. He'd been a busy little boy, promoting his app everywhere he could. I invented a new handle of my own—Pandora, just to keep with the theme. Then I used it to send Hermes a direct message on TorChat. It was the safest way I knew to open a cryptographically secure line of communication without compromising my own identity.

It was like putting a worm on the hook. Now I just had to wait and see what I caught. Or not.

To: Hermes

From: Pandora

Subject: FNC actual?

Hello. I'm interested in knowing more about this app of yours. How much are you asking for FNC access? And more important, what assurances can you give me that this is legit? If we're not talking about FNC actual, I'm not interested.

Let's talk.

Tx.

Pandora

CHAPTER 61

THE NEXT DAY, between working at home and another session at Eve's, I squeezed in an early dinner with Mom and my sisters. For more than a week, I'd been begging off their invitations to come home, usually saying that I was too busy at work.

The full truth was, there was no way I could show up at my parents' house with a security detail in tow and not worry Mom and Dad to death. Especially Mom. So this was the compromise, even if she didn't know it.

We met at the Oceanaire, a few blocks from the office, and got a table near the bar.

For a while my sisters did most of the talking, which kept the spotlight off me, happily enough. I heard about field hockey, and SATs, and some boy named Neil, who was "almost definitely" on the verge of asking Sylvie to go out with him, once and for all.

"But what about you?" Hannah eventually asked. "Are you, like, a spy now?"

They knew I couldn't say too much about work, but I also

saw that hungry look in my littlest sister's eyes. Unlike Sylvie, Hannah actually wanted to be like me, and in the meantime, she wanted to know as much as possible. Unlike my mother, who I think was stuck between wanting to know everything about my job and nothing at all, since it stressed her out so much.

"Not really a spy," I told Hannah. "It's more like Hansel and Gretel. I spend a lot of my time following virtual bread crumbs to see where they lead."

"Cool," Hannah said.

The bread crumb analogy was for Mom's benefit, given her professional focus on fairy tales and my own desire to shift the topic away from me as subtly as possible.

"What do those crumbs symbolize, anyway?" I asked, as though the question might give me some needed insight—which, for all I knew, it might.

"In fact, that's an easy one," Mom said. She picked a piece of focaccia out of the basket on the table and sprinkled some crumbs across the cloth, in a little winding path.

"Bread is food, and that represents life," she said. "As long as those crumbs are there, Hansel and Gretel have a way back, literally, but also figuratively." Then she started picking the crumbs back up, just like the birds in the story. "However, when the crumbs are gone, there's no way home again. And that represents the threat of death."

"Something tells me there's a lesson coming," I said.

"There's *always* a lesson," Sylvie said knowingly. Hannah and I tried not to smile.

"So, is that what's happened?" Mom asked me. "Did you lose the trail back home? Because God knows I've tried to get you out there for weeks, and it's been like pulling teeth."

So much for changing the subject, I thought. My mother has never been easily deterred. Maybe that's where I get it.

"I've just been busy," I said. "You know that, right?"

Mom reached across the table and put her hand on mine. "You look tired, Angela. This work is changing you, and not in a good way," she said.

"I *am* tired," I told her honestly. "But we're doing *good* work, Mom. We really are. And I'm exactly where I want to be—at the Bureau, working with Eve, the whole thing. I'm just on a steep learning curve, you know?"

"Hmm." Mom narrowed her eyes at me and sat back. "Why do I still feel like there's something you're not telling me?"

I could only shrug and avoid her stare by looking down at my menu. The alternative was to tell her she was right. There *were* plenty of things she didn't know about. Things I had no intention of telling her.

Like, for instance, how the homicidal maniacs at the center of this case had singled me out, by name. Or how the retired FBI agent quietly having a burger at the bar was there for my own protection.

Or how if she knew everything there was to know it would only kill her with more worry.

And nobody needed that.

BACK AT EVE'S that night, I was disappointed to find that Hermes hadn't replied to any of my messages. I was surprised, too. This guy seemed like he really did thrive on attention, and exactly the kind I was trying to give him.

Maybe Hermes was just some highly skilled nerd playing in his basement somewhere, I thought. It wouldn't be the first time. Some of the most surprising hacks had come from ridiculously young people.

I sent a couple of follow-up messages from my own alter ego, Pandora, but I wasn't holding my breath for it to yield me anything useful. Once that was done, I turned my attention back to the usual: tearing apart the app one piece at a time.

That took me all the way up to eleven o'clock, when Eve said good night and went upstairs. I told her I'd let myself out by midnight, which was as late as I wanted to keep George waiting outside in his car. He never complained. I knew this was his job, but still, I felt bad for keeping him waiting like that.

In any case, the next hour flew by, the way it always did when

I was working. This app's code was seemingly endless. All I could really do was plug away at it one subroutine at a time and hope to get an overall better understanding of what it could do—and, by extension, a better understanding of whoever had written it.

I was just on the verge of shutting down for the night when I heard my new burner phone ping with a text notification.

Only three people had that number: Eve, A.A., and Justin Nicholson. But what I saw instead on the screen was a short message from an unknown caller, with a number I didn't recognize.

Hello, Angela.

What the hell? I was deep enough into this that I knew something strange had just happened. But what, exactly?

Who is this? I wrote back.

We've never quite met, but I think you know who it is, came the reply.

My heart was thudding, and I wasn't sure what to do.

Why are you contacting me? I asked.

Isn't that what you wanted? I got back.

My next thought was, *Hermes?* I doubted it, but then again, nothing seemed certain these days.

I reached for Eve's landline to call Keats next. It seemed like a prudent thing to do, but before I even got that far, another message came through, on top of the last one.

By the way, how's George?

Jesus Christ! How did this guy know about George? Much less what his name was.

I ran over to the window and looked down at the street. From there, I couldn't see anything except the top of George's car. Nobody else seemed to be around. The block was quiet.

Even so, I didn't feel reassured.

My phone chimed with another message, but I ignored it as I bolted down the stairs and threw open the front door.

I could see George in his car, and for half a second, I felt a flood of relief.

"George?" I called out, but there was no response. It looked like maybe he was sleeping.

Except—of course—he wasn't.

There was blood, I realized. I could tell even in the low light, from the way his white collar had been stained dark.

The sight of it scrambled my brain. There were no cogent thoughts in my head now, as I moved around to his side of the car, terrified of going another step but unable to stop myself.

And there he was. His eyes were wide-open and unseeing. Two holes in the windshield lined up with the gunshot wounds to his forehead and neck where he sat, still upright.

I realized with another rush that whoever had done this was also keeping an eye on me. Maybe with the same gun sites.

Reflexively, I dropped to my knee and leaned against his car.

911.

The number passed through my head. I knew I had to call, but it seemed to take forever to get the message to my frozen hands.

And when I finally lifted the phone to dial the number, I saw the most recent text that had come in—the one I had ignored on my way down the stairs.

It said, Aren't you forgetting someone?

And even in the blurred frenzy of thoughts competing for my focus, I realized what had just happened.

Oh, my God.

Oh, my God.

No.

Not Eve, too.

CHAPTER 63

I RAN BACK to the front door, my mind searing with more wordless thoughts.

"Nine one one. What is your emergency?"

I heard the voice on my phone and realized I'd already dialed. My focus was on the keypad outside Eve's door. I had to let myself back in. I had to get to her before they could.

Unless I was too late.

"This is 911. What is your emergency?" the voice repeated. "Is anyone there?"

"I need help!" I screamed as I ran up the first flight of stairs. "A man's been shot in his car at this address. And my friend's in trouble!"

"We're sending help right away," the dispatcher told me. "Please stay on the line..."

I didn't hear what else she said. What I heard now—in fact, all I could hear anymore—was the sound of the baby crying from one more floor up.

"Eve!" I screamed, but there was no answer.

I took the next flight of stairs three at a time. It was dark in the hall when I got there, but I could see a line of light under the bedroom door.

"*Eve?*" I tried again. "Are you there?"

Why wasn't she answering? I was terrified that I knew the reason, and conscious that I might have been walking into the exact same trap. But nothing was stopping me now. I couldn't wait for the police, even if I wanted to.

I tore open the door and scanned the room, trying to focus past the blur of my own terror.

Marlena was there, wailing in her crib.

Eve's bed was unmade and empty.

The bathroom was dark.

A window in the back had been left open. The curtains were wafting with the breeze it let in. I ran to it now and looked out, but there wasn't anything to see. The neighborhood was quiet, as if nothing at all had just happened.

As if George weren't dead.

As if Eve hadn't been taken.

Almost as if, before it even began, it had already been over.

WHEN I HIT the sidewalk with Marlena still crying in my arms, a small crowd of pajama-wearing neighbors and passersby had already gathered. Several people were holding each other, some of them crying. I saw George dead in his car, again, and my knees buckled. It brought me down hard on Eve's front step. I knew this was real, but I couldn't make it into a fact. Not in my head. All I could manage was—

Hold the baby.

Soothe this little girl.

I clung to those thoughts, and to her, until the police arrived to secure the scene. Suddenly, cruisers and personnel were everywhere. One of the officers took Marlena and swaddled her in his jacket. I hated to hand over the baby, but it wasn't my choice, and besides, I was in no position to take care of her myself. It all went by in a dark blur.

Soon after that, I saw Keats, Obaje, and the rest of their team pulling up. I had no idea how they'd gotten there so fast. For that matter, I had no idea how much time had passed by now, but I was glad to see them.

Billy took my statement first, slowly and deliberately, making it as easy as he possibly could as I walked him through what I knew. After that, he poured me into the back of a manned police cruiser and brought me my things from inside. I wrapped my arms around my messenger bag like it was some kind of surrogate for the baby. Anything to hold on to.

"I've got someone coming to pick you up, an Agent Lisa Konrad Palumbo," Keats said. "She'll take you where you're going."

"What do you mean?" I asked. "Where am I going?"

"Somewhere safe," was all he said. "You need to disappear for a little while. Are you okay waiting here?"

"Why wouldn't I be?" I asked. It was a ridiculous answer, considering what I'd just been through, but I didn't want Billy worrying about me. He'd already spent enough time on that. I wanted him out there looking for Eve.

Keats knelt by the open door and put both arms on the frame of the car, closing us in a little huddle. When he spoke, it was a low murmur, just for me, and I could tell I was about to hear something confidential.

"She's still alive, Angela," he said. "I can tell you that much."

"How can you know that?" I asked. "How can you possibly—"

But then I realized. Whoever was behind this must have notified the Bureau that it was about to happen. It was exactly the kind of move these attention-seeking scumbags had been pulling all along. The more they accomplished, the more they flaunted their position.

"They told you ahead of time, didn't they?" I asked.

"Just not enough to do anything about it," Keats confirmed.

"Jesus."

"For all we know, Reese Sapporo's abduction in Portland was some kind of dry run for whatever this is supposed to be," Billy said. "My guess is they drugged her before they took her out that upstairs window. But Angela? Look at me."

I took a shaky breath and looked him in the eye.

"If they wanted to kill her, she'd already be dead. Okay? Trust me. We've got the whole city lit up with surveillance. We've already spun up a task force at the field office, and we're covering every known route out of the city. Believe me, we're going to find her. *Do not* give up hope."

I gave him a nod, which was as much as I could manage.

"Go," I said. "Do what you have to do."

And then he was gone.

That left me alone with the cop in the front. I didn't even know the officer's name. He'd kept his eyes forward the whole time, like he didn't want to intrude. Which was just as well. I didn't feel much like chatting.

I hated to think about the hell Eve was in. Not to mention how out of her mind she'd have to be, worrying about Marlena. But Keats was right. Eve had to be alive. Otherwise, why take her? Reese Sapporo had been returned unharmed. Maybe this was just another version of the same maneuver. With any luck, we'd have Eve back by morning.

But where was she now? What did these people want? And why? It was like a shifting constellation of questions, one moving target after another, with no clear answers.

"Hey, excuse me? Are you hearing that?"

I glanced up. The cop had twisted around to look at me from the front seat. He chinned down at the messenger bag on my lap.

"Sounds like your phone's going off," he said. "You seemed a million miles away, but I wasn't sure if that might be important."

"You must have heard something else," I told him. "I don't

have a phone on me." I'd dropped my burner inside the house, and it had already been tagged for evidence.

But even as I finished saying it, an unmistakable ping sounded from somewhere inside my bag. I looked down and back up at the cop, totally confused. He just shrugged and left me alone.

I had to rummage through my usual collection of junk to find where that sound had come from. And there, at the very bottom of the bag, I found a silver Android phone I'd never seen before. It had a charger rubber-banded to it and a white bar on the screen that read 5 NEW MESSAGES.

What in the blue hell?

When the cop caught my eye in the rearview mirror, I wasn't sure what to say. So I punted. "It's my friend's phone," I told him. "I forgot I had it with me."

But whoever had planted that Android there was no friend of mine. That much was clear. They must have dropped it in my bag while I was outside losing it at the sight of George's murder.

I tapped the message bar with a shaking finger. It opened the phone right up without any unlock code and took me straight into the app.

The app. The one I'd been seeing everywhere I looked, ever since this case began.

And there, in the familiar three-color interface, I saw my five waiting messages, all of them sent within the last minute.

Hello, Angela.

Don't say a word.

Don't even look around.

One wrong move and Eve dies.

Hit me back when you're ready for more instructions.

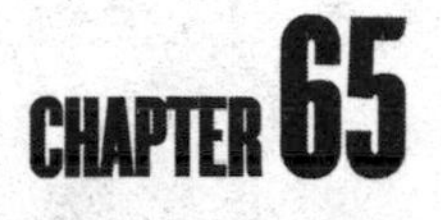

IN MY HAND, I now had a phone with the capability to listen, watch, and track my every move down to the square meter. I knew as well as anyone what that app could do.

So I kept my eyes down, heart thundering, and texted back right away.

What have you done with Eve? I asked.

The reply was almost immediate.

If you want to find out, start walking up West Broadway.

I eyed the cop in the front seat, but he'd gone back to leaving me alone. My thumbs flew over the keyboard, sending another question.

Why would I do that?

At first, nothing happened. Then I got back a photo instead of a text. It was nearly identical to the one they'd sent just after Reese Sapporo's abduction. It showed Eve in a blurry close-up, eyes wide, with silver tape over her mouth. And there, at the edge of the frame, was the unmistakable black barrel of a gun, pointed at her head.

I slapped a hand across my own mouth to keep from blurting anything out. It was almost as if I was looking at someone other than Eve. She barely looked like herself, and I had no context for seeing my friend and mentor, this woman who had been more of a rock to me than anyone I'd ever known, trapped in this horrifying state.

Outside the cruiser, police and agents were buckling down the scene. Yellow tape had already gone up in front of Eve's house and around George's car. The crowd had swelled, and a few officers were starting to corral everyone up the block.

How am I supposed to walk away from this? I texted.

You're the genius, Angela. You figure it out, he wrote back. And then, You have one minute.

With that, a digital timer popped up on the Android's screen, counting down from sixty seconds.

Maybe it was a bluff, but I couldn't assume that. These people had shown themselves more than willing to kill for no reason. There was no time to come up with a work-around, either. I was already down to forty-five seconds.

And whatever they wanted from me, I was the one who had set it all in motion. There was no way I could let Eve pay for my mistakes. That realization cut through everything else, including my panic.

"Hey," I said to the cop in front. "I forgot to tell Agent Keats something."

"I don't have him on my radio," he told me.

"No, I didn't think so," I answered, and looked down at the phone again. There were thirty seconds left. Half a minute to get out of that car. My hand was already on the door handle and I took out my credentials for show.

"I'm just going to run in and find him. I'll be right back," I said.

"I can get one of my guys to—"

"Don't bother, I've got it," I told him.

Before the officer could say anything else, I slid out of the car and shut the door behind me with about fifteen seconds to spare. I knew I might have been making the worst mistake of my life, but given the alternative, I can only say that I'd do it again if I had to.

No question.

CHAPTER 66

I FORCED MYSELF to walk away from the cruiser at a casual pace. I couldn't afford to draw any attention to myself, and I was terrified someone might pull me back.

I saw Obaje standing outside Eve's front door, but he was talking to someone. Billy was nowhere in sight. Everyone was too busy to notice as I slipped up the block and away from the scene.

As soon as I turned off of Eve's street and onto West Broadway, I started running. I didn't know where I was going, but my body needed to move. My mind was a seething mess of confusion and I was terrified about whatever came next. But at least my feet knew what to do.

Once I'd gotten around that first corner, the phone pinged three times in my hand. I looked down to read the incoming messages without slowing my pace.

Carlito's Coffee. Five blocks on your left.

Order something and wait at the counter.

You have two minutes.

The on-screen timer had already reset and started counting down again. It felt like this was some kind of game for them. Like they were toying with me, and I had no choice but to play along.

I knew exactly where Carlito's was and broke into a sprint the rest of the way. I focused on speed, focused on my feet, focused on getting there—and tried not to think about what might happen if I didn't.

When I reached the coffee shop, I stumbled as much as walked inside. It was after midnight by now. Most of the tables were empty and there was nobody waiting at the counter. I ordered a latte, gave my name, and shoved some money at the aproned dude staring back at me.

Then I looked down to check the Android. Nothing new had come in.

What now? I wrote, and hit Send.

At nearly the same moment, a chime of some kind sounded from across the room. My eyes snapped up to see a guy in a red and black Northeastern hoodie, just picking up his phone.

I held my breath. I watched as he read whatever was in front of him and set the phone back down without ever looking my way.

So I sent another message.

Hello? Are you there?

And again, the guy's phone dinged.

Maybe it was a coincidence. Phones are constantly going off in a place like Carlito's. But tell that to the adrenaline pumping like white water through my system just then.

Before I could think about it—or think at all—I was plowing my way across the floor. A few empty chairs tipped over in my wake, and the guy looked up just in time to see me bearing down on him fast.

He jumped up with his phone and backed away.

"What were you just doing?" I demanded.

"What the bloody hell?" he asked in a clear English accent.

"Show me your phone!" I screamed, half out of my mind. I lunged for it and he stepped back again. Someone grabbed my arm from behind.

"Whoa, whoa! What's going on here?" one of the staff asked.

"This nutter's trying to take my phone," the Brit said.

"Where is she?" I yelled at him. "What have you done with her?"

"Calm down, miss!" he shouted back, just as I heard a new message dinging into my own phone. Then another, and another.

If anything was going to re-rack my focus, it was that. I tore my arm free from the barista and looked down to see what I had.

One block north. Right on C Street.

Wait at the corner of C and Cypher.

You have two minutes.

The digital timer was back and had started its countdown all over again.

When I looked up, the Brit was staring at me like I was some kind of lunatic. And in fact, it was just hitting me that I may have made a horrible mistake. Maybe even a fatal one, where Eve was concerned.

But that didn't mean I was wrong about this guy. He could have been just one part of a larger team. Some kind of diversion, or test.

As I stared back, I could swear I saw him fighting off a smile. His eyes crinkled, like he was taunting me, silently daring me to make the wrong move.

When I checked the timer on my phone, twenty seconds had already evaporated. That left a minute forty to cover the next leg. I had to leave now if I was going to go at all.

I gave the Brit one last look, committing his face to memory—strong nose, sandy-brown buzz cut, cleft chin—and turned to head for the door. The last thing I heard before I hit the sidewalk was "Latte, single shot, for Angela?"

But I was already gone.

CHAPTER 67

IT WAS GETTING surreal. I felt like I was slogging through mud and fog as I covered the next several blocks, texting back and forth on the fly with the architect of my own nightmare.

Where are you taking me? I asked.

Just keep going, he said.

Are you going to release Eve if I do?

Yes.

How do I know that?

You'll have to take my word for it. Or not.

And then what? Kill me?

Of course not.

Then what? Talk to me!

The replies had been coming in as fast as the questions I sent, but now they stopped. When I reached the designated corner, I stared at the screen, waiting for something to happen.

Hello? I texted.

I looked up and down both streets. There was nothing out of the ordinary to see, and nobody to catch my attention. The intersection was deserted.

I tried again. Where did you go?

My breath caught in my throat as I started to imagine the worst. Was it over? Had I pushed too hard? Was Eve gone?

Then, as suddenly as it had stopped, it started again. A flurry of pings sounded and a series of messages scrolled in fast.

> Change of plans.
>
> Pocket the phone.
>
> Keep it on you at ALL TIMES.
>
> One word about this to anyone and Eve dies.
>
> If we lose track of you, Eve dies.
>
> Do not test us.
>
> Do not forget these instructions.
>
> We'll be in touch.

I blinked several times, frozen in my spot. What in God's name was that supposed to mean? They'd be in touch? When?

What do you mean? I wrote back, just before I heard my name.

"Angela!"

I turned 180 and saw Keats. He'd just jumped out of a cruiser, parked diagonally in the intersection behind me, lights flashing. I hadn't even heard the car coming. Now Billy was sprinting toward me with one hand on the gun at his hip.

I didn't know what to do. My options were extremely limited, in any case, and I slipped the phone into my pocket as surreptitiously as I could. This was insane, but I couldn't stop now. I had to protect Eve. And to do that, I had to keep the phone a secret, at least for the time being.

"I'm okay, I'm okay!" I said, just as Billy got to me.

"What the hell are you doing out here?" he shouted. "Have you lost your mind?"

It was a struggle to synthesize everything into one response.

Anything I said to Billy might be overheard through that Android. And any mention I made of the phone itself would almost certainly get Eve killed.

"I thought I saw them taking her!" I said. The lie burst out of me in a panic. "I didn't know what to do...and I just...ran after the car. I'm sorry! I shouldn't have done that. I was wrong. It wasn't even them!"

"Okay, okay," Keats said, his voice easing. He put an arm around my shoulder and shepherded me toward the cruiser as it pulled up the block. "It's done now. But Jesus, Angela, you scared the crap out of me."

I could barely look him in the eye. I felt terrible for lying, but the alternative was worse. The bulge in my pocket felt conspicuous as hell, even if nobody else seemed to notice. What I needed was a few minutes alone to think this through and not make any rash decisions. For once.

In the meantime, all I could do was stick to the story, take it one thing at a time, and pray that this sick little game hadn't just come to an abrupt end.

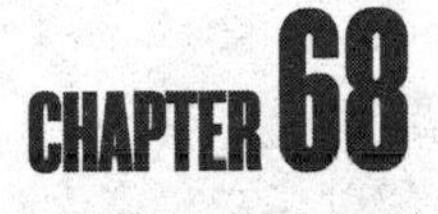

WHEN WE GOT back to the street outside Eve's house, an unmarked black van was waiting to take me wherever I was headed next. I assumed that meant some kind of safe house. What little I knew about these kinds of things told me I'd be unreachable for the foreseeable future. But that was just a guess.

"Can I at least call my parents?" I asked Billy. "I can't just disappear on them."

"Yeah, yeah," Billy said. "Of course. But just one call, and it's going to have to be quick."

It felt like I was getting arrested as much as going into protective custody.

"Hello?" Mom answered. It was nearly 1:00 a.m. I could hear the confusion mixed with concern in her voice.

"It's me, Mom," I said. "I'm on Agent Keats's phone."

"What is it, sweetheart? What's wrong?" she asked.

I took a deep breath and my chest shuddered. Everything that had just happened was too much to think about at once.

"We've had a situation at work," I said, trying to sound as

level as possible. "All I can really tell you is that I'm okay. They're taking me somewhere safe."

"What?" Mom said, her voice rising. I'd given her too much, too fast, I could tell. "Who's putting you up? For how long? What happened?"

"I'm so sorry," I told her. "I can't say any more than that, and I don't have time to talk. But I *promise* you I'm safe. That's all you need to know for now. I'll be in touch just as soon as I can, I swear."

"At least tell me where they're taking you," Mom demanded.

"I don't know," I said. "And it's actually better if you don't know, either."

Keats was motioning at me to wrap it up. I could tell he hated having to hurry me, but this transfer wasn't a whenever kind of thing. We had to go. And meanwhile, I'd just stoked every fear Mom had ever had about me and this job.

"Angela..." She was crying now and running out of words, which was unusual for anyone in my family.

"I love you, Mom," I said. "Please tell Dad and the girls that I love them, too."

There was no easy good-bye. No good way to finish that call. So I told her I was going to hang up, and then handed the phone to Keats to do it for me. I just couldn't. Not with my own mother still crying on the other end.

Billy seemed to understand. "I'm sorry about that," he said. "The work is goddamn heartless sometimes. But I promise you, this is for the best."

"I know," I said, and I did, but it was still overwhelming. I felt horrible for what I was putting my family through, on top of everything else.

Billy opened the van's sliding door for me so I could get in the back. I assumed the woman in the driver's seat was my assigned agent, Lisa Konrad Palumbo, but there were no introductions. I wasn't even sure what to call her.

"I'll check in with you tomorrow," Billy said. "Try to get some sleep."

My mind was flying. All I had was more questions. What about Justin Nicholson? Who was going to look in on him at the hospital? And George's family—what about them? Would they be taken care of?

Most of all, though, I was thinking about Eve. What was the investigative plan there? How much in the loop would Billy be able to keep me? And what came next?

I couldn't afford to ask any of it. The more I said, the more information I'd be passing to whoever might be listening through that Android in my pocket. Chances were I'd have to come clean, maybe sooner than later, since there was no real hiding from them anymore. But until I could think through this more clearly, my default remained the same: *Keep Eve alive.*

"I'll talk to you soon," Keats told me. When I didn't answer, he gave me a tight smile. Then he slid the panel door closed and banged on it twice from the outside. Agent Konrad Palumbo hit the gas, the van lurched, and we took off into the night, heading for "somewhere safe."

Whatever that meant anymore.

WHEN I THINK *safe house,* I think about remote cabins in the woods and unassuming little places tucked deep in the suburbs. But that's probably because I've seen too many movies and bad TV shows.

In fact, Agent Konrad Palumbo took me to the last place I expected.

As we pulled into the sally port behind the federal building where I worked, I thought maybe we were stopping to change vehicles.

But no.

"Here we are," Konrad Palumbo told me.

"You've got to be kidding," I said, even though she obviously wasn't.

In fact, this was good news. I still hadn't worked out what to do about the de facto tracking device in my pocket and whoever was now following my every move. But if there was one place they couldn't physically get to me, it was going to be here.

Once the inner garage door had closed behind us, we got out of the van and onto a freight elevator. Konrad Palumbo took us up to the sixth floor, one story above my own office and the CART.

"So, Agent Konrad Palumbo," I said on the way up. "Is there—"

"Call me Lisa," she said with a reassuring smile. I didn't think she knew about my specific circumstances, but I appreciated that she was trying to make this as easy for me as possible.

"Lisa," I said. "Can you tell me anything about what's about to happen here?"

"I'll do better than that," she said. "I'll show you."

The elevator doors had just slid open and she gestured for me to go ahead of her.

It was coming up on 2:00 a.m. by now, but the checkpoint just off the elevator was staffed with two uniformed guards. It was exactly like the station I passed going to work every day on the fifth floor, usually with a flash of my ID. This time, though, we had to empty our pockets, walk through the metal detector, and get a hand scan and a pat-down from one of the guards.

Immediately, my pulse ticked up. I knew I didn't have a choice about the phone. I'd have to take it out of my pocket, but I also couldn't afford to tip my hand here. Was this the end of the charade, before it had barely begun?

I waited for Agent Konrad Palumbo—Lisa—to go through first. When she wasn't looking, I dropped the phone into an empty gray tub and covered it with my keys, ID, and jacket, then set it all on the moving belt, along with my bag.

I barely breathed during the pat-down. One guard searched me while the other watched the monitor, scanning my things on their way through.

Please, please, please—

"Okay, you're good to go," the first guard told me. "Grab your stuff and follow the agent inside."

I kept my poker face and slid the phone into my pocket. Then I followed Konrad Palumbo onto the sixth floor's main hallway as they buzzed us through.

Just inside, she swiped her ID to get us past yet another security door. This one led to an enclosed staircase. It was just a single flight, up to the seventh floor and back out again.

We came into a much shorter corridor than the one below. I counted five beige steel doors on the left and four on the right, with an alarmed fire exit at the far end. It was easy to imagine this little wing as a kind of secret compartment within the much larger federal building. I didn't even know that the Bureau had offices on seven.

I followed Konrad Palumbo down to the last door on the right. She held her ID up to the card reader. The little red light turned green with a click, and she pushed the door open.

"This is you," she said. "Home sweet home... ish."

Inside, there was a carpeted space with a platform bed, a couch, a bathroom, and a tiny kitchen, including a full bag of groceries on the counter. It was basically a little studio apartment, minus the windows.

"More like cave sweet cave," I said. "How long am I going to be here?"

Konrad Palumbo shrugged. "I'm not going to lie. You're going to get bored."

I wish, I thought, and fingered the phone-shaped bulge in my pocket.

"Write me up a list of things you'd like from your apartment," she said. "Support staff will check in with you about incidentals, and psych services will be by first thing in the morning."

"Psych services?" I asked.

"It's protocol, with the death of an agent," she said. "And listen, I'm really sorry about George. It's a horrible thing that happened to him."

"Whoever did it deserves to die *a slow, painful death,*" I said for the benefit of whoever was listening in through that phone. "I'd kill them myself if I could."

Agent Lisa Konrad Palumbo narrowed her eyes at the intensity in my voice. She was trained to pick up on small changes like that, I'm sure, but she didn't call me on it, which I appreciated.

I started scribbling down a quick list for her. Clothes, shoes, a few toiletries, laptop...

"Can this include my bike and indoor trainer?" I asked.

"I don't see why not," she said.

It was the one thing I knew I'd want, if I had to be cooped up. Without some kind of exercise, I was going to go completely mental in there.

"Now try to get some sleep," she said.

"I will," I told her.

But that was just another lie. I had no intention of getting any sleep. Just the opposite, in fact.

This was going to be the all-nighter of my life.

CHAPTER 70

AS SOON AS I'd locked the door behind Agent Konrad Palumbo, I took out the phone and checked for messages. There were none.

Anyone home? I tried.

There was no immediate answer, and no reason to wait around for one, either. They knew how to reach me, obviously, and they were taking their time doing it. I had no idea what to expect from them, or for that matter, when to expect it.

My best move was to get as much done as I feasibly could in the meantime. That meant not letting myself get overwhelmed with worry about Eve. Yes, there was sufficient cause to be afraid that the very worst could happen—that she wouldn't be coming back again. That was possible for any number of reasons, including the ones I could think of and, even more frighteningly, some endless number of reasons I couldn't even begin to foresee.

But obsessing about all that wasn't going to do a thing to up Eve's chances of getting through this. Logically speaking, Eve and I would both be better off if I kept myself focused and productive.

So I moved on to the next thing I knew how to do. I went looking for Hermes.

The Android was fully functional, which meant I could get online as much as I wanted. I just had to do it consciously. I was living in a virtual fishbowl now, but if these guys were as smart as they seemed, this was exactly what they'd expect me to do.

I worked from memory, going back to every technology board, every chat space, and every seamy little dark net hangout I could think of where I'd seen signs of Hermes before.

The last time I'd tracked him, he'd all but advertised himself as a key player in this case. There had been signs of him everywhere I looked.

Now it was just the opposite. I spent a tedious three hours going page to page without finding a single indication that Hermes had ever existed. It was like someone had gone around scrubbing out every footprint and eating every bread crumb that had been all over the trail before.

Which meant one of two things to me: either our killers had pulled up stakes and moved their operations yet again, or the supposed connection between these sext murders, Hermes, and the Free Net Collective was just an elaborate bit of fiction.

My money was on the latter. Hackers do it all the time, laying down false leads as a smoke screen while they go about their real business elsewhere.

And Hermes hadn't just been some garden-variety smoke screen, either, I realized. He'd been a trap. One that I'd fallen for, just like the half-baked wannabe they'd probably pegged me for.

I hated myself for the position we were in. Eve never would

have fallen into this if it hadn't been for me. Her words came filtering back into my mind now. *If it's this easy, it means they wanted you to find them,* she'd told me. And she'd been right. Devastatingly so.

With any luck, Keats's team was way ahead of me on all of this. Maybe by dawn, they'd have Eve home again and the killers would be in custody—or dead, for all I cared.

But until I knew any better, this little covert operation of mine was full steam ahead.

CHAPTER 71

I DIDN'T MEAN to fall asleep.

When I jerked awake, it took me a second to recompute where I was, and why. Everything flooded back in a nasty rush. The phone, set to vibrate, had woken me up. A new message had just come in.

Hey Angela. Wanna talk?

They'd been watching me sleep, hadn't they? It was a disgusting feeling. But I also knew that any contact was better than none.

I'm here, I wrote back.

Any luck finding Hermes? he asked.

No, I answered. But you already knew that, didn't you?

You were pretty obvious.

I wasn't trying to hide. I was trying to get you to talk to me.

Well here I am. Did you get much sleep?

Where is Eve? I wrote.

I asked you a question first.

According to the Android, it was just before 9:00 a.m. The last

I remembered, it had been coming up on seven. I could feel the last forty-eight hours dragging on me like a literal weight.

I slept a little, ok? Where is Eve?

She's right here with me. Safe and sound.

WHO ARE YOU? I pounded out. If we'd been talking on the phone, I would have been screaming at him by now.

I'm nobody! he wrote. Who are you? Are you nobody, too?

A chill razored up my back. Even I recognized that line. It was from an Emily Dickinson poem.

This wasn't the cold, authoritarian voice of whoever had sent me running around the city the night before. This was the poetry lover. The chameleon who had seduced Gwen Petty, and Nigella Wilbur, and Reese Sapporo by becoming whoever they needed him to be online.

We'd known for a while that there was more than one of these guys. Now the picture was becoming clearer. This was the chatty one. And the other guy was... what? The engineer? The executioner?

What do you want? I asked.

Send me a pic, he said. I'll make it worth your while.

This app is programmed to take a picture every 10 seconds, I wrote. Why do you need me to send another one?

Don't play dumb, he said. That's not the kind of pic I mean. You know what I like.

It was getting seedier by the second. He was right. I did know what he liked. I'd seen more than enough of it in the leering, predatory sexts he'd traded with his young victims.

At the same time, I thought, if that's what got this guy off, it meant there was something he wanted that I could control. That meant leverage, and even a tiny bit was more than I'd had up to now. So I tried to work it.

I need proof that Eve is still alive, I said. Then we can keep going.

What kind of proof? he asked.

Let me speak with her.

That's not going to happen. But since you've been good, hold on.

I'm not sure how long I sat there, waiting to hear back. I thought about what Billy had told me on my very first day with this case. *The clock is* always *ticking*, he'd said.

It had never felt truer than it did just then. Every minute that passed now was one more minute Eve had to spend in hell.

Finally, just when I started to wonder if he was playing me—was he ever going to come back?—I got word. Instead of a text or a photo this time, an audio file scrolled into the Android's chat thread, and I hit Play right away.

What I'd received was a recording of Eve, her voice flat and emotionless as she read back the most recent text exchange.

"'I need proof that Eve is still alive. Then we can keep going.' 'What kind of proof?' 'Let me speak with her.' 'That's not going to happen. But since you've been good, hold on.'"

That was it, only eight seconds long. But it meant she was alive! Just hearing her again filled me with the energy I needed to keep going.

I listened to the recording three more times, straining for any background noise that might give me some clue about where they'd taken her. There was nothing to extract, and before I could try a fourth time, the screen refreshed, the audio file disappeared, and a new text took its place.

Satisfied?

Why are you doing this? I asked.

Not so fast. It's your turn.

For what? I asked, even though I knew.

It's called show and tell, he wrote. You show, I tell. Every pic buys you a new question. Fun, right?

I could feel my desperation, rising inside me like mercury. I didn't want to go down this path, but I had to be able to say I tried everything, for Eve's sake.

Before I could respond either way, a sharp knock came at my door. I flinched, then went to look through the peephole. A woman I'd never seen before was standing in the hall.

"Who is it?" I asked.

"Angela, I'm Dr. Ann L. Johnson," she called back. "I'm here from psych services."

Dammit! I'd forgotten she was coming. And it wasn't like I could send her away, as much as I would have liked to.

"Just a minute!" I said as a quick series of new messages scrolled onto the phone in my hand.

Sounds like you have company

We'll play later

This is just getting interesting

Don't blow it now, Angela

CHAPTER 72

DR. ANN L. JOHNSON had an easy, chic kind of vibe going on, with her pleated pencil skirt, three-quarter-sleeve cardigan, and a beautiful floral print scarf that would have made my mother jealous. I could easily imagine her as the headmistress at some tony New England boarding school.

After some initial chitchat that I figured was meant to put me at ease—like that was ever going to happen—we sat down at my little kitchen table for the psych evaluation I assumed she was there for.

She asked how I was feeling about George, about Eve's disappearance, and about the case in general. I answered honestly but superficially, never forgetting that someone else could be listening in. The whole thing was as uncomfortable as it was unavoidable.

And then, inevitably, Dr. Johnson wanted to talk about my least favorite subject: me.

"I've spoken a bit with your superiors here," she said. "It sounds like you're quite an eager learner."

"Is that a euphemism?" I asked.

"It is, a little bit," she acknowledged.

I'm not a fan of shrinks. I'd been sent to a few in my adolescence, probably to make sure I wasn't child-geniusing my way to a career as a psychopath. And while I'm sure they were all perfectly good docs, they always made me feel like an animal in a zoo.

Still, I knew what Dr. Johnson was looking for. So I cut to the chase for both of us. The sooner we got this over with, the better.

"What can I say? Some people overeat. Some people gamble or drink," I told her. "I over*do*. I overthink, and always have. But that's also part of what's gotten me this far, especially for someone my age."

"It's true. Your resume is extraordinary," she said.

"That wasn't a dig for compliments," I told her. "What I'm saying is that I wouldn't walk away from that part of myself, even if I could."

She only smiled at that, which made me want to scream.

"Angela, let me start over with you," Dr. Johnson said. "You tend to go all in, on just about anything. Am I right?"

"Fair enough," I said.

"Has anyone ever spoken to you about impulse control? Or prescribed any medication for that kind of thing?"

I paused, actually taking it in. Impulse control? Medication?

"I thought we were supposed to be talking about George and Eve," I said.

"I'm merely suggesting that it's possible you've succeeded so spectacularly in *spite* of these tendencies, not because of them," she went on. "In which case, just imagine what you might accomplish without them."

I couldn't argue with that and wasn't going to. Her logic

wasn't the problem. It was her timing. I just didn't want to be having this conversation.

She went on. "I'm not telling you to pretend there's no crisis," she said. "But maybe this sequestration will help you pull back on the throttle a bit. Just take a conscious breath or two. Give your mind some space to process all of this."

"Do I have a choice?" I asked, looking around my little cave. "I'm in the ultimate time-out here."

"That doesn't mean it's lost time," Johnson told me. "It's just a matter of what you want to do with it."

On that we agreed fully. I couldn't wait for her to leave.

She stayed a little longer anyway, offering something to help me sleep (no, thank you) and asking about a convenient time for her to "drop by" again. Like I was going anywhere soon. The fact that I got all the way to the end without completely losing my shit felt like as much of an accomplishment as I could hope for.

Finally, she got up to go. I walked her out to the hall and promised that I'd think about everything she'd said. Then I shut myself up in my room and turned back to the real task at hand:

Hacking my way out of this corner I'd gotten myself into.

CHAPTER 73

ANOTHER STRING OF messages was waiting for me after my session with Dr. Johnson.

The first one just read FYI.

Then came a screen capture from a Twitter account under the name JustCuz.

> Hey @FBI! Any luck finding #EveAbajian? Didn't think so.

The tweet, stamped for five thirty that morning, had been posted with the picture of Eve they'd sent me the night before, mouth taped and eyes wide. It gave me the same hollow feeling in the pit of my stomach as it had the first time I saw it.

And there was more. The third message was a link to a CNN story with the headline FBI ABDUCTION TWEETED BY ALLEGED KIDNAPPERS.

> Authorities are following up on a disturbing tweet that appeared briefly online Wednesday morning. The single

posting, from an account held under the username JustCuz, referenced the unconfirmed kidnapping of a Boston-area FBI employee and included a graphic picture of the alleged victim. The tweet has since been taken down by Twitter.

CNN has learned that the victim in question is Eve Abajian, a cybersecurity analyst and consultant with the FBI's Boston field office. Witnesses confirmed that police were called early this morning to the street outside of Abajian's home in South Boston, where the body of retired federal agent George Yates was found in his car, following an apparent execution-style shooting. Calls to the FBI for comment were not immediately returned.

My little safe house was starting to feel like a bomb shelter. Everything was blowing up out there and I was stuck inside, listening to the explosions.

These guys knew exactly what they were doing. They knew the tweet would be taken down, and they knew it wouldn't matter. Once it got out, the media machine would treat it like the catnip it was meant to be.

What do you want from me? I messaged back.

I didn't expect a quick answer, but I got one.

We want you to help us disappear.

Disappear? What did that mean?

How? I asked.

Cable this phone to any networked computer at the FBI. We'll take care of the rest.

That's when I knew I was talking to the other guy. The one I'd started to think of as the Engineer, as opposed to the Poet. This one was all business and no chat.

What about Eve? I asked.

You do your part and she walks away.

Why should I believe anything you say? I wrote.

Not my problem, he answered. Your call.

They had to be making this up as they went along. They couldn't have known ahead of time where I'd be taken. But now they were trying to capitalize on it.

Or at least this guy was.

Were the two of them even talking to each other at this point? Were they deliberately trying to confuse me? Playing me off of each other?

For that matter, were these two even in the same location? I had no way of knowing.

The only sure thing was that I couldn't give in to this latest demand. Not even for Eve. It was one thing to compromise my own safety. It was another to allow them access to the Bureau's servers. That would put far too many other people in jeopardy. And if I knew Eve at all, I knew she'd back me up on this. There was simply no way.

But the Engineer didn't have to know that.

I'm stuck here, I wrote. How do you suggest I do this?

You have six hours, he answered. Already, that damn timer of his had popped up again and started counting down.

I need more than that, I wrote.

This is not a negotiation, he told me. In six hours, we find our own way to disappear. Then Eve stays put and she can starve to death while you look for her. Think on that.

A bolt of rage shot through me. I forced myself to set down the phone rather than hurl it across the room. Then I picked up the mug I'd been drinking from and threw that instead. It smashed into a shower of blue shards and coffee, dripping down the wall by the door. And no, I didn't clean it up. Or care.

I took up the phone again.

Please give me more time, I wrote.

Silence.

Hello? We need to talk about this.

Still nothing. He'd said all he was going to say, and I was left there with no more than the sound of my own shaky breathing. Clearly, the next move was mine to make.

But I had no idea what it was going to be.

AT AROUND TEN, Billy came by. He had an FBI duffel full of my clothes, along with my bike, my indoor trainer, and everything else on my list, with one exception.

"No laptop?" I asked.

"You're officially off-line as long as you're here," he said. "I know that's like cutting off your oxygen, but you understand."

There was so much I couldn't say, and even more on my mind. I wasn't even sure if I should feel guilty for hiding so much from Billy. It was like a complex moral equation and I didn't have the skills, much less the presence of mind or the time, to balance it out. All I could do was take this one thing at a time.

"What about my family?" I asked.

"I went by your folks' place this morning. They're concerned, of course, but they're doing okay," he said. "What about you? How are you holding up?"

"Never better," I said. Billy didn't even try to smile at that. "Okay, I'm horrible," I told him. "I'm going crazy in here. I want to cry and kill someone at the same time."

He nodded with the calm understanding of a Bureau vet, even if he didn't know all the particulars of my personal hell that morning.

"Listen," he said, "I can't tell you much, but since part of this has gone public, there's no reason to keep it from you."

He navigated his phone to a page and handed it to me. What I saw was the *Globe*'s website, with their own version of the CNN story from that morning. The headline this time was TWEETED FBI KIDNAP CONFIRMED.

"Oh, my God!" I said. I tried to seem genuinely surprised and took a minute to scan the article for anything I didn't already know. Apparently, the FBI had held a press conference to confirm Eve's kidnapping, but they weren't sharing any details about the case.

"We figured we might as well own it," Billy said. "It wasn't a bell we could unring." Then he thumbed toward the door. "But come on. I can at least show you around before I go."

"Really?" I wasn't even expecting to get out of the apartment that day.

"Don't get too excited," he told me. "It's the world's shortest tour."

The hall outside my room was as empty as it had been the night before. All the closed doors looked exactly alike except for the fire exit, which had an alarmed crash bar and a surveillance camera mounted above.

"Your ID card will get you into your apartment, and into the admin office during business hours," Billy said. "Other than that, you're not to go anywhere."

"Admin office?" I asked.

He pressed his own card to the reader on the door directly opposite mine. The little red light clicked to green, and Billy pushed the door open.

"Welcome to the end of the tour," he said.

I followed him into a cramped, windowless office. A woman was sitting alone at a U-shaped workstation, and she stood up as we came in. I couldn't help noticing her desktop computer, as well as the ASUS laptop sitting on her return. I wasn't sure what that might mean for me, but it was something.

"Angela Hoot, this is Rena Partridge, one of our operations coordinators," Billy said.

"Angela, hi." She shook my hand with a reassuring smile. "If there's anything you need—drugstore run, a message for Billy Boy here, or even just some kind of favorite foods—I'm your gal."

With her short salt-and-pepper hair and the red glasses on a chain, she seemed like someone's elderly babysitter, not a high-security-clearance FBI employee. I liked her right away.

"I'll probably have to take you up on that," I said. "Thank you in advance."

If I needed to get online without the Android, this office opened up some possibilities, I thought. Maybe not with Rena's desktop, which would be hardwired into the building's network. But the laptop was an option—

"Angela?" Keats said.

I snapped back to attention. They were both looking at me like I'd missed something. Which, for all I knew, I had.

"Hon, you should get some sleep," Rena said. "You look exhausted."

I didn't argue with that. I just thanked her again and followed Billy back out to the hall. He wasn't kidding about the world's shortest tour, either. Three steps later, we were standing outside my door like it was the end of some strange date.

Our night together in Portland seemed about a century ago.

A past lifetime. Maybe a future one, too, but I couldn't think about that right now.

"I've got to run," Billy said.

"Of course," I told him. "Thanks for bringing my stuff."

He hesitated and tilted his head to catch my eye. "You know this isn't your fault, right?" he said.

"That's a complicated question," I told him. "Maybe one for another time."

"Right." He looked at his watch. The clock was ticking for both of us. "I'll check back when I can," he said.

And one tick later, he was gone.

CHAPTER 75

NORMALLY, THE BEST way for me to get my head on straight is by hitting the trail with my bike. But "normal" was off the table right now, so I set up my trainer in the middle of the room and started riding in place.

I left the Android where I could see it, in case anything new came in. Then I got a good crank going, put my head down, and tried to synthesize everything I knew into a cohesive plan of attack.

As I turned the various factors over and around in my head like a Rubik's Cube, I kept coming back to the same idea: *geolocating malware.* If I could sneak the right kind of self-loading program onto one of the devices these guys were using on their end, I could get back an IP address, and from that a physical location.

Which meant there was a possibility that I could actually find Eve without ever leaving the building.

The real question was how to get this done without them noticing, much less in the next four and a half hours.

I thought about what Eve said to me once: *Sometimes you have to look past the code and into the coder.* With people like Darren Wendt, that was easy. Darren had all the intellectual depth of a kiddie pool. He couldn't have been more oblivious to the hacks I sent his way.

These guys were different. Maybe they were typical ego cases for hackers, but they were also smart as hell and well resourced.

Lucky for me, I was smart as hell, too.

I downshifted several gears and cranked the trainer's resistance until I was riding up a virtual thirty-degree incline. It put an exquisite kind of pain into my quads and glutes, and I told myself there was *no stopping* until I'd figured this out or reached pure muscle failure, whichever came first.

Sticking with the malware idea, it made sense to target the Poet, not the Engineer. He was the one I knew for sure was in the same location as Eve, since he'd recorded her voice and sent it to me. He also seemed more human. Less focused. More distractible.

I hated to think about what it was going to take to distract him. As he'd said himself, I knew what he liked. But I'd deal with that when I had to.

In the meantime, I focused on the tech aspects of this hack, laying out contingency plans like a flowchart in my mind.

I don't know how many miles I covered. My thoughts were spinning as fast as those pedals, and I barely noticed as I went from smooth, even strokes to jerky, sporadic pulls. When I couldn't manage one more rotation, I eased back the resistance and coasted into a cooldown, arms overhead and sweat streaming.

I knew what I wanted to do now. Or at least I knew what I wanted to try. There were no guarantees, but as that ticking timer made abundantly clear, I couldn't afford to sit around on my ass, waiting for a better idea.

Ready or not, it was time to flip this game.

CHAPTER 76

I DISMOUNTED MY bike, muscles singing, and peeled off my sweaty tee and bra. Then I put on my hoodie and left the zipper down just far enough to make it look like I was trying to start something with this guy.

I turned the Android's camera on myself then and did what I could to keep from looking completely disgusted. The truth was, I was about 90 percent fearless, but this was well inside my 10 percent.

Before I could change my mind, I snapped a selfie and posted it into the app's chat thread.

Are you there? I texted.

Even if he responded soon, I figured I could afford a minute away from the phone. That's what I needed for the next step. It was a gamble, but there was no way through this without taking some kind of risk.

I picked up my card key, slipped silently out of the apartment, and let myself into the admin office across the hall.

"Hey, hon. What can I do you for?" Rena asked, looking up from her keyboarding as I came in.

"I'm really sorry to ask," I said, "but I was just working out, and it reminded me that I was supposed to pick up my asthma prescription yesterday."

And no, I don't have asthma. There was no prescription.

"Are you okay?" Rena asked with the immediate concern of a mother. "Do I need to call someone?"

"I'm fine," I told her. "But I'd feel better if I had that inhaler, just in case. It's at the CVS on Mass Ave."

Already she was stepping out of her low heels and into a pair of Keen slip-ons. "Don't give it another thought," she said. "I'll go now and knock on your door as soon as I'm back."

"Thank you so much," I said. I hated lying to this nice lady, but it couldn't be helped.

Back in my apartment, I closed the door, turned around, and pressed my eye to the peephole.

Rena came out a second later. I watched her head up the hall and gave it another slow ten count, just to make sure she was gone. Then I went right back to her office, grabbed the laptop, and returned to my apartment in one quick loop. The daily security logs would record every time I used my key card, but hopefully that wouldn't matter by the time anyone noticed.

I checked the Android as soon as I was back. There were no new texts for me, which was just as well. I still had some humps to get over.

I input my work password to hop on the laptop's Wi-Fi and then used my credit card to buy a copy of the software I was going to need for this. Twelve hundred dollars down the drain. Oh well. It was the least of my worries right now.

The program was called Stego. That's short for steganography, which is the practice of digitally hiding information in plain sight. In this case, it was going to be one of the selfies I'd send the Poet, embedded with a bit of geolocating malware. As soon as it reached his phone or laptop, it would self-detonate and send back all the information I'd need.

God willing.

Next, I went looking for the malicious code itself. The dark net is full of spyware libraries, if you know where to look. And geolocation isn't exactly rocket science in that world. It took me all of two minutes to find something I could use, and a few seconds more to drag it into Stego's source window.

Now I needed the carrier file. A.k.a., the distraction.

I stood up and positioned myself in front of the laptop's camera. This time, I lowered my zipper all the way, keeping my breasts covered but showing a full highway of skin down the front. If he wanted more than that, he could go screw himself. Literally.

I set the camera to a three-second delay, clicked the shutter, and stood back. After a quick countdown, it snapped the photo I needed. Then I dropped it into Stego alongside the code I'd already delivered and clicked Run.

The software took it from there, knitting my geolocator right into the image, pixel by pixel. A status window opened up a few seconds later to indicate its progress: 5 percent and counting.

For a few minutes, nothing more happened. Then, just as the image clicked over to 36 percent complete on the laptop, a new text scrolled into the Android's chat screen.

That's not much, he said. Presumably, he meant the modest little selfie I'd already sent. You can do better.

I wrote back right away, making sure to keep the laptop out of sight of the phone's camera.

Of course I can, I said. Isn't that how the game works? It gets better as it goes along.

Why don't I believe you? he responded.

Believe it. I don't have time to be shy anymore. If I play along, will you do everything you can to get Eve out alive?

Absolutely, he said. I'm in charge. Don't worry.

It wasn't that I trusted his word. Not even a little. It was all about taking a page from this guy's book and turning myself into the person he wanted me to be. Or at least letting him *think* that's what was happening. It was the best way I knew to draw him into a trap of my own making.

Okay then, I said. Let's play.

CHAPTER 77

THE SOFTWARE WAS reporting in at 68 percent complete by now. I needed to draw this out for however long it took.

I want to see more this time, he said.

Not so fast, I said. It's my turn to ask a question.

Go ahead.

Are you Hermes?

I knew you were going to ask that, he said. No. Hermes never existed.

So you have no connection to FNC? I asked.

Clever girl. This is why I like you, Angela, he said. Now you go.

I hated to think about what he might be doing with himself right then, but I stayed focused on the big picture. I was spinning a web here. And first chance I got, I was going to suck the lifeblood right out of this bastard.

So I pulled my zipper down a few inches from where it had been in the first shot and posted a new pic.

That's about a 6, he wrote. I'm still looking for a 10.

Be patient. We'll get there, I wrote back. My turn. Why are you doing all this? What's the bigger objective here?

Why do you think there is one? he asked.

Seems like a lot of trouble for nothing.

Who said anything about NOTHING? he wrote. Ever hear of George Mallory?

I hadn't, and I took a second to look up the name. Wikipedia told me that Mallory had been a mountain climber in the 1920s. The thing he was most remembered for was his famous quote about why he wanted to climb Mount Everest. "Because it's there," he'd said.

And weirdly enough, it made perfect sense. Black hat hackers lived by that credo, in their own nihilistic way. They were motivated by doing things that had never been done before, often just for the sake of doing it.

It also echoed the Twitter handle from that morning: JustCuz. This was starting to add up.

So you wanted to kill those people because they were there? I asked.

Basically.

Does that mean this app is your Mount Everest?

It was, he said. But now YOU are.

And a thousand invisible spiders went crawling through my stomach. Jesus Christ, this guy was all over the map.

I don't know what to say to that, I told him.

You don't have to say anything, he wrote back. Next picture, please.

THE GOOD NEWS was, my Stego image was just about there. I watched the status window as it clicked from 99 to 100 percent complete, and a throbber started cycling on the screen while the software did its final processing.

Anyone there? the Poet texted. I warned you, Angela. Don't bore me. It won't end well for Eve if you do.

I'm just deciding how much to show you, I wrote back quickly.

That's easy, he said. Show me everything.

Finally, a new window opened on the laptop, and I had my finished image. It looked exactly like the original. He'd have to blow it up to wall-size before he'd be able to see any impact from the embedded code.

None of which was my immediate concern. The most vulnerable part of this whole process was in the next step: transferring that infected photo from Rena's laptop to the Android.

I had no idea if the app would detect that granular a file change or not. If it did, then I'd just wasted two days of hell and was about to lose everything, including Eve. But there was no stopping now.

I turned off the laptop's Wi-Fi first. Then I slid the phone across the table, keeping it flat, with the camera aimed at the ceiling. I plugged its charger cable into a port on the computer and transferred my spyware-laden selfie to the Android's photo library as quickly as I could.

Once that was done, I yanked the charger cable and posted my image on the Android so he could see it. Then I turned the laptop's internet back on and started watching for any incoming reports.

Within seconds, I had confirmation that the spyware had rooted. So far, so good.

HOT, he wrote me. THIS IS WHAT I'M TALKING ABOUT.

You like that? I asked. It nauseated me just to write it, but I had to string him along.

Let's just say you earned your next question, he said.

As I watched the laptop, the screen blinked twice, repopulated, and spit out an IP address, followed quickly by an actual street location.

147 Condor Street, Boston MA 02128

I didn't need another Q and A with him, but I did need more time. So I kept going.

Why did you take Eve? I asked. Why not me?

As he worked on his answer, I tore back onto the laptop and mapped the address I'd been given. Condor Street was over by the Chelsea River in Eastie. Only 2.9 miles from my current location. Easy striking distance.

I wanted to see what you could do on your own, he texted. You depend on Eve too much, you know that?

That's not true, I typed back even as I was scanning the route on the laptop, committing as much as I could to memory.

Moving on, he said. I want to see more now. And I do mean MORE.

I was ready for this, too. I'd known I was going to need a big stall at some point. I also knew this guy was a horny son of a bitch.

I'm all sweaty from my ride, I told him. If we're going to keep going, I need a nice hot shower first.

Excellent. Can I watch? he asked.

No but you can listen, I said. And you can see when I'm done.

No clothes this time. And no towel.

Give me fifteen minutes.

Hurry up, he said. I won't wait forever.

You won't have to, I told him. It's like I already said. The game gets better as it goes along.

And I meant it. Just not in the way he might have thought.

It was time for me to snap this trap, once and for all.

CHAPTER 79

I CARRIED THE Android into the bathroom and set it on the sink, without a view of the shower. Then I turned on the hot tap and let the bathroom start to steam up.

I draped a towel around the showerhead so it would sound like someone was in there.

And I slipped out of the bathroom, closing the door behind me.

A few seconds later, I was back in Rena's office. I grabbed the phone and dialed Billy's number, but it went straight to voice mail. Dammit! It felt like forever just getting to the beep.

"Billy! It's Angela! I don't have time to explain, but I know where they're holding Eve. It's 147 Condor Street in Eastie. God, I hope you pick this up soon."

I couldn't call the police. If they got to that address without instruction, Eve was screwed. Someone needed to head them off or get there first. So I ran back along the hall and down the stairs to the guard station on six.

One of the guards stopped me right away with a hand out. "Hold it right there," he said.

"I need to get hold of anyone on Agent Keats's team," I told him. "It's an absolute emergency. An agent's life is at stake."

The other guard picked up the phone. "I'll try Agent Keats right now," he said.

"He's not picking up!" I told him. "Call Audrey Gruss's office. Call whatever emergency contact you need to, and get them over to 147 Condor. Have you got that? They need to go in carefully. Keats will know why, but if you can't get him, I need to be there, or I need to talk to someone myself—"

"You're not even authorized to be on this floor," the first guard said. "Go back to your quarters. As soon as we have contact, we'll let you know—"

"Are you even listening to me?" I yelled at him.

"Miss, you need to calm down."

"Let me go to the fifth floor and find someone myself," I said. "You can escort me, if you need to."

I reached for the elevator button, but he wasn't having it and stepped in my way.

"Please don't make me remove you from this area," he said. "We're on it, okay? Now turn around and go. I'm not going to ask again."

I felt like I was in a nightmare within a nightmare. They were only following protocol, but that wasn't good enough. And I couldn't waste any more time spinning my wheels with them.

So I made a decision. I went back upstairs, down the hall, and quietly into my apartment.

I could hear the shower running as I grabbed my bike and turned to leave. But then I stopped. I pulled a small paring knife out of the kitchen drawer and sheathed it in the laces of my sneakers, just in case. It was a gut move, not a rational one. But who the hell knew what might happen?

Wheeling my bike into the hall, I turned right instead of left this time. I went straight for the fire exit and used my front tire to break through the crash bar. A second later, I was humping that bike down seven flights as fast as I could, while the high-pitched wail of an alarm echoed up and down the stairwell behind me.

When I reached the ground floor, there was only one way out. I hit another crash bar with my tire and burst onto the sidewalk, like some kind of escaped convict.

I jumped on my bike, hopped the curb down to the street, pointed myself east, and started pedaling like hell.

CHAPTER 80

IN BOSTON, ANYTHING under three miles is faster on a bike than it is by car. For me, anyway. If I reached Condor Street first, I wouldn't go rushing in like some kind of action hero, but at least I could keep whoever showed up from doing the same thing.

With any luck, I could still keep Eve alive.

I kept my eyes up for traffic and ground the pedals as fast as I could. What I needed was another phone. And when I saw the business-suited gentleman standing just off the curb with his nose buried in his screen, I made a split-second decision.

"Hey!"

I'd grabbed it out of his hand and was halfway through the next intersection before he even spotted me.

If this didn't work, and maybe even if it did, I was going to end up in jail. Meanwhile, I should have stopped riding long enough to call this in, but I just couldn't bring myself to do it. No stopping now. No turning back. No nothing. I kept on pedaling as I checked the road ahead, looked down long enough to dial 911 for the second time in three days, and kept heading east.

"Nine one one. What is your emergency?"

"My name is Angela Hoot and I'm with the FBI," I shouted into the phone. I was shooting up the narrow space between the slow-moving traffic on my left and the sidewalk on my right, just hoping nobody threw open a car door without looking. "I need emergency responders to 147 Condor Street immediately. Tell them to call Agent William Keats at the FBI for instruction. They have to proceed with extreme caution. Do you understand?"

"I'll do what I can, ma'am," she said. "Please hold."

But I couldn't even do that. My quickest route was through the Callahan Tunnel, which doesn't allow bikes, much less have a bike lane. I needed both hands for this, and it was coming up fast. The dispatcher was going to have to get this done without any more input from me, I thought, and shoved the phone back into my pocket.

I hung a right onto New Chardon Street, then right again, down toward the tunnel entrance. It was like a cattle chute at this point. The tunnel itself was a mile long, which meant three minutes at the speed I was going, and I'd already lost any wiggle room on the shoulder.

Bring it, I thought. If I could ride six-inch-wide trails in the woods, I could thread this needle, too.

As I passed inside, daylight gave way to a sickly green glow from the electric fixtures, mixed with a red blur of taillights ahead. I mostly kept my eyes on the cars, checking to the right every few seconds to keep from crashing into the side wall. There was a raised walkway above me, but I couldn't get to it.

Drivers kept edging past my bike. A few yelled, and several of them blared their horns, which were amplified by the tunnel's acoustics. It was an all-out war on my senses. I had no choice but to gut it out.

Eventually, the road curved right, and I could see a tiny square of daylight several hundred yards ahead. I focused on my breathing, in and out with the rhythm of the pedals, counting as I went.

On the twenty-fourth breath, I broke free, into the daylight again. Thank God. Not that I could feel relieved for long. I was getting close now.

The traffic only got hairier outside of the tunnel, with everyone suddenly changing lanes. I swerved right onto Porter Street to avoid getting shunted up to the expressway, where I would have *really* been screwed.

Then a quick left onto Chelsea for a couple of blocks, and another left, onto Brooks, for one last stretch before I reached the river.

The closer I got, the more my thoughts turned to what might happen next. The police were on their way. Hopefully word had filtered over to someone at the Bureau as well.

I pulled the phone back out of my pocket to try Billy again, but it had locked up in the meantime. The only thing I could manage from the lock screen would be another emergency call, which was better than nothing—

But I never got that far. I didn't even see the car coming until it was too late.

He'd pulled out from between two buildings, both of us moving too fast. I swerved into the middle of the road to try to avoid him, but it didn't do me any good. His bumper caught me from the side, full on.

An explosion of pain shot up my leg. I flew sideways, leaving the bike behind. My body was airborne just long enough for me to register that fact, before I came down hard on the cement. Ears ringing. Head spinning. Vision blurred.

Game over.

CHAPTER 81

I HEARD VOICES before anything else.

"Oh, my God!"

"I'll call 911."

"Is she okay?"

Someone came around the front of the car. I saw a pair of feet, then felt a hand on my shoulder.

"Can you stand?" he asked.

"I... I think so," I said. I needed to get back on my bike. Some part of me knew that wasn't going to happen, but I wasn't letting go of it yet.

"Go slow. Let me help you."

He put an arm around me and got me onto my feet. As soon as I put any weight on my right leg, the pain came screaming back, and doubled down on itself. Jesus, what had I done? My leg buckled, and he boosted me up again, all but carrying me toward his car. I felt like I was going to puke.

"I need to call someone," I slurred.

"My phone's in the car," he said. "I'm taking you to the hospital right now."

"Ambulance is on the way," someone else said from a distance.

"I've got her," the guy said. "Can you open that passenger-side door for me? I think she's going to pass out."

"Got it."

"Thanks."

It was all happening without me. I couldn't think straight. I vaguely caught sight of my bent and twisted bike in the middle of the street.

"Eve..." I croaked out.

"Yes, we're leaving now."

"No. *Eve*..."

"I've got you," he said. And then from in close, right next to my ear, "Poor Angela. Did you really think you were going to pull this off?"

That's when I looked up and saw his face clearly for the first time. It was the Brit. Or whoever he was. Strong nose, sandy-brown buzz cut, cleft chin. The one from the coffee shop, but there was no accent now.

Before I could even speak, I felt a sharp stab under the arm. My scream didn't even form. All I heard was a rasping sound from my throat, like air escaping a ruined tire.

I felt weak. And then weaker again.

"She's losing consciousness," he said.

"No," I said. "Help..."

"Yes, we're getting you help."

"No."

"There she goes," I heard him say. I knew he'd injected me with something, but it was the last thought I had before everything slid sideways again. Daylight turned to a wash of gray, followed quickly by a descending blackness.

And then there was nothing at all.

CHAPTER 82

I WOKE UP in the dark. There wasn't anything to see, and I didn't know where I was.

Then a bump. And another. Each one jolted my body, bringing me wide awake with a pain that seemed to be everywhere.

We were moving. I was in the back of a van of some kind.

And I wasn't alone. As my eyes adjusted to the dark, I realized someone else was there, sitting across from me.

Jesus! My panic turned on like a switch. When I screamed, I realized my mouth had been taped. My wrists were taped, too, crisscrossed behind my back. I couldn't stop myself from speaking, even though the words never made it past my gag.

"Eve? Eve!"

It was her, I could tell. I recognized the shape of her, filling in what I couldn't see with what I knew from my gut.

She wasn't stirring, and I realized all at once that she might be dead. The possibility grabbed hold of me like an icy hand. I couldn't reach her. I was lashed to some kind of brace or upright, holding me against the side wall of the van. I kicked with my two bound feet, trying to nudge her awake, desperate to see her move.

And then she did, barely. I saw the rise and fall of a breath. *Thank God.* She was unconscious, but she was alive. That was all that really mattered. Still, it opened up a whole cascade of other questions.

Where were we headed? How long had I been out? How many miles had we covered?

I remembered the Brit then. Or whatever he was. He hadn't been driving a van when he hit me. That meant I'd been out long enough for him to change vehicles.

My bike was long gone. My stolen cell phone, too. I'd left both of them lying broken in the street.

But the knife! It might still be there, I realized, tucked into the laces of my shoe.

I twisted around, pulling against the tape and the mesh straps that had me stuck in one position. I couldn't lean forward enough to reach my feet, but with some effort, I bent at the knees and brought my feet toward my hands instead. It was just enough for me to feel around the laces, where my fingers closed on the plastic hilt I was looking for. *Thank God.* The blade was bent but still usable.

With some more maneuvering, I got the knife wedged between the floor and the tape around my wrists. I had to rock back and forth to create a sawing motion. Each stroke sent up a throb from my leg, watering my eyes with the pain. I had no idea how mobile I was going to be even if I could get out of these bonds. The pain was nearly overwhelming, but the adrenaline was doing its own bit to keep me conscious and focused. I'd drag myself through this if I had to, but there was no use even thinking about that until I'd gotten through the tape.

After a little more sawing, I heard a welcome ripping sound.

It was just enough. I pulled with both hands, and the rest of the tape gave way.

I tore the gag off my mouth and sucked in a desperate lungful of air like I'd been drowning. Then I started sawing away at the mesh straps that still kept me lashed to the wall.

"Eve!" I tried again, in a hoarse whisper. She didn't respond. Whatever they'd knocked her out with had clearly been more than I'd gotten.

The van was sealed. I could see some kind of molded industrial plastic wall at the front. I had no idea if anyone could hear us or not, but it made sense to be careful. The one thing I might have left on my side was some element of surprise.

That, and the knife.

I sawed even harder at the straps around my torso now. They were far tougher than the tape, but with my hands unbound, I was making decent headway. I'd be free of them soon. I didn't know how much longer this drive was going to be, or where we were going, but whenever we got there, I intended to be ready.

CHAPTER 83

THE RIDE WENT on for at least another hour. It's hard to say how long. I lost track of time, but I eventually felt a change as the van went from the highway to some kind of lower-speed roads with several turns. After that, the hum of concrete disappeared completely and the bumps came harder and faster.

It was all the worst possible news. We had to be well outside the city by then. I had no idea what kind of weapons they might be carrying, or even how many people were in the front of that van.

Finally, we came to a stop. I heard movement on the other side of the front wall for the first time. One door opened, then the other, followed by two slams. Then voices, but I couldn't hear what they were saying.

Eve was still out. I'd left her bound up, since the alternative had been to have her rolling around unconscious inside that moving van. It had been hard enough for me to manage myself, holding on and gritting my teeth against the nonstop throbbing in my leg.

This was all on me. I had to do whatever I could. The knife in my hand was my life now. Eve's life. Marlena's future. I tried to breathe slowly as I waited to see what would happen next.

More footsteps told me that one of them had come around the back. I heard a jingle of keys. Then the sound of one key snugging into a lock.

One chance. That's all I'd have. I positioned myself against the side wall of the van where they'd left me and arranged the straps as best I could to keep up some appearance that I was still tied. The knife was in my right hand, tucked behind my back, out of sight but ready to swing.

As the door opened, I dropped my chin and rested it against my chest, my eyes closed. I felt a flashlight play over my face.

"She still out?" a voice said.

"Looks that way," said another.

The second voice was the familiar one. I recognized it from our run-in at the coffee shop. It was the Brit—or whoever he was. The voice was the same, but the accent was gone. The whole thing had been some kind of charade within a charade.

I heard one of them climb into the van. It was almost impossible to keep my eyes closed. I had to work by sense here. And pray for luck.

"I'm going to wake her up," the familiar voice said. He was almost close enough to reach with my knife.

I held my breath and waited another beat, until he was bent over me. That's when he seemed to notice that something was wrong.

"What the—?" he said. And I moved.

My eyes popped open. My right hand came up fast, aiming the tip of the knife for the shadow of him. For the very center.

Let it find his heart, I thought in that flash of a moment.

He moved fast, too, and deflected my swing with his arm. For a second, I thought I had him, but all I caught was the fabric of his sleeve. I heard a ripping sound, and he jumped back, stumbling over Eve's legs. There was no room to maneuver in there.

The knife jerked in my hand, its bent blade caught on the cloth, but then it tore free. I lunged toward him and swung again. He was ready for me this time and took a swing of his own. His fist knocked the knife right out of my grip, and I heard it skitter across the metal floor of the van, toward the back.

I had no choice but to keep trying. I dove after it. The blade glinted in the beam of the flashlight, and I half-expected him to get there first.

Instead, he reversed his tactic. He moved in the opposite direction, away from me. At the same moment that I got a grip on the knife again, I felt his hands on my ankles from behind. Before anything else could happen, he was dragging me straight out of the van, past Eve, arms trailing.

He pulled me all the way out. I fell onto the ground on my stomach. By the time I'd flipped over, he already had a foot on my chest, pinning me to the dirt. I could just make out his stance against the last of the twilight and what looked like the gun he now had pointed at my face.

"Hello, Angela. Have a nice nap?" he asked. "Actually, don't answer that. Just drop the damn knife."

I didn't have a choice and loosened my grip, letting the knife fall out of my hand. Even as I did, the other guy was there, slapping a fresh piece of duct tape over my mouth.

"Smile," he said. A camera flash popped, blinding me to what little I'd been able to see in the first place.

I'd blown it. I'd missed my chance. All I saw was shadows and bright spots as the flash ghosted across my eyes.

But I'd seen enough to know that probability had turned

against me long before this moment. As soon as I'd laid eyes on the Engineer's face, back at the coffee shop and again in the street that afternoon, I'd lost any chance I had of making it out of this place alive.

They had nothing to gain by letting me go anymore. And everything to gain by killing me.

CHAPTER 84

THE ENGINEER, OR whoever he was, wasted no time re-taping my wrists. He was big, and way too strong for me. With no trouble at all, he got me sitting up and lashed to a tree before he took the tape off my mouth again.

The sun was all but gone now. Twilight was turning into night, and I could hear spring peepers nearby.

We were deep in the woods, I realized. Somewhere far enough out that he didn't care if I made any noise or not.

"Did you like the British accent?" he asked just before a flashlight beam seared into my eyes. I squinted hard, trying to see around it. "We've got a million of them. Southern, German, whatever. Not that it matters. Just a little something to muddy the water."

When I tried to speak, a wave of nausea stopped me. I heaved, but nothing came up.

"That's the propofol," he said. "It'll wear off."

I could hear the other one—the Poet?—moving around in the dark. A van door opened and closed. Music came on, muted from inside the vehicle. Some kind of guitar rock. The kind I hate.

"What about Eve?" I said, trying again. I couldn't see her from where I was, but it didn't seem as though they'd moved her, or even paid her any attention yet.

"She's down for the count," he said from the other side of the flashlight. "I like to take things one at a time."

"You told me you'd let her go," I tried.

"And *you*"—he took three fast strides toward me—"said you'd play by the rules. So I guess neither of us got what we wanted."

He was standing over me now. The gun was still there, close enough that I could see the black nib of a sight on his barrel.

I didn't know how he'd intercepted me, but I could think of a few ways. It had been days since I really took stock of that app. For all I knew, he'd spotted my malware before it could ever pose a serious threat. Maybe I'd been shortsighted, or careless. It was hard to say anymore. But what choice did I have?

"You were never at that address on Condor Street, were you?" I asked.

"Oh, we were there," he told me. "We lost a perfectly good apartment, thanks to you. The cops are all over it now. I should shoot you just for that."

"So that's it? You're going to kill me?" I asked. I'm not sure why I wasn't incoherent, because I *was* terrified.

"Nah," he said, and stepped back again. "Not my department."

"What does that mean?" I asked.

The music from the van bumped up in volume as the Poet stepped outside again.

"You all set?" the Engineer called over his shoulder.

"Yep." The other's voice came out of the dark. I could hear him walking closer better than I could see him. "I was just putting Angela's picture up on Twitter. Hey, Angela, guess what? You're famous now!"

The Engineer turned toward his partner. As he did, the flashlight beam swung out of my eyes and gave me my first real look at the Poet.

Justin Nicholson had described his shooter as a short man with, he thought, a Southern accent. Presumably, this was him. The accent had been a fake, for sure. But now I wasn't so sure about the "man" part, either.

This kid was impossibly young. He didn't look any more than eighteen, and probably wasn't even that. Hell, he barely looked old enough to drive.

"Ready for me here?" he asked.

"She's all yours, little brother," the other one said, handing off the flashlight. "I'll just be in the van, if you need me."

"I won't," the Poet said.

"I know," answered the other as he disappeared into the dark and left us alone.

Dear God, what had I fallen into?

CHAPTER 85

"SO . . . HI," HE said, putting down the case he'd carried over. As he sat cross-legged on the ground facing me, he seemed like any other average white kid. Baggy pants, ring tee, and a mop of shaggy hair. The kind you hide behind when you don't fit in.

Everything about him was young. Exactly as young as I thought he'd been *pretending* to be online.

"How old are you?" I asked.

"How old do you think?" he said.

My impulse then was the same as it would have been for any boy this age: round up. Don't offend him by shooting low.

"Nineteen?"

"That's exactly right," he said, but I knew he was lying.

"And you two are brothers?" I asked.

"That's not important right now."

Oddly enough, he was right.

He opened his case and took out a pistol, then set it on the ground. That was followed by a large hunting knife, which he set next to the gun. The flashlight was on the ground, too.

The details of everything were sketchy there in the dark, but he seemed to be putting on some kind of show. I could tell he wanted me to see this, one bit at a time. Like maybe he had something to prove.

Finally, he took out a phone and started texting something.

"Did you really think that piece of crap malware was the way to go?" he asked without looking up. "It was pretty rookie for someone like you. We're not idiots, Angela."

"No," I said. "I didn't think you were."

"You had six hours. I could have coded something better from scratch in half that. You probably could have, too. Maybe even gotten away with it."

He wasn't wrong. The truth of it cut into me. I hadn't thought this through.

And then, another realization.

"Is that your app?" I asked. "Did you write it?" I'd assumed all along that the other guy was their coder.

The kid smiled down at his screen, thumbs still busy. "Duh," he said. "What do you think of it?"

"I think anyone would love to have fifteen million copies of their work out there," I answered honestly.

"Seventeen million now," he said. "And don't tell me you've never wanted to hack at that level."

"The difference is, I never wanted to kill anyone," I said.

"Are you sure about that?" He stopped and looked up from his phone for the first time since he'd taken it out. "What about Darren Wendt?"

The name hung there in the air. I wasn't even sure how to respond.

"Oh, yeah," he went on. "I know all about you. Ever since that day at Boston Latin. You completely changed the game then. You should be proud."

I was processing everything as fast as I could. There was a lot to take in. When he went back to his phone, I thought he was still texting, but then he held up a picture for me to see.

"Remember this?"

It was an image of Billy and me standing outside Mass General, taken from across the street. "Ever wonder how we got the number of that burner phone?"

"I assumed you hacked Justin Nicholson's account," I said. "He was one of the only people I gave it to."

The kid's face lit up. There was an odd innocence to his smile, like he was genuinely happy to be sitting here, talking to me.

"I love that you know that," he said, already navigating to the next image. When he held this one up, I saw a picture of myself getting into George's car outside the Bureau field office.

"Poor George," he said. "You may have changed the game, Angela, but George paid the price."

It was a struggle to keep my anger down. "You didn't have to kill him," I said.

"See, that's where you're wrong," he told me. "There are lots of people we didn't *have* to kill. But George? He was in the way."

"Of what?" I said. "Of me?"

The kid rocked his head side to side. "That's a bit simplistic. But as a binary question, let's say yes."

It was all coming together, in its own twisted way. As far as I could tell, he'd created that app just to see if he could. Then he killed those girls and their families because they were there.

Now he'd turned his micro attention span on me. Which begged the question, *How do I keep this kid distracted?*

How long could I survive?

CHAPTER 86

THIS GUY WAS the genius of the future. He seemed to know a little bit about everything, and everything about nothing.

I hated people like him. Even the sane ones.

He scooted closer then, coming onto his knees. From there, he leaned in so his face was practically touching mine. When he put a hand on my leg, I shuddered, imagining the worst.

"Do you want me to kill Darren for you?" he asked. "Because I will, you know."

"I don't want you to kill anyone," I said. "Including Eve. Or me."

He squinted and tilted his head, like he was trying to figure me out. When his hand slid farther up my thigh, I bucked, trying to shake him off.

"Don't fucking touch me," I said.

He froze for an almost imperceptible moment. Then a smile hit his face and he rocked back to sit on his heels.

"You know, my one disappointment is that you're not as good-looking in person," he said. "You don't have much of a body, either."

It was bizarrely typical. Yes, he was probably insane, and definitely homicidal. But he was also like any number of other guys I'd known in my life. The ones who are all bluster until they get cornered and have to perform. Then suddenly, it's nothing but fumbling, excuses, and, with the real assholes, blame.

He was back on his phone now, looking at something else, like our little exchange hadn't even happened.

"Can I ask you a question?" he said. "When did you know you were a genius?"

That actually gave me pause. I'd been asked a million things about my IQ, my brain, and my academic chops over the years, but no one had ever put it that way. And since conversation was the least threatening thing I could hope for out there, I rolled with it.

"I guess it depends on what you mean by *genius,*" I said. "I've known I had a high IQ as long as I can remember."

"But when did you know you were different?" he asked. "Special."

"Fourth grade," I said. "That's when they started separating me out from kids my age."

"Not until fourth?" He seemed genuinely surprised. He even looked up from his phone again. "Was your family supportive? Did you get special classes, or whatever?"

I nodded. "I took high school calculus that year."

"And are your parents smart?" he asked.

"Yes," I said.

"But not like you."

I had to pause, even though I knew the answer.

"That's right," I said. Instinct was driving me to be as honest as I could. It seemed obvious he had some history of his own with this kind of thing. Maybe it would help humanize me in his eyes. I'd heard somewhere that that's the first thing you should do with a captor of any kind. Never let them forget you're a person, as opposed to some object or plaything.

Meanwhile, the phone still had at least half of his attention. He wasn't texting, though. It looked like he was watching something now. For what little time I'd been around him, I had yet to see him settle and focus on one thing.

"My parents didn't know what to do with me," he said, his eyes still on the screen. "But I sure knew what to do with them."

"Did you—"

The question started out of my mouth before I thought better of it, but then I shut up just as quickly.

"I sure did," he said anyway, and looked at me again. "You know, we can't all grow up in perfect little suburban homes—"

"That's not what I meant," I said.

"—with just the right Mommy and Daddy—"

"I'm sorry," I said. "I didn't mean to—"

"—and two perfect little sisters," he added.

"Wait... What?" I said.

The realization of what he'd been leading up to settled over me now, like a horrible, heavy weight.

"What did you just say?" I asked again as he tooled endlessly with that goddamn phone.

"What's the matter, Angela?" he asked. "I thought you were proud of your family."

"No," I said, as it all fell into place, and I saw exactly where this was headed. "No... no..."

"We just want to meet them," he said. "Don't you think that's sweet?"

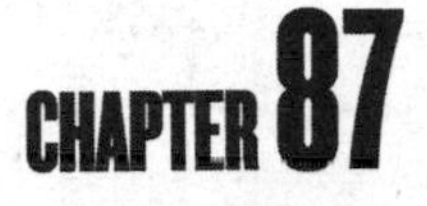

CHAPTER 87

"NO, NO...NO..."

It was all I had, like some kind of infinite loop in my brain.

"Hey, Mikey!" the kid shouted.

Mikey? Mike? Michael? The name cut through my panic and registered, just in case. A second later, the older one got out of the van and came over.

"What's going on?" he asked.

"I just told her where we're going," he said.

"You can't do this," I said to them, focusing on the Engineer now. "Be reasonable. He's your brother, right? Your younger brother. Talk some sense into him! Don't you need to get away? Just...leave. Go. For your own sake."

"I agree with you," he said. "But tell that to him." He thumbed at the Poet. "This is his operation. He calls the shots."

"Wait," I said, looking from one brother to the other. "He...what?"

It wasn't an impossible idea, but it was so opposite what I'd been assuming, it seemed almost nonsensical for a second. This *kid* was the one in charge? Really?

"Oh, yeah. Once he gets his mind set on something, there's no talking him out of it. He's the genius, not me. But you knew that already, didn't you?"

"Of course she did," the kid said confidently. He'd started repacking his case, going about his business as if I weren't right there, freaking out.

"Any other day, and you'd like him," the older one said. "Swear to God. He's very much your type."

"Well, intellectually, anyway," the Poet added, and stood up next to his brother. "Ready to go?"

A scream ran through my mind, but I kept it where it was. "This is crazy!" I said instead. "Neither of you are thinking straight. You can't go to my house."

"It's a done deal, Angela," the kid told me. "Come on. It'll be fun."

But the words kept spilling out.

"My family won't even be there," I said. "You have to know that. They're off at some safe house by now."

"In fact, they're not," the Poet said.

He was right. I was flailing for anything to say—and then doubled down on the lie, too, because there was no reason not to. "I'm telling you, they're under federal protection. I swear!"

I didn't expect it to get me anywhere, and it didn't. All he did in response was turn his phone around to show me what he'd been watching all that time.

It was a video feed of some kind.

From my family's house, I realized all at once.

There, on the screen, I saw my sister Sylvie. She was slumped on the couch at home, leaning over the camera in her own phone, obliviously texting away or playing a game. The app had been watching her, too. All this time.

"And let's not forget Hannah," the Poet said. He ticked something on his screen and the view switched. Now I saw my other sister from the vantage point of my mother's laptop, which usually lived on the kitchen counter.

Hannah was in her pjs, eating a bowl of cereal at the table. She always ate cereal before bed.

"Looks like everyone's hunkering down for the night," the Poet said. "Think they miss you? Not that it matters. You'll all be together again soon enough."

His words blurred in the air. What little I could see in the gloom around me seemed to blur, too. And that scream I'd been holding down came up before I could stop it.

"Help!" I shouted. *"Someone, please help me!"*

"Don't do that," the older one said, but I couldn't stop. It was like falling down a hole with nothing to grab on to. I knew it wouldn't matter, but I had to try.

"There's no way I'm going with you!" I told them. "You can just kill me right now and get it over with. Go ahead! Shoot me, you asshole! Do it!"

The words were coming with a clarity I didn't even know I had. I wasn't afraid to die anymore. Not in that moment. The thing that scared me most now was getting in that van and letting them take me where they wanted to go.

The older one leaned down and pressed both of my shoulders against the tree. I tried to push back, but it was an impossible situation.

"Help!" I screamed again. *"Please! Someone!"*

Then another stab of pain ignited under my arm, just like the last time. My mind fired up with a fresh wave of panic, mostly because I knew what was coming. It wouldn't be long now.

The drug took hold almost right away. It started with the fuzziness around the edges. I think I might have mumbled one last protest, but then came the gray blur. The slipping away. And finally, the black.

I WOKE UP in the van again. Not because we were moving, but because we'd just stopped. A single line of light was cutting between the back doors, and I could see Eve across from me.

Her eyes were open.

I bolted up and got caught short against my own bindings. My head snapped back against the wall of the van. It took me another few seconds to refocus.

Eve's mouth was taped like mine. I could just see the whites of her eyes. I leaned toward her, babbling her name incoherently from behind my gag, but all we could really do was stare at each other. Tears were streaming from my eyes now.

I knew where we were, and I knew what was about to happen.

Images rushed through my mind. Crime scene photos of Gwen Petty, and the victims before her, all asphyxiated in their bedrooms. Family members, too, shot in their beds. Horrible stuff, like I'd never imagined.

Now it was all about to come very much to life, right in front of me.

The back of the van opened, and I got a better look at Eve as more streetlight streamed in. She was pale and drawn, and barely even looked like herself. I could see her trying to make some noise, kicking with her feet, but she was too weak even for that. God only knows what she'd been through since I'd last seen her.

The older of our two captors climbed in and went to Eve first. He bent over her, doing something I couldn't see. A few seconds later, she went slack, and he dropped the hypodermic he'd been carrying. That was it. She was out again.

Then he turned to me. "Time to go," he said, and a fresh wave of panic erupted all through me.

No, no, no, no! I tried to scream, uselessly.

He leaned in and used his hunting knife to cut away the straps that held me in place. I rolled away from him instinctively, but I knew there was nowhere to go.

"Hey, get in here," he whispered to his brother. "We're going to have to light her up."

Light me up? What the hell did that mean? I was still using my heels to push myself away, but then my back hit the rear wall of the van, and I was truly cornered.

The Poet climbed in with his briefcase. All I could do was watch as he opened it on the floor and took out the gun I'd seen before, although I could tell now that it wasn't actually a pistol. It was chunkier than that.

A Taser.

No sooner had I figured it out than I heard a snap and a buzz. My body jerked, then seized, with an electric pain unlike anything I'd ever felt before. It seemed to reach every extremity, freezing all of my muscles at once, and even erasing the throb I'd been feeling in my leg since the bike accident. Which was basically trading one burden for another. All I could feel now was the paralyzing current and the full-body jolting pain that went with it.

"Let's go," the Engineer said. His arm hooked under mine and I unfolded off the floor like a rusty chain as they hauled me out of the van. I got one more look at Eve, out cold, before they closed the door and dragged me away.

They'd backed into my family's driveway, I saw. That part was no surprise. We passed my father's old Saab, parked closer to the house. The front-porch light was on, but all the windows were dark.

I had nearly zero strength left. Still, I resisted with everything I had. I writhed out of the Engineer's grasp and dropped to the ground, but they scooped me right back up.

The Poet took my legs now, and they carried me like an old rolled-up rug around to the back of the house. The parked van gave them all the cover they'd need from the street. Not that anyone was passing by at this hour.

These guys had obviously cased the house, and they knew just what to do. When we came to the kitchen door at the back, they set me down again. I could see the gun in the Engineer's hand, a knife sheathed at his side, the Taser in the Poet's hand, and his own knife as well. Only in my worst imaginings could I guess at how they intended to use them.

This was all my doing. I'd promised my mother that everything was going to be okay. I'd told her that there was nothing my family needed to worry about.

And now, I'd brought the monsters right to their door.

CHAPTER 89

"WHERE'S THE HIDE-A-KEY, Angela?" the older one whispered to me. "There's always a key somewhere. Just nod if I'm getting warmer."

He used his pointer finger to sweep left and right, watching me the whole time like this was some kind of game.

In fact, the key was in a magnetic box on the back of the outside spigot, five feet away. I knew that he'd probably figure it out on his own if he tried, but the longer this took, the better.

He still had hold of my arm, and after a few more passes, he leaned down to speak into my ear.

"Listen to me. We're going in, one way or another. If you help, we make it easy for your sisters and parents. Quick and done. But if you make this harder than it has to be? Well, then we're going to take our time. Up to you."

"Go to hell," I said—or at least tried to say, from the inside of my taped mouth. I think he got the gist, anyway.

I was out of my mind. I had no rational thought left. Even if it did make sense to take his threat seriously and give him what he wanted, I still couldn't bring myself to do it. Not with my family on the other side of that door. The longer I made these guys wait, the more chance there was for a miracle. Which was what I needed now.

It didn't buy me much time, in any case. "Screw it," he said, and elbowed a glass panel out of the back door without any trouble. A few seconds later, he'd reached in and undone the lock from the inside.

They carried me through the kitchen, and this time I didn't struggle. I kept still, letting my eyes focus on the room around me, ranging from side to side, hoping to make some kind of physical disturbance or loud noise to wake up the others.

The knives in the big wooden block were out of my reach. The china cabinet in the dining room wasn't close enough for me to throw myself against it, even if I could get free of them. And a few seconds later, it was moot, anyway. It didn't take more than a moment to pass all the way through the house, to the bottom of the stairs.

They moved quickly now, up the steps with silent feet on the carpet runner and then down the hall to my room. They knew exactly where it was.

When we got there, they dropped me on the bed, right next to the white-painted nightstand where I used to keep my endless stack of reading. Now it was repopulated with a sampling of my academic trophies from high school and further back. My parents had made a shrine to me, in my own room.

Soon it would be my memorial.

None of my yelling and screaming rose to more than a low hum from behind the tape on my mouth.

"Stop it!" the younger one whispered fiercely. And I felt the electric seizure of the Taser once more. A grunt came from somewhere deep inside me. In my head, it was another scream.

By the time I could martial any motor skills at all, they'd taped me to the bed, one wrist on either side, lashed to the posts. With a little more energy, I might have been able to rip free, but that wasn't happening.

"Don't make me do that again," the Poet whispered in my ear.

He climbed onto the bed and then on top of me, straddling my waist with his legs. It stirred the bile in my stomach. I was afraid for a second that I might actually throw up behind my gag.

"This needs to be quick," his brother told him. "You know what to do."

"Just go," the kid said, staring me in the eye. "Take care of the others."

He flipped on the bedside lamp as his brother left the room and closed the door. I could see his face clearly again in the light. He looked eerily peaceful. Happy, even. This was what he'd been waiting for, I could tell. This was what he did to salve that writhing, insane, genius brain of his.

And it wasn't sexual, either. Not anymore. He wasn't even trying to touch me.

No, this was about killing some part of himself. Even I could see that.

"So, I guess this is going to have to be quick," he said. "But I want to thank you, Angela. It's been a pleasure. I mean that."

He reached around my head now and pulled the pillow out from underneath me. I bucked and twisted on the bed with everything I had, though it wasn't much. All I could really do was watch as he brought the pillow down over my face.

It had been hard enough to breathe already. Now it was impossible. There was no air anywhere that I could find. And I knew it was finally close to over.

In every way.

CHAPTER 90

THE PANIC OVERTOOK me. I twisted, side to side, straining against the tape. I whipped my head around as if that was going to fight him off. There was nowhere to go and nothing I could do.

I felt the full weight of his body on the pillow now, pressing into my face, while his hands sought out my throat. One finger at a time, they closed around me, trembling and tightening, both.

I couldn't breathe. Not even a little.

Dear God, I was going to die.

Blue sparks, or something like it, shot across my dark field of vision. My head swam. Even as I struggled, my body was losing the strength it needed to move at all.

A loud bang of some kind sounded in the background. It was my bedroom door, I realized, slamming open.

Then the Engineer's voice.

"Something's wrong! We have to go, now!"

But the pressure around my head and face only increased. The hand on my windpipe tightened its grip.

"What are you talking about?" I heard. "Get the hell out of here!"

The hand on me slipped away, and the pressure eased. I sucked in a breath, and another. The pillow slipped off my face, and I saw the older of the two trying to pull the kid off me. With my wrists taped to the bedposts, there was still nothing I could do.

"I'm not screwing around with you!" the older one said. "Nobody's home. Understand? We have to go. This one's my call. Bring her if you want, but we're leaving."

Another loud slam sounded, this time from downstairs.

"FBI!" someone shouted.

Klieg-bright lights blazed to life outside my bedroom window. I heard feet on the stairs. Flashlight beams danced and crisscrossed in the hall.

The Poet had already started cutting the tape around one of my wrists. He was still on top of me and looked back fast over his shoulder as the raid came closer.

I moved just as fast. My hand ripped free and landed on the first thing I could reach—an old Mathlympics silver cup from ninth grade on the nightstand.

I swung it as hard as I could. This time, I connected. One of the cup's handles sunk with a nauseating crunch right into the side of his skull.

The effect was instantaneous. He slumped and rolled halfway off the bed, blood already seeping from the wound in his head before he slid the rest of the way to the braided rug on the floor below.

I tore the tape from my mouth. "In here!" I screamed just as the older one grabbed me off the bed.

My other wrist, still bound, felt like it was going to snap.

But the tape gave way, and he had me now. We stumbled back against the wall farthest from the door even as he was pulling me in front of him like a shield.

At the same moment, the doorway filled up.

"FBI! Drop your weapons!"

Black-suited cops in tactical vests and helmets were there, AK-47s raised. They came in formation, one agent in the lead, with two others flanking him from behind. Red and blue flashers were running outside now, casting bits of color around the walls of my room.

"Don't even think about it!" the Engineer yelled, pulling me closer. He had one arm snaked around my neck and was using the other to press the barrel of his pistol into my scalp just above my right ear.

Shouts reverberated and blended in the room.

"Let her go!"

"Back off!"

"Don't do this!"

"I'm warning you!"

I could feel the gun scraping painfully against my head. A line of blood trickled into my ear. I wasn't even sure where to look.

"Back off!" he screamed at them again. "I'll kill her, and you know I will!"

As fast as it had all happened, it seemed as though he'd suddenly realized his own advantage. The entry team did, too.

"That's right!" he shouted. "Guns down, right now!"

My body was blocking any clear shot they had. The lead agent put up a hand for the others, and they moved, almost in slow motion, lowering their weapons.

"Now back up, out of the room!" the Engineer told them. "And give me someone I can talk to! Unarmed!"

"That'd be me," said a voice from somewhere in the back of the pack.

As the others cleared out, I saw Billy standing in the doorway. He still had his vest on, but his helmet was off and his empty hands were raised in the air as he took a tentative step past the others, into the room.

CHAPTER 91

"I'M AGENT KEATS from the FBI," Billy said.

"I know who you are," the Engineer said. "What authorization do you have?"

"I'm the lead investigator on this case," Billy said. "Tell me what you need for us to de-escalate the situation."

His hands were still up. He used his foot to kick the bedroom door closed behind him, and he flicked on the overhead light.

Our eyes met for a second before he put his gaze back on the man holding me hostage.

"Don't do anything stupid," Billy said. "Just tell me what you want."

"I want you to get us the hell out of here," the Engineer said. "And I mean out of the country."

"How do you propose that?"

"Just...shut up! Give me a minute to think. Jesus!"

He seemed to be on the edge of a complete meltdown. For all I knew, he was lost without his genius brother.

Not that I wanted to test his limits. I could just see out of the corner of my eye where his gun hand was shaking, his finger still on the trigger.

"What about your guy here?" Keats said. A pool of dark blood had spread past the edge of the rug and as far as the door. "He doesn't look so good. Can we bring in an EMT?"

"No! You get him out into the hall," the Engineer instructed Billy. "Nobody else comes in."

Billy spoke into the radio on his shoulder. "I need EMTs to the second-floor hallway, right now," he said. Then he moved slowly, picking the kid up in his arms and handing him off to someone in the hall. It was a long, slow pass-off. Nobody was making any false moves, but the Engineer dug the barrel of his gun that much farther into my skin anyway.

"Close that door again," the Engineer told Billy, and he complied, keeping his hands spread out in front of him. I could hear the med techs starting to work on the wound I'd sunk into the other one's skull. I hoped the kid wasn't dead. Even now, I didn't want that on my conscience.

"Okay, talk to me," Billy said. "Where are you trying to get to?"

"Mexico City," the guy said. It sounded to me like he was making it up, improvising now as much as he and his brother ever had.

"Okay," Keats said placatingly. "That's doable, but you're going to have to give us a little time. You planning on taking your man out there, too?"

"Of course," he said. "Have your people get him ready for travel. No hospital. They do what they have to here, and then we're out."

Keats obediently relayed the information.

"We're working on a chopper," he said then. "How soon can you let Angela go?"

"She's coming too," he said.

That was no surprise. I knew Billy had to ask, but it was obvious where this was going. They needed me as an insurance policy, all the way out of the country.

"Okay, let's take this one thing at a time," Keats tried again. "What about Eve?"

"She's in the van outside!" I blurted. I got it out before the Engineer could stop me.

"Shut up!" he screamed, and moved the gun around to my face. His free hand grabbed me by the jaw and wedged my mouth open so he could stick the barrel of his pistol inside.

I tasted metal and my eyes watered.

"Hey, *hey!*" Keats said. "Jesus Christ, stop it! Nobody's coming for you, okay? Just ease up, brother."

"I'm not your goddamn brother," he said. "And you don't give the orders." But he took the gun back out and held it to my cheek instead. "Not another word," he told Billy. His voice was rough and shaky. I'm not even sure which of us was more desperate. Everything felt somehow slow-motion and rushed at the same time.

"Check the van in the driveway," Keats said into his radio.

"Already there, sir," a voice came back. "We have Ms. Abajian."

If it was possible to breathe a sigh of relief, I did just then.

Keats looked at the Engineer again. "All right. It's going to be at least twenty minutes before we're mobile. See if you can find a more comfortable position."

"Don't worry about me," he said.

"I'm not," Keats said, and stuck out his chin at me. "I'm worried about her. You can't keep that stance for twenty more minutes. You're already exhausted. I can tell."

For a second, nothing happened. Then the Engineer yanked me by the shoulder, pushing back and downward, pressing me into a kneel. I tried to do it, but my right leg had stiffened way up. I came halfway down instead, landing on my left knee.

At the same moment, a loud popping sound came, like a stun grenade, from out on the lawn. I saw a flash of blue light from the corner of my eye and turned to look. So did the Engineer.

Everything happened fast. I saw the red dot of a laser site appear on his forehead. On instinct, I dove out of the way as much as I could in that small space. It was a blind move and I crashed into my own nightstand, bringing the lamp down on top of me.

At the same time, I heard a small sound of breaking glass. The Engineer's head cocked back, like someone had punched him in the face. His knees bent first, but the rest of him followed.

"Shot fired!" Keats was saying into his radio. The bedroom door opened and personnel were flooding back in.

Billy was there in a second. He scrambled across the bed to reach me.

"Are you okay?" he practically shouted, shielding me against anything else that might come flying.

"I'm okay!" I said. I really was.

Because over Billy's shoulder, I could see where the Engineer had come to a rest on the floor. A dark, impossibly round circle showed on his forehead, and his eyes seemed frozen wide open.

He was dead already. The sniper's bullet had found its mark.

And the longest night of my life was finally over.

CHAPTER 92

THE NEXT SEVERAL minutes are a blur in my memory. There were EMTs to check me out. Billy wrapped a blanket around my shoulders and helped me walk out of the room after I flat-out refused the gurney they wanted to use for me.

He explained a few things as we slowly made our way down the stairs.

"We assumed some kind of home invasion was a possibility as soon as you disappeared," he said. "Your family was under guard the entire time. It turns out your parents are just as stubborn as you are, and they insisted on keeping up appearances for as long as possible. But it worked."

The house had been surreptitiously vacated just after lights out, he told me. All of the previous home invasions had taken place between midnight and 4:00 a.m., and this one had been no exception.

As soon as we made it out to the front lawn, my mother, father, and sisters rushed up from the curb to enclose me in the most welcome group hug in the history of group hugs.

"My God, Angela, you're bleeding!" Mom said.

"I'm okay," I told her.

"You're not the judge of that," she said. A second later, my mother was literally grabbing an EMT to take another look at me. It was my knee that needed attention, but I didn't say that out loud in front of Mom.

"How are you still alive?" Dad asked, kissing my head over and over, hugging me as gently as he could. My sisters were clinging on either side of me, crying happy tears.

In the midst of that, I caught sight of Eve, laid out on a gurney in the back of an open ambulance. I gently extracted myself from the family cluster and climbed in to see her.

"Look who it is," she said groggily.

"Billy told me they're bringing Marlena to the hospital," I told her. "You'll see her soon."

A tear rolled out of the corner of Eve's eye. It was the first time I'd ever seen her cry, if that even counted. And it broke the seal on my own tears, too.

"Eve...I'm so sorry," I said, choking it out through a sob. There were no definitive words for what I was feeling. Regret, relief, joy, love, and everything in between.

"Don't be sorry," she told me. She put a hand under my chin and got my eyes to meet hers. Maybe it was the narcotics, but she'd never touched me so tenderly before. I waited for some sage piece of wisdom from her.

"Remind me not to get you any more internships," she said.

I laughed through my tears and blew snot down my shirt without giving a hoot.

"Duly noted," I said, and kept the rest of my mushy feelings to myself. Like for instance, I sent a little prayer of thanks up to God for bringing Eve Abajian into my life in the first place.

And for making sure the two of us weren't done with each other yet.

CHAPTER 93

IT TOOK ME several days to get all the info I'd been dying for, but there was finally an unofficial team meeting on my first shift back at work.

We had it in SAC Gruss's office, marking the first time I'd been invited to the top of the pyramid like that. Not bad. She had a killer view of the harbor, a private bathroom, and the kind of imposing mahogany desk you might expect. She seemed to fit perfectly behind it. Audrey Gruss wasn't afraid to lead, and I admired that about her.

I sat on one of Gruss's two couches, listening to the debrief and looking over the file of materials Keats had passed around.

The killers in this case were Aaron and Michael Dion, legitimate biological brothers, ages seventeen and twenty-three. They'd been left behind by two very wealthy parents whose double murder had never been solved—until now.

Back at that time, the brothers had been separated by the foster system, both passed from home to home, until the older one, Michael, had aged into his trust fund at twenty-one.

The younger one, Aaron—the Poet *and* the Engineer, as it

turned out—was a bona fide genius in his own right. He'd been a prodigy all his life, graduating high school at age thirteen, well ahead of my own accomplishments.

He'd also been in and out of psychiatric care, until the system lost track of him. In classic fashion, his known file was hip-deep in reports on his inability to attach to anyone beyond his brother. It all tracked with everything I knew about him from our brief time together.

Michael was dead, I knew by now. But Aaron was going to pull through.

"I think Hoot put a permanent dent in his head," Keats said, trying not to smile. "What did you use on him, anyway?"

"Brute strength," I said with a straight face. Several of the others, including Gruss, seemed to approve.

The truth was, none of it sat entirely well with me. Aaron had been right about one thing: he and I shared some common ground. I know what it's like to live inside a crowded mind like that. It can manifest in all kinds of ways, but history is littered with the miserable lives of brilliant people. It was tragic, in a way.

"So what happens to him now?" I asked.

"He'll be in psychiatric custody at least until he's eighteen, and then his case can be retried," Gruss reported. "Let's just say my hopes aren't too high for this kid."

Mine weren't, either. But in a way that I never could have predicted, some small part of me was pulling for him. He was all alone in the world now, and nobody deserves that.

No exceptions.

Then, as the meeting was breaking up and I was turning to go, Gruss called my name.

"Angela? Got another minute?" she said.

Of course the answer was yes. I sat back down while she closed the door and resituated herself across the desk from me.

I couldn't help getting a little case of nerves. Unlike most people, Ms. Gruss intimidated me.

"So tell me," she said. "You've been through quite a lot in a short time. What are your feelings about continuing on?"

Oh, man. Here it came.

"I'd like to finish out the internship very much," I said. "If you'll have me, I mean."

"Actually, I was asking about the longer term," Gruss said. She took a packet of some kind out of her drawer and slid it across to me. "So when your six months is up, I'd like you to consider our training program at Quantico."

I coughed out a little laugh before I could help myself.

"I'll be honest," I told her. "That's not what I thought you were going to say."

"I can tell," she said.

I tried to maintain eye contact with her, but it was hard not to jump into that packet right away. It looked like some kind of pre-application.

"Thank you, ma'am," I said. "Thank you very much. I'll be filling this out the first chance I get."

"I'm glad to hear it," she said. "Just make sure you're ready. This training program isn't the easiest thing you'll ever take on."

"Considering the last few weeks, I'm pretty sure it won't be the hardest thing I've ever done, either," I said. "With all due respect."

She smiled then, as briefly as ever, but warmly, and dismissed me back to my desk.

As I headed out of the room, I could feel my thoughts turning toward the future in a whole new way. Most of all, I just kept thinking, *What next?*

Because I was all out of predictions.

THE CRAZINESS AROUND the case went on for nearly a week. The press coverage was absurd, and I had to lie low for a while.

But finally, I got to have a nice dinner, one-on-one, with my bestie, A.A.

And by dinner, I mean I brought a loaded pizza and a bottle of Jameson to our old apartment. That's where life could start to feel something like normal again.

I'm not naive enough to say that everything I'd been through meant never sweating the small stuff again. But I wasn't going to waste any more opportunities, if I could help it.

So once A.A. and I got through all the brouhaha about this case, I brought the subject around to her.

And me.

And us.

"Listen," I said. "There's something I've been wanting to do for a while now. I should probably ask you about it first, but . . . I don't know. I guess this whole experience has left me in a 'Just go for it' kind of mood."

"Excuse me?" she said. "Since when have you *not* been that way?"

"Good point," I said.

So I leaned in, put a hand on her cheek, and kissed her. I did it lightly and slowly. Then I lingered. And she let me. The whole thing sent a swimming feeling through my body before I leaned back again.

"O . . . kaaay," she said. "Was that for real? Or are you just—"

"It was for real," I told her. "And maybe a little late in coming."

There were a million other things in my head, but nothing that actually needed saying.

A.A. took a swig of Jameson from the bottle. "I didn't even know you were bi," she said. "I mean . . . are you?"

"I don't know," I said. "I'm not really down with the label, if that's what you're asking. But does it matter?"

"God, Piglet, I'm not sure what to say," she told me. "Believe me, if I was going to go for a girl, you'd be at the top of the list. Actually, scratch that. You'd *be* the list."

Her smile was warm, like the whiskey glow I could feel in my chest. This wasn't a rejection. It was just loving honesty, the kind you're lucky to get once or twice in a lifetime.

"Don't take this the wrong way, okay?" she said. "I just don't think I'm interested. But if you tell me we can't be friends now, I'm totally going to hunt you down, take you captive, and tie you up in the woods."

"Very funny," I said.

"Too soon?"

I shook my head. "For anyone else, maybe. Not you."

"Friends, then?" she asked, putting her hand on top of mine.

"Sisters," I said. "For life."

CHAPTER 95

AT MY FAMILY'S insistence, Keats came to the house in Belmont for dinner that Saturday night. It didn't stand for as much as I think they all wanted it to.

"Come outside for a second," he said when I answered the door. I followed him down to the curb, where he was parked. He popped the hatch on his car.

In the back was a brand-new, twenty-seven-inch Giant Talon. It was exactly like my old bike, but newer, better—and double suspension. Those puppies aren't cheap.

"I figured you deserved it," he said.

"But *you* didn't have to buy it," I said.

"It's from all of us at the office," he told me.

"Oh."

I was a tiny bit disappointed, in a way that I wasn't going to admit to myself, much less to Billy.

"Well, I'm overwhelmed," I said. "Thank you. Really. In fact, maybe I'll skip dinner and go out for a ride right now."

"And leave me alone with your family?" he said. "Move. Inside, Hoot. That's an order."

Dinner was actually a lot of fun. I liked watching Billy squirm under the Hoot microscope.

"Are you the one Angela dropped out of college for?" Sylvie asked.

"She didn't drop out," Hannah said. "She was kicked out."

"Drop-kicked, maybe?" Billy tried, which scored a couple of huge grins at the table.

Not from Mom, though. She still had no sense of humor about my MIT debacle. If she had her choice, I'd be out of the FBI and back at school.

But lucky for me, that wasn't up to her.

"Angela's going to make an excellent trainee at Quantico," Billy said. "We'll miss her at the office while she's gone, but then it'll be great to have her back."

"Angela 2.0," Hannah said. "Superagent extraordinaire."

"Next subject?" I said. It was crossing into embarrassing territory now.

"So, Agent Keats," Mom started in as she poured some cabernet. "What's your favorite fairy tale?"

"Excuse me?"

"Sleeping Beauty? Snow White?" Mom asked. "Which story stuck to you most from your childhood?"

Billy looked at a loss, like the question was some kind of personality test. Which it basically was.

"I don't know," he said. "I've never been much into fairy tales."

A round of knowing looks circled the table as my mother reached out to take Billy's hand.

"I can help," she said. "Don't worry. Everything's going to be fine."

It was funny, but also true. Because deep down inside, my mother knew exactly what she was talking about. Everything *would* be fine one of these days. Even if Billy wasn't the happily-ever-after type.

Then again, neither am I.

ACKNOWLEDGMENTS

Special thanks to Kevin Swindon and the staff of the Computer Analysis Response Team at the Boston FBI field office.

ABOUT THE AUTHORS

JAMES PATTERSON is the world's bestselling author and most trusted storyteller. He has created many enduring fictional characters and series, including Alex Cross, the Women's Murder Club, Michael Bennett, Maximum Ride, Middle School, and I Funny. Among his notable literary collaborations are *The President Is Missing*, with President Bill Clinton, and the Max Einstein series, produced in partnership with the Albert Einstein estate. Patterson's writing career is characterized by a single mission: to prove that there is no such thing as a person who "doesn't like to read," only people who haven't found the right book. He's given over three million books to schoolkids and the military, donated more than seventy million dollars to support education, and endowed over five thousand college scholarships for teachers. For his prodigious imagination and championship of literacy in America, Patterson was awarded the 2019 National Humanities Medal. The National Book Foundation presented him with the Literarian Award for Outstanding Service to the American Literary Community, and he is also the recipient of an Edgar Award and nine Emmy Awards. He lives in Florida with his family.

CHRIS TEBBETTS has collaborated with James Patterson on nine of his previous titles, including the Middle School series and *Public School Superhero*. He lives in Vermont.

ALEX CROSS ENTERS
THE FINAL SHOWDOWN
WITH THE RELENTLESS KILLER
WHO HAS STALKED HIM AND
HIS FAMILY FOR YEARS.

TURN THE PAGE FOR A PREVIEW OF THE
NEWEST ALEX CROSS THRILLER.

FEAR NO EVIL

COMING IN NOVEMBER 2021.

CHAPTER

Washington, DC
Late June

MATTHEW BUTLER COCKED HIS HEAD to one side, considering the big-boned blonde in front of him. She was handcuffed and shackled to a heavy oak chair bolted into the concrete floor beneath bright fluorescent lights.

If the woman was anxious about her predicament, she wasn't showing it in the least. She was as chill as the yoga outfit she wore. No sweat on her pale brow. Beneath her warm-up hoodie, her chest rose and fell calmly, each breath measured. Her shoulders were relaxed. Even her eyes looked soft.

Butler adjusted the strap of his shoulder holster.

"I know they've trained you for this sort of thing," he said in a voice with the slightest of Western twangs. "But your training won't work against me, Catherine. It never does."

A fit, balding man with a hawkish nose, Butler had

workman's hands and wore black jeans, Nike running shoes, and a dark blue polo shirt. He crossed his thick forearms when she smiled back at him with brilliant white teeth.

"Whoever you are, you are going to be destroyed for what you're doing," Catherine Hingham said. "When they find out—"

Butler cut her off. "You know, in my many years as a professional, Catherine, I have come to rather enjoy the delicate process of breaking into hearts and minds. They are very much interlinked, you know—hearts and minds—and I have found that one is almost always the key to the other."

"Langley will annihilate you," Hingham said, studying Butler as if she wanted to remember every line in his face.

"Your operators won't help you today," Butler said, gesturing at a pile of blank paper and a pen on the table before her. "Tell me the truth and we can all move on with our lives."

"I'll say it again: You have no jurisdiction over me."

Butler chuckled, gestured around the room. "Oh, but in here, I do."

"I want to see a lawyer, then."

"I'm sure," he said, sobering. "But we're talking about a serious threat to our national security, Catherine. A few rules of engagement can and will be broken in order to thwart that threat."

"I am not a national security threat," she said evenly. "I work for the Central Intelligence Agency, with the highest clearances, in support of my country's freedoms. Your freedoms as well."

"That's what makes your traitorous actions so hard to understand, Catherine."

Her face reddened and she shifted in her chair. "I am no traitor."

Butler took a step toward her. "The hell you're not. We know about the Maldives."

Hingham blinked, furrowed her brow. "The Maldives? Like, the islands in the Indian Ocean?"

"The same."

"I have no idea what you're talking about. I have never been to the Maldives. I've never even been to India."

"No?"

"Never. You can talk to my case officers about it."

"I plan to at some point," Butler said, taking another step toward her. He reached down to touch the back of her left hand before letting his finger trail across her wedding band and modest engagement ring. "Does he know? Your husband?"

"That I work for the CIA?" she said. "Yes. But he has zero idea what I actually do. Those are the rules. We play by them."

Butler sighed as he gently took hold of her left pinkie with his leathery hand, thumb on top.

"Do you know the surest way to sever the connection between the body and mind, and therefore the heart?"

"No," she said.

"Pain," Butler said. He gripped her little finger tight and levered his thumb sharply downward until he heard a bone snap.

CHAPTER

2

CATHERINE HINGHAM SCREAMED IN AGONY, fighting against her restraints, then yelled at him, "You cannot do this! This is the United States of America and I'm a sworn officer of the Central—"

Butler broke her ring finger, then waited for her to stop screaming and crying.

"You have eight fingers left, Catherine," Butler said calmly. "I will break them all and if you still do not tell me what I want to know, I will have your five-year-old daughter brought here and I will begin breaking *her* tiny fingers one by one until you confess."

The CIA officer stared at him in disgust and horror. "Emily has cerebral palsy."

"I know."

"You wouldn't. It's...monstrous."

"It is," he said and sighed again. "And yet, because there is so much at stake, Catherine, I will break your little girl's fingers. But only if you make it necessary."

The CIA officer continued to stare at him for several moments. He gazed back at her evenly until her lower lip trembled and she hung her head.

"The costs," Hingham whispered hoarsely. "You have no idea what a child like Em..." She could not go on and broke down sobbing.

"The heart wins again," Butler said. He pushed the pile of blank pages in front of her. "Start writing. The Maldives. The numbered accounts. Their connections. All of it."

After a few moments, Catherine Hingham calmed enough to raise her head. "I need witness protection."

"I'll see what I can do," Butler said and held out the pen to her. "Now write."

The CIA officer reached out with both handcuffed hands shaking. She took the pen. "Please," she said. "My family doesn't deserve what will happen if—"

"Write," he said firmly. "And I'll see what I can do."

The CIA officer reluctantly began to scribble names, addresses, account numbers, and more. When she'd moved to a second page, Butler had seen enough to be satisfied.

He walked behind the CIA officer and nodded to a small camera mounted high in the corner of the room.

A gravelly male voice came through the tiny earbud Butler wore in his left ear. "Mmmm. Well done. When you have what we need, end the interview and file your report, please."

Butler nodded again before moving in front of Catherine Hingham. She set her pen down and pushed the pages across the table at him.

"That's it," she said in a hoarse voice. "Everything I know."

"Unlikely," Butler said, using the nail of his index finger to lift up the first sheet so he could scan the information she'd provided on page two. "But this looks useful enough for now. It will give us leverage. Was that so hard, Catherine?"

She relaxed a little and said, "Okay, then, I've given you what you wanted. Now I need a doctor to fix my hand. I need witness protection."

With his fingernail, Butler scooted the confession pages to the far right of the table. "You're a smart woman, Catherine. Well educated. Yale, if I remember. You should know your history better. We don't protect traitors in the United States of America. From Benedict Arnold on, they've all had to pay the price. And now, so will you."

The CIA officer looked confused and then terrified when Butler took a step back and drew a stubby pistol with a sound suppressor from his shoulder holster.

"No, please, my kids are—" she managed before he took aim and shot her between the eyes.

CHAPTER 3

FROM THE TIME WE'D MET as ten-year-olds, John Sampson, my best friend and long-term DC Metro Police partner, had been stoic, quiet, observant. Since his wife, Billie, had died, he'd become even more reserved and was now given to long bouts of brooding silence. I knew he was still wrestling with grief.

But that late-June morning, Big John was acting as wound up as a kid about to hit the front gates of Disney World as he bopped around my front room, where we'd laid out all our gear for a trip we'd been talking about taking for years.

"You think we'll see a grizzly?" Sampson asked, grinning at me.

"I'm hoping not," I said. "At least, not up close."

"They're in there, big-time. And wolves."

"And deer, elk, and cutthroat trout," I said. "I've been studying the brochure too."

Nana Mama, my ninety-something grandmother, came in wringing her hands and asked with worry in her voice, "Did I hear you say grizzly bears?"

Sampson glowed with excitement. "Nana, the Bob Marshall Wilderness has one of the densest concentrations of grizzlies in the lower forty-eight states. But don't worry. We'll have bear spray and sidearms. And cameras."

"I don't know why you couldn't choose a safer place to go on your manly trip."

"If it was safer, it wouldn't be manly," I said. "There's got to be a challenge."

"Glad I'm an old lady, then. Breakfast in five minutes." Nana Mama turned and shuffled away, shaking her head.

"Checklist?" Sampson said.

"I'm ready if you are."

We started going through every item we'd thought necessary for the twenty-nine-mile horseback trip deep into one of the last great wildernesses on earth and for the five-day raft ride we'd take out of the Bob Marshall on the South Fork of the Flathead River. An outfitter was providing the rafts, tents, food, and bear-proof storage equipment. Everything else had to fit into four rubberized dry bags we'd use on the river after he dropped us off.

We could have signed up for a fully guided affair, but Sampson wanted us to do a good part of the trip alone, and after some thought, I'd agreed. Six days deep in the backcountry of Montana would give Big John many chances to open up and talk, which is critical to the process of coping with tragic loss.

"How's Willow feeling about our little trip?" I asked.

Sampson smiled. "She doesn't like the idea of grizzly bears any more than Nana does, but she knows it will make me happy."

"Your little girl's always been wise beyond her years."

"Truth. Bree liking her job?"

Thinking of my smart, beautiful, and independent wife, I said, "She loves it. Got up early to be at the office. Something about a possible assignment in Paris."

"Paris! What a difference a career change makes."

"No kidding. It was like the gig was tailor-made for her."

"Maybe we should think about going into private-sector investigations too."

"Pay's better, for sure," I allowed.

Before he could reply, my seventeen-year-old daughter, Jannie, poked her head in and said, "Nana says your eggs are getting cold."

I put down my dry bag and went to the kitchen, where I found my youngest child, Ali, already finishing up his plate.

"Morning, sunshine," I said, giving him a hug. He ignored it, so I tickled him.

"C'mon, Dad!" He laughed, then groaned. "Why can't I go with you?"

"Because you're a kid and we don't know what we'll be facing."

"I can do it," he insisted.

Sampson said, "Ali, let your dad and me scope it out this year. If we think you're up to it, we'll bring you along on the next trip. Deal?"

Ali scrunched up his face and shrugged. "I guess. When do you leave?"

"First thing in the—"

My cell phone began to ring at the same time Sampson's chimed.

"No," John protested. "Don't answer that, Alex. We're supposed to be gone already!"

But when I saw the caller ID, I grimaced and knew I had to answer. "Commissioner Dennison," I said. "John Sampson and I were just heading out the door on vacation."

"Cancel it," said the commissioner of the Metro DC Police Department. "We've got a dead female, gunshot wound to the head, dumped in the garage under the International Spy Museum on L'Enfant Plaza. Her ID says she's—"

"Commissioner, with all due respect," I said, "we've been planning this trip for—"

"I don't care, Cross," he snapped. "Her ID says she's CIA. If you want to continue your contract with Metro, you'll get down there. And if Sampson wants to keep his job, he'll be with you."

I stared at the ceiling a second, looked at John, and shook my head.

"Okay, Commissioner. We're on our way."

JAMES PATTERSON
RECOMMENDS

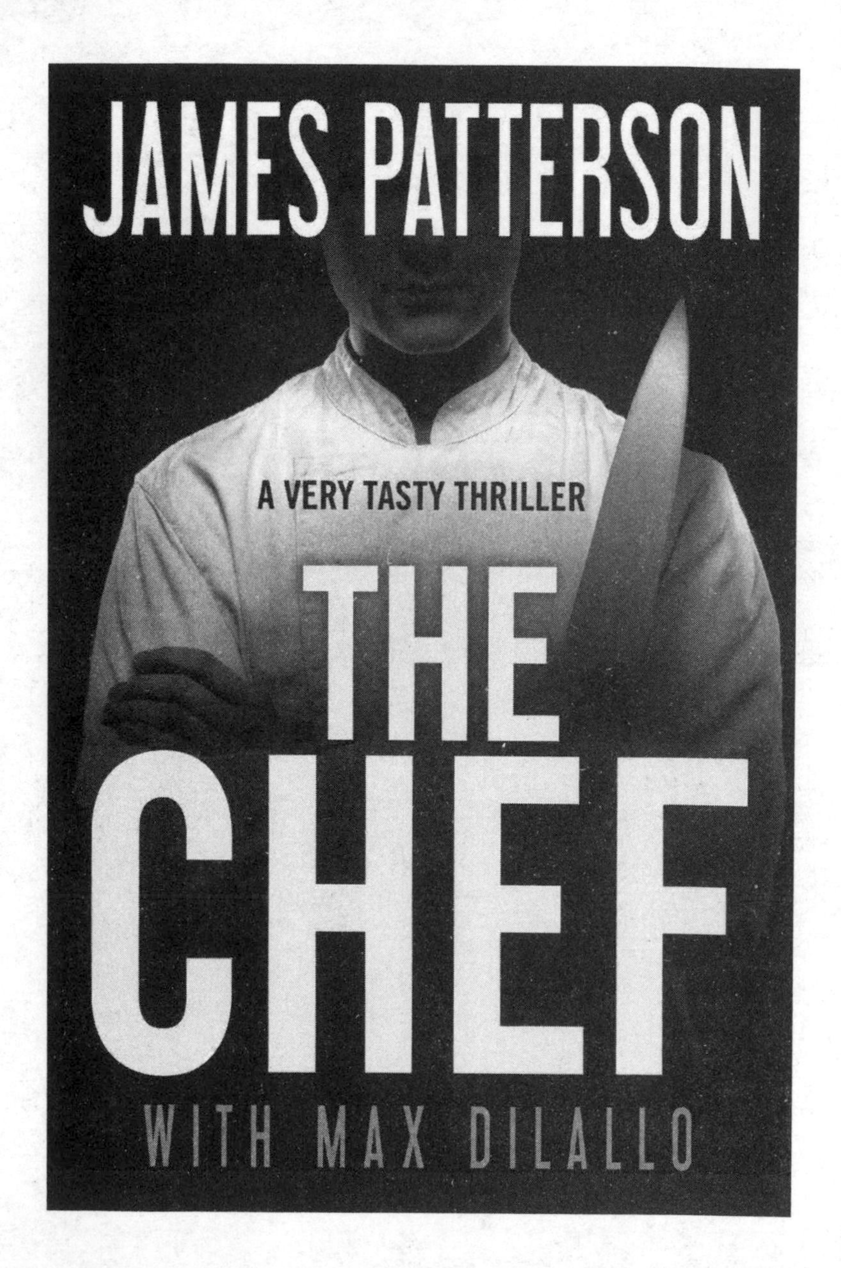
JAMES PATTERSON
A VERY TASTY THRILLER
THE
CHEF
WITH MAX DILALLO

THE CHEF

In the Carnival days leading up to Mardi Gras, Detective Caleb Rooney is accused of murder—committed in the line of duty, of a major crimes investigator for the New Orleans Police Department. I know what it's like to love your home, so Rooney is in anguish as his beloved city is under attack. And the would-be terrorists may be local.

Amid crowds of revelers, Rooney follows a fearsome trail of clues, racing from outlying districts into the city center. He has no idea what—or who—he'll face in defense of his hometown, only that innocent lives are at stake. This might be my most delicious thriller yet.

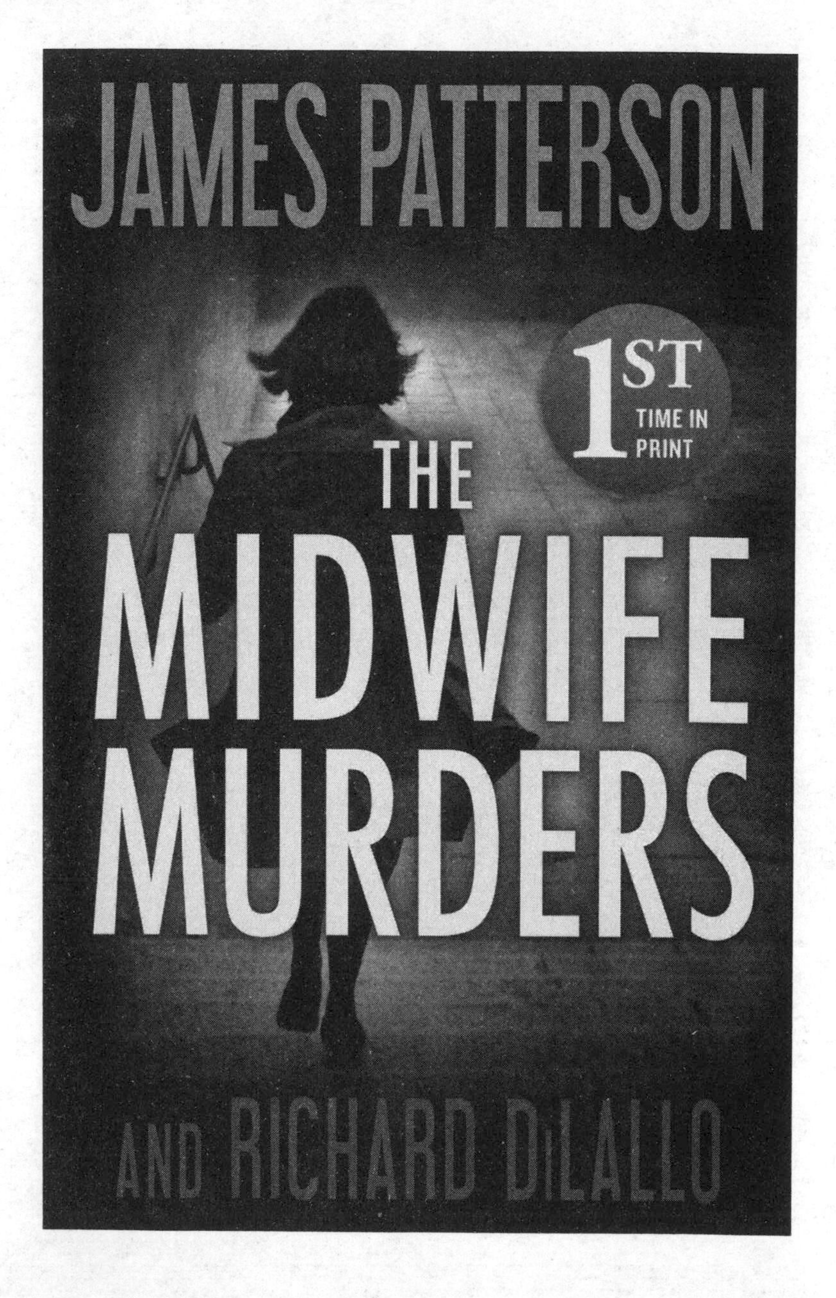
JAMES PATTERSON
1ST
TIME IN
PRINT
THE
MIDWIFE
MURDERS
AND RICHARD DiLALLO

THE MIDWIFE MURDERS

I can't imagine a worse crime than one done against a child. When two kidnappings and a vicious stabbing happen on Lucy Ryuan's watch in a university hospital in Manhattan, her focus abruptly changes. Something has to be done, and senior midwife Lucy is fearless enough to try.

Rumors begin to swirl, with blame falling on everyone from the Russian mafia to an underground adoption network. Fierce single mom Lucy teams up with a skeptical NYPD detective, but I've given her a case where the truth is far more twisted than Lucy could ever have imagined.

JAMES PATTERSON

1ST TIME IN PRINT

THE FIRST LADY

& BRENDAN DUBOIS

THE WORLD'S #1 BESTSELLING WRITER

THE FIRST LADY

The US government is at the forefront of everyone's mind these days and I've become incredibly fascinated by the idea that one secret can bring it all down. What if that secret is a US President's affair that results in a nightmarish outcome?

Sally Grissom, leader of the Presidential Protection Division, is summoned to a private meeting with the President and his chief of staff to discuss the disappearance of the First Lady. What at first seemed an escape to a safe haven turns into a kidnapping when a ransom note arrives along with what could be the First Lady's finger.

It's a race against the clock to collect the evidence that all leads to one troubling question: Could the kidnappers be from inside the White House?

JAMES
PATTERSON
& ANDREW BOURELLE
THE
WORLD'S
#1
BEST-
SELLING
WRITER
TEXAS
RANGER
OFFICER
RORY
YATES
COMES
HOME—
TO A
MURDER
CHARGE

TEXAS RANGER

So many of my detectives are dark and gritty and deal with crimes in some of our grimmest cities. That's why I'm thrilled to bring you Detective Rory Yates, my most honorable detective yet.

As a Texas Ranger, he has a code that he lives and works by. But when he comes home for a much-needed break, he walks into a crime scene where the victim is none other than his ex-wife—and he's the prime suspect. Yates has to risk everything in order to clear his name, and he dives into the inferno of the most twisted mind I've ever created. Can his code bring him back out alive?

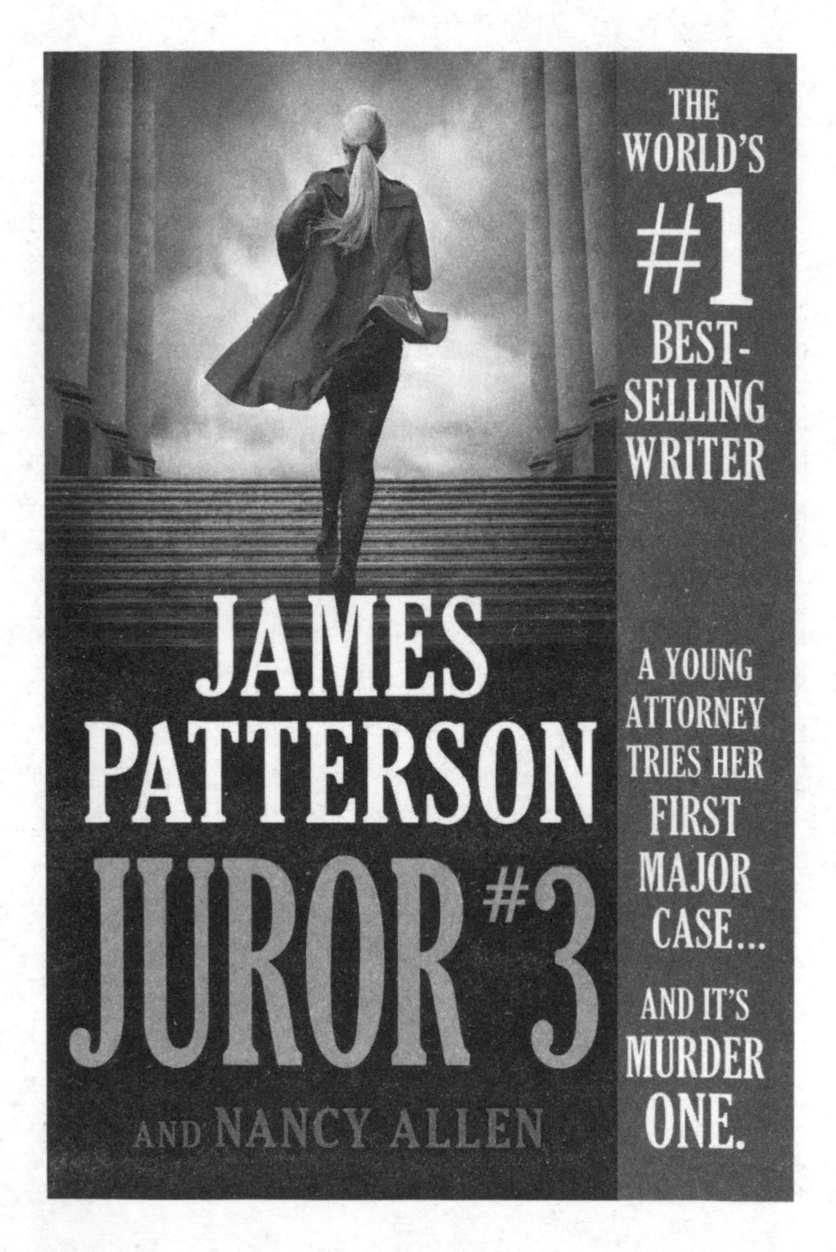
THE WORLD'S #1 BEST-SELLING WRITER
JAMES PATTERSON
JUROR #3
AND NANCY ALLEN
A YOUNG ATTORNEY TRIES HER FIRST MAJOR CASE...
AND IT'S MURDER ONE.

JUROR #3

In the deep south of Mississippi, Ruby Bozarth is a newcomer, both to Rosedale and to the bar. And now she's tapped as a defense counsel in a racially charged felony. The murder of a woman from an old family has Rosedale's upper crust howling for blood, and the prosecutor is counting on Ruby's inexperience to help him deliver a swift conviction.

Ruby is determined to build a defense that sticks for her college football star client. Looking for help in unexpected quarters, her case is rattled as news of a second murder breaks. As intertwining investigations unfold, no one can be trusted, especially the twelve men and women on the jury. They may be hiding the most incendiary secret of all.

For a complete list of books by

JAMES PATTERSON

VISIT

JamesPatterson.com

Follow James Patterson on Facebook

@JamesPatterson

Follow James Patterson on Twitter

@JP_Books

Follow James Patterson on Instagram

@jamespattersonbooks